PENGUIN BOOKS
GROUND MONEY

As well as *Ground Money*, Rex Burns has written six
other Gabe Wager mysteries – *The Alvarez Journal*,
winner of an Edgar Award, *The Farnsworth Score*, *Speak
for the Dead*, *Angle of Attack*, *The Avenging Angel* and
Strip Search – and sees the series continuing as a fictional
biography. In addition, he has published several other
novels. He writes reviews for newspapers and teaches at
the University of Colorado at Denver.

REX BURNS

GROUND MONEY

PENGUIN BOOKS

PENGUIN BOOKS

Published by the Penguin Group
27 Wrights Lane, London W8 5TZ, England
Viking Penguin Inc., 40 West 23rd Street, New York, New York 10010, USA
Penguin Books Australia Ltd, Ringwood, Victoria, Australia
Penguin Books Canada Ltd, 2801 John Street, Markham, Ontario, Canada L3R 1B4
Penguin Books (NZ) Ltd, 182–190 Wairau Road, Auckland 10, New Zealand

Penguin Books Ltd, Registered Offices: Harmondsworth, Middlesex, England

First published in USA by Viking Penguin Inc. 1986
Published simultaneously in Canada
Published in Penguin Books 1988

Printed and bound in Great Britain by
Cox & Wyman Ltd, Reading

To Richard Houghton Burns

CHAPTER 1

I guess . . . I guess what I'm asking, Gabe—dammit all—is if you'll help me out."

The plea came hard through Tommy Sanchez's wrinkled mouth, and Gabe Wager, sharing Tommy's embarrassment, stared at the rows of brightly lit whiskey bottles behind the bar. He could tell Tommy no, and Sanchez would understand. There would be neither begging nor blame; they'd finish their beers and argue a little over who got to pick up the tab, and then the cowboy would mash out his cigarette and shake hands and say, "Thanks, anyway, Gabe," and stump out of Wager's life forever. Or he could say yes and it would be pretty much the same except Wager wouldn't lose a friend. But he might get kicked out of the homicide unit of the Denver Police Department for sticking his nose in places it didn't belong.

"I'll try, Tommy," was the most Wager could say. It sounded as bad as a politician before election day. "Let me see what I can find out, anyway."

"Appreciate it, Gabe. *Muchas gracias.*"

"*De nada.*" That was it; agreement sealed, they talked a little about quarter-horse racing and a lot about rodeo, about people Tommy had seen lately on the circuit and some of the old-timers who were only vaguely echoing names to Wager. After so much time, it was hard to reach back to Wager's fourteenth and fifteenth years, when Tommy had been—let's see, twenty-one? twenty-three?—old enough, anyway, to be a hero to Wager and every other kid in the long-gone Auraria barrio. One of the best all-round rodeo cowboys in Colorado, Vaquero Tommy Sanchez, as they called him then, had taken time to talk with Gabe and the others as if they were truly the men they hungered to be. Wager could remember the local rodeo grounds west of town in what was now a sprawling suburb with its own office towers and blank-walled factories and tangle of streets and traffic. Then it had been ranch land, and on one corner of it, off old Highway 6, was the rodeo grounds: a collection of sagging bleachers warping in the summer sun and winter snow. Dust—that's what Wager remembered—and the heat; the sting and smell of dust kicked up and dragged over by sweating, straining cowboys and the white-eyed animals who fought them with speed and strength and savagery: man against untamed nature. And Vaquero Tom, one of the few Mexes to earn his way into the professional ranks of the sport they invented, roping and riding through four or five events. God, he seemed so tall and wide-shouldered when he came to the barrio to visit his grandparents; it was always an occasion—"I just saw Tommy Sanchez"—and, in ones and twos, Wager and the other kids would drift over to old Elias Sanchez's backyard as if by accident and just happen to find Tommy and his grandfather drinking iced tea in the rustling shade of the cottonwood. You knew then it was rodeo time, one of those punctuations that marked the almost unnoticed glide of long summers that began with Cinco de Mayo, was marked halfway by Fourth of July, and ended with the smells of new school Levi's and fresh pencil shavings and the World Series on the radio. There were also lesser fiesta days—those of the church—and better nights when the carnival pitched its neon rides, and the oily-smelling tents filled with the sticky aroma of cotton candy riding on the musty odors of caged animals. Or the stock-car season with its championship races at the dirt track in the bug-filled glare of spotlights. But for three or four years, the best time had been rodeo, and you knew it was here when Tommy Sanchez came to town.

In his rookie year he was good enough to be sponsored as a steer roper, sharing purses with the man who provided the horse, the entry fees, and a lot of good advice. Wager still remembered the excitement when Tommy fired out of the chute after a sprinting and twisting longhorn. The rising blare of the loudspeakers—"Here comes Vaquero Tommy Sanchez"—lifted Wager with the same feeling he got when the big roller coaster out at Elitch's tipped over that first screaming peak.

"Andy Shaw—I ain't heard from him in a long time. I wonder if he's dead."

"Wasn't he a steer roper, too?"

"One of the best. I learned a lot from him. He won him some good money, too, when there wasn't that much to win."

The trick was to angle your horse against the path of the steer, and the horse had to be smart enough and quick enough and have enough balance to outthink, outtwist, and outrun a half-wild steer that knew exactly what that man wanted to do to it. Then the rope whipping out to settle quickly over the horns and yank tight while the horse, bunching against the oncoming shock, turned and lunged away. With a twang, the rope jerked stick-tight as the cow went one way and the horse another. If everything was right—the timing, the riata, the equipment, the angles of the running animals—the steer would be yanked into the air, to spin heavily against its own speed and plummet solidly into the arena's dust, stunned, sometimes its neck broken, occasionally a leg shattered. If things went wrong, the horse and rider would go down; and the same things could happen to them. All of this against the clock, and prize money to only the fastest four riders and their horses. Tommy made his best living that way until he lost his horse down in Prescott. "Broke her neck when she went over— damn mean cow and a smart one. Rope-wise. I had to put Dolly Bee down. Damn, she was a good horse." Tommy broke his leg in two places that time, Wager remembered. When he mended, he concentrated on the riding events instead of the timed ones. "Hell, I'd raced quarter horses until I got too heavy. The barebacks and broncs wasn't much different from some of them I raced. And bulls— hell, there's not much you can do with them anyway except hang on." Besides, the purses were getting bigger, the competitive times faster, and Tommy was getting older. It just made sense to specialize in events that had the least overhead. "I had to rent horses after that, and some of them I wasn't sure of. It would have took me three years to train another cow horse of my own. And then it wouldn't have been as good as Dolly Bee." Moreover, steer-roping was a fading event because of damage to the animals.

But by then, at sixteen years old, Wager faced his own challenges in the Marine Corps. He and his mother lied to the smiling recruiting sergeant about his age, but there was no lying to anyone about how scared he was later, stamping his numb boots against the frozen mud of a bunker and listening to the Chinese bugle calls drift and toss on the north wind from loudspeakers somewhere out in that cold dark. More than once the memory of Vaquero Tom had blotted out minutes and even hours from those empty nights of staring into the freezing blackness and waiting for another "incident," waiting for them to come and try again to "straighten out the line" before all the talking finally stopped at Panmunjom.

Now, of course, Tommy didn't ride anymore. He was a horse handler—a stock hand for the contractors who pro- vided animals for rodeos whose size and glitter outdis- tanced anything he ever dreamed of when he was healthy enough to ride. Now, he walked on legs broken in half a dozen places while his panting lungs pushed against his ribs that had strange angles and bumps. He worked the animals with knotted, swollen knuckles whose sprains and breaks were becoming arthritic. But he was still in rodeo. "Hell, Gabe, I'll die in it if they let me."

"You don't have anything to retire on?"

"Aw, I got a little ranch down near Antonito. It's about as

much as a dog can piss across. But who wants to quit what they do for a living? *Jijole*—you quit that and you start digging your own grave! No, I reckon I'll hold on as long as I can. And there's this thing about the boys. . . ."

John and James. The two left alive, and the ones he wanted Wager's help with. "Just exactly what did you hear about them?" Wager asked.

It wasn't anything concrete. A rumor, a meaningful silence, a nod of the head and uneasy eyes from people who used to grin and grab for his hand when they saw him. "That's the damned problem, Gabe. It's like everybody knows something but me."

"But you think they're in trouble?"

"Well, there's smoke; that's all I can say. I don't know for sure that there's anything to it, but I want to find out. And if there is . . . well, I want to help them before they screw themselves up." He fumbled for his cigarettes and stared at the package before drawing another one out. "I seen too many kids mess themselves up by doing dumb-ass things."

"Have you seen them lately?"

"No. I reckon they were up at Cheyenne for Frontier Days. But, hell, that's a big rodeo. And a couple young kids in all that excitement—they got better things to do."

From a large speaker at the rear of the bar, the thud of an electronic bass quivered their shirts and a nasal voice groaned, "My life is just an empty road and people walk on me."

"Have you heard anything from their mother?"

"Only when she wrote to tell me James was rodeoing and to say it was all my fault."

"So you haven't actually seen them with anyone?"

"No."

"You haven't tried to write or call?"

"I never was much of one for writing. And the only phone number I've got is their mother's."

"When was the last time you talked to either of them?"

Tom shrugged and pulled at his beer; his lip made a squeaky noise in the bottle. "Couple years now. I wanted to go to John's high school graduation. But I knew his mother'd be there . . . and I wasn't sure what the boys would think about it anyway. So I called him instead. He said he was glad to hear from me."

"Has either written you since then?"

"Christmas card. It was signed 'Love, James.'"

"That was before you started hearing about the people they were running around with?"

He nodded. "It caught up with me here in Dever at the National Western."

"Last January?"

"Two Januaries ago by now, I guess." He drank again. "I just been over to look at the old neighborhood. Hell, I couldn't even find it. *Carajo*, Gabe! Even the streets are gone!"

"Urban renewal. They put a university there."

"I saw the Tivoli Brewery and Santo Cajetanos. But, man, that's all. If it wasn't for them, I wouldn't of known where the hell I was."

Wager let the man talk about his bewilderment in trying to find his way around what had become an entirely new city. It was Tom's means of escaping the lingering ache of his failed family life, and Wager could understand both the failure as well as the need to bury it. In fact, just as Wager had seen in the younger Vaquero Tommy an idol that, in his own way, he once tried to follow to excitement and adventure, so now he felt in Tom's isolate, wandering life, anchored only by his job, a chill of premonition about his own future. And that, too, was a thought better pushed back rather than brought out for examination. "Their mother really blames you for the boys going with the rodeo?"

"She still blames me for Elias."

The oldest boy, the one killed when a horse hung up coming out of the chute and rolled on its rider—nineteen-year-old Elias. "She wrote to tell you James was rodeoing. But she didn't say anything else? Who he was with or anything?"

"We don't have a damn thing else to talk about."

Wager rephrased it. "Has she written to you before

about them? Where they were or who they were running around with?"

"Once or twice, I guess. John was working a ranch down near Lubbock awhile back after he graduated from high school, and she wrote and told me. I didn't get a chance to see him, though. You know how it is—a man gets busy, and time goes by so damn quick."

"Any other time?"

"Just when she found out James was rodeoing."

"And that was the last time?"

"That's it."

"Do you have any names? Any idea of who they're supposed to be with?"

"No."

It was Wager's turn to drink his beer and wonder how to live up to his promise. He'd check the computers, of course; and then ask around among friends in agencies which had statewide jurisdiction to find out if either Sanchez boy was a name they'd heard. But beyond that, he didn't know what to do. "Why don't you just look them up and ask them, Tommy?"

"Ask them what? If they're getting in trouble? Who those *culos* are they're running around with? Christ, Gabe, I'm the last one they'd tell anything to."

Besides, Wager knew, there was Tommy's fear that neither would want to see their father. Not after so many missed chances.

"That's why I come to you. I turn this thing over every which way, and I don't see no way I can look into what's going on without them finding out. Too many people know who I am. They know them, too—they know about me and Elias, and who John and James are." He lit another cigarette. "I got a few people I can ask, but, hell, they're old-timers like me—they're not in the middle of things no more."

"Maybe there's nothing at all."

"I'd be mighty happy if that's what you find out."

He promised again, "I'll see what I can do."

Out on the sidewalk, they stood a few moments in the

waves of heat from the sun-scorched concrete and talked about the unseasonable weather. Tommy plugged another cigarette into the corner of his mouth and lit it with the old one. Flipping the smoldering butt into the littered gutter of Colfax Avenue, he asked, "Whatever happened to all the *chinga* shows you used to have along here?"

"Closed them down. Denver's a clean town, now."

"That's too damn bad."

It wasn't all true, either. "How do you feel about the boys rodeoing?"

He spat a shred of tobacco toward his pointed boots. "It's OK for a little while. But I hope they don't try it for a living. There's no way in hell they can make any money in it now."

"Why's that?"

"They're trying the old way, and you can't do that no more. Now you got to start when you're nine or ten. You go to Little Britches rodeos and to rodeo schools. Now most of the pro-rodeo cowboys are college graduates." He spat again. "Intercollegiate rodeo, for God's sake."

"I didn't know it was that big."

"There was almost fifteen million dollars prize money won last year. But there's a hell of a lot more people going after it now. *Caga*—they got training machines and seminars and goddam gurus running around teaching meditation to bull riders! It's a big business now, Gabe. It sure as hell ain't what it was when I started. You got to have a potload of money just to get into it, now. There's no way in hell for two raggedy-assed ranch hands to step in and make a go of it."

"Are you going to tell them that?"

"They wouldn't listen. I don't think they'd listen." The cigarette spun toward the curb. "I want to straighten out this other stuff, first. Without them knowing anything about it, if we can."

"How do I get in touch with you in case I do find something?"

Tommy lifted his brown Stetson with its high crown and

the feathered band and ran twisted fingers through hair that was still mostly black. "Well, I'll be over in Oklahoma for a while—I'm supposed to look at some horses at a place near Sturgis. Damned if I know the address there, though. Know how to get there, but I don't know how to send a letter there."

"It'll take at least a couple weeks." If he was lucky.

"By then I should be back at my place." He borrowed Wager's pencil and notebook to print a rural route number. "There's a telephone sometimes. I'll give that to you, too."

"If I find out something, you'll hear from me."

Tommy's palm was dry and thick as knotted leather, and popped slightly as he clasped Wager's hand. "Appreciate your help, *amigo*—I really do. See you on down the road."

Wager watched the silver-and-blue pickup with its high camper shell pull away from the curb and into the heat-shimmered traffic of the summer afternoon. On the cream-colored bumper, a tattered sticker read "I'm a Roper Not a Doper," and another said "Tony Lama Boots and American Rodeo—Best of the West." There were a few others, but they were ragged and faded with age and dirt, and Wager guessed Tommy had stuck them on as much for laughs as for statement.

He got into his Trans-Am, the trapped air of a hot spring day wrapping him like warm cotton, and worked his way across the one-way streets that carved Denver into a grid of semi-isolated neighborhoods. He had promised Jo he would be over right after the shift ended, but that was before Tommy had called him. Now he was almost two hours late. But what the hell, Jo was a cop, too, and she would understand. Or pretend to, which was good enough for Wager.

.   .   .

It was a new apartment for Jo, the back half of a duplex, and Wager still felt like *un perro en barrio ajeno*—a dog in a strange neighborhood—as he went up the pitted concrete walk to her front door. On this side of Washington Park, the old houses were small and the streets lined with the overflow of cars parked by tenants who shared single-family homes and apartments in violation of the law. But people had to live somewhere, and with the cost of houses and especially of the money to buy them, not many singles could afford the American Dream anymore. And, in fact, all over Denver Wager had seen a larger number of couples, many with children, setting up life in apartments and sharing houses with others. There was a touch of irony about that, for these were Anglos, the children of those who had taken their tax money out of the city to fill the surrounding suburbs with split-levels parked on lanes and drives and circles. Here their offspring were gradually developing the same kind of crowded and noisy neighborhood Wager had grown up in. Now all they had to do was put in a corner grocery store and a cantina, and call it progress.

Jo unlocked the screen door and took his coat; her black hair—longer than regulations allowed—was gathered for coolness into a loose braid down her back. A brief hug, comfortable in its familiarity: "Beer's in the refrigerator—but it smells like you've already had some."

Wager told her why he was late.

"What does Tom want you to do?"

"See what I can find out without letting his kids know about it." He finished pouring the Killian's into a half-empty glass as he lounged against the kitchen sink and watched her stir things into a salad.

She blotted her forehead with the back of her wrist. "That's a long way from the homicide business. Do you know anyone you can talk to?"

"I might. I'll see what I can find out, anyway." He shrugged. "I told him I would."

It was Wager's job to grill the steaks in the tiny backyard, and he built up the charcoal fire that had burned to ash as Jo waited for him. This time she sat while he worked, the freckled shade of a locust tree playing across that jet-black hair and the gold-brown eyes that watched him. He seared the meat on one side and then flipped it and coated it with Wager's Own Peculiar Picante Sauce. When, twelve minutes later, the steaks were done, the two of them sat at the round picnic table covered with a red-and-white-checked cloth and toasted each other with a glass of Bardolino.

"I like your new house, Officer Fabrizio."

"And I like having you here, Detective Sergeant Wager."

Standing, she was almost as tall as he was; but when they sat he gained a couple of inches. That was because of her long legs, the second thing he had noticed about her that day a few years ago when, leaning across the counter of Records, he watched her bend to take a file from a lower drawer. The thing he noticed first had been covered by her skirt. And the thing he noticed third was the laughter in those golden eyes when she straightened and turned and caught his stare.

They hadn't dated then—she had a boyfriend and Wager a recent divorce—but later, when he finally asked her out for a beer, the laughter had come back when she told him, "I remember the first time I saw you." Now he felt the kind of comfort with her that he never thought possible with any woman, and certainly had never felt with his wife. Which wasn't her fault, but his; as Jo had said one night, when a man goes into the military at sixteen and comes out twelve years later, he probably knows a lot about life, but not much about women. Wager had never thought about that himself; it hadn't seemed important and it didn't contribute much to his job. But occasionally now he wondered what else he might have lost by spending his teen years on the end of one war and his youth at the beginning of another. But if he knew it all, he'd be a different person; and he might not be sitting here learning to drink fancy imported wine and gnawing a steak bone across the table from a woman with the best-looking legs in Colorado. Among other things.

"When are you putting your grape vine in?"

"What grape vine?"

He held up his glass. "I thought all you Italians had to hava da grape."

Jo looked around the tiny backyard bordered by chest-high wooden fences. An untended flower bed ran down one side toward the garage and alley beyond; a scattering of water-starved zinnias made bright explosions here and there. Along the other fence, dead vines from last year's zucchini crop tangled among the tall grass. "What I need is a Mexican gardener to clean this place up first. You've got some vacation time coming—want to moonlight?"

"I tried growing a petunia once. It died."

"In your apartment, I can understand it. You even have a photograph of a dead tree."

"That was from a case. Besides, I like it."

"I do too: Noble Defiance Even in Death. It says something about you. That, and the sword on the wall."

Wager hadn't given much thought to that, either; the wall had looked blank and the old NCO's sword kept falling out of the closet, so it just made sense to put them together. Which is what he told her.

"Uh oh, I stepped on his Mexican macho." She uncovered a bowl of sliced melons and fruits. "Here—have something to sweeten up your disposition. And don't try to hardnose me, buster; I'm a cop, too."

And Wager guessed that was why he liked her. No, more than liked—but that was an area he wasn't ready to delve into. And as long as she was willing to do without definitions, so was he.

They spent a lot of the afternoon watching the sun drop below the trees and feeling the day's heat cool into the freshness of evening. They talked about the people in Records and in Homicide, the various lieutenants and captains, and the political shifts and alignments of the new city administration. Every now and then one of them—Jo, usually—would say, "That's enough shop talk," and they would grope for some other topic, occasionally finding one. But inevitably it led back to the world of the department, because that was where they both felt most alive and most comfortable. It wasn't until much later when, warmth to warmth under the light blanket that kept off the chill air of a late-spring night, Jo again mentioned Wager's long-delayed vacation.

He lifted himself on an elbow and peered through the dimness at the oval of her face. "Have you been building up to this? Wine, dinner, a fine evening—was all this a setup?"

He didn't know whether or not he meant the accusation, and she must have heard that in his voice, because when she finally answered, she was only half joking, too. "That's a pretty crummy thing to say, Wager. It crossed my mind, and I said what was on my mind. I'm not trying to manipulate you and I'm not trying to emasculate you."

That wasn't exactly what he meant, but since she mentioned it, he'd clarify things: "I had a woman who never let on what she was really after, and I sure as hell don't want another like that."

"You arrogant bas—"

"She'd hint around and I was supposed to guess what she meant. Then she'd get pissed when I wouldn't play her game."

"I'm not playing a game. And you don't have me, Wager. Nobody has me."

"I didn't say I did. But by God, I don't see why a man has to be on his guard around a person he . . . he . . ."

"I wasn't trying to hint anything. I was trying to talk to you. It seemed like a good idea at the time. But if you're so damned defensive and insecure that you want to go looking for plots and accusing me of trying to manipulate you, well, Sergeant Wager, maybe you'd better get your shoes out from under my bed!" She sat up too, now, the vague shadows of eyes and mouth staring hotly at him and the fall of her dark hair straight down over both shoulders where her pale breasts lifted to part it. "Go on, dammit—either apologize or get out."

His lips felt like a line between the fingers of a clenched fist, and the inertia of stubbornness stifled any apology. Silently, he swung his feet to the floor and groped for his clothes. Silently, she stared across the foot of the bed into the darkness.

When he had his jacket on and his tie stiffly in place, he managed to say, "I'm sorry."

"So am I."

But he went, nevertheless; and she did not try to stop him.

CHAPTER 2

What's with you, Gabe?" Max Axton rose from his desk, his wide torso darkening the windows that looked out over Denver with its changing skyline of growing office towers.

Wager looked up from the scrawled report he had been attempting to complete. "What's that mean?"

"Hey, partner, take it easy. You've been talking to yourself for half an hour."

"Have I?" He looked with surprise at the crumpled sheet. It dealt with a domestic shooting, a familiar story of ex-husband walking in on ex-wife and blowing away her now ex-boyfriend with a sawed-off shotgun. And then saving the state money by using the other barrel on himself. Maybe it was supposed to make the woman feel sorry, but from what Wager had seen, she was glad to be rid of both of them. You'd think the dumb son of a bitch would've known when to let go.

His partner, Max the Axe, as he didn't like to be called, glanced at the yellow tablet with its smears of pencilings and lines through words here and there. "Just put down what happened—at about seven forty-five a.m., Mr. Otis Neal Smith walked into the kitchen where he found his ex-wife and her boyfriend having breakfast et cetera et cetera." He slid several papers onto the desk. "Here's the responding officer's letter and the witnesses' statements. You want to package it up when you're through? I've got to be in court in half an hour."

"Right." Wager scratched out another word and added "alleged" in front of the killer's name. He felt Max gaze at him briefly before the big man turned to telephone the police photographer and find out if the pictures had been developed yet. The call had come in at 8:05, just after the shift began, and could be filed for the captain by noon if information from all the other units could be gathered together by then. Not that there was any rush to clear the case today—the murderer wasn't at large in this world. But there was no reason to let it drag, either, when a telephone or the radio might call them to another one before the shift was out. Besides, this one would count on the daily case load, the ten to fifteen folders assigned to each of the homicide detectives now that the new administration had stopped pooling them under the "team approach," where everyone—and no one—was responsible for all the cases. Other types of requests could come in, too, at any minute: "We got a rape and some clues and a witness—can you come and take over the investigation?" Homicide cops, like all members of the Investigations Division—Assault, the bomb squad, others—had backup duties for the uniformed division. Street cops had the same Procedure Manual, which they were supposed to read, but a lot of them didn't or wouldn't. It was easier to call out the detectives. And they went. Because that might be the difference that got a conviction. But things could be worse; Wager could be in Assault, the pressure cooker, where 90 percent of the crimes had a suspect and witnesses right there, and every suspect had to be charged or cleared within seventy-two hours. Now that was paperwork.

Wager finished his report and glanced over the dry paragraphs that it all boiled down to. Then he put it in the basket for the typist. "I'm going down to Records."

Max was shrugging into a sport coat that was too tight across the shoulders. "Say hello to Jo for me."

"Right."

He started that way, taking the stairwell instead of the oversized elevators. But the closer he came the slower he walked, because he wasn't quite sure what he wanted to say and, more important, he wasn't sure what she would say. That had been the problem with that routine report—rather than focusing on the shootings and the woman's broken statements, his mind had been framing words to Jo. And, the thought twisted the corners of his mouth, both narratives, the one on the page and the one in his mind, had the odor of death to them. Finally his feet stopped on the gray pebbled rug that hushed the constant traffic and tried to hide the street dirt that was tracked in by pair after pair of black shoes. He still hadn't answered his own question of what the hell he had to apologize for. She was the one who got wound up over what he said—and he hadn't meant it all that seriously anyway. But the way she took it, well, that indicated she probably did mean something when she kept harping on his accumulated vacation time. He damned well knew he stood to lose it; he'd lost more than a few weeks of vacation over the years because it seemed to pile up so quickly. And besides, he didn't like vacations; he'd tried one once and it was lousy. Lorraine never could understand that, either, so now she was married to a guy who was always taking vacations—some kind of stockbroker or something. And one thing Wager didn't need in his life was another Lorraine nagging about his damned vacation time.

With mingled loss and relief, Wager turned from the glass-faced entry of the records section and trudged back to the homicide office. Max was gone, the stand for the radio-pack empty on his desk, and Wager was glad. All morning he had felt the questions the big man had been on the verge of asking. And whenever Max neared Wager's desk, he would hunch lower over the scattered papers and memos and quick-reference telephone numbers to fend off Max's curiosity. Nosiness he'd call it in anyone except his partner. But Wager was having enough trouble trying to explain his feelings to himself without having to explain them to someone who had no business in it anyway.

He stared at the telephone on his desk; the records section was four numbers away—that close: just dial four numbers and ask for Officer Fabrizio. But first he had to make his arm move, and he felt the same kind of palsy that had silenced him last night and which had just slowed his steps outside her office. If he called and apologized, she would win that vague but very real thing Wager felt was threatened—the thing she labeled his insecurity or his macho. And all those complexities would be back again. He had been given this opportunity to regain a simple, untangled life. Now, if he wanted to, he could live without a schedule that accommodated someone else. It was a chance to get back to a life as free and alone as Tommy Sanchez's. All he had to do was nothing—just let enough time pass.

When he finally dialed a number, it was not to Records but to the Organized Crime Unit, an outfit he'd served in several years ago before coming to Homicide. The voice that answered gave him that peculiar feeling of stepping back to a place he had left long ago, and finding that not only was everyone else the same, but so was their view of him.

"Hello, Suzy—this is Gabe Wager."

"Gabe! I mean Sergeant Wager—how are you?"

"Fine. How are things over there?"

"Oh, golly, don't ask. It's budget time again—you know what that means."

"I sure do." And he also knew of the pressures the new city administration had brought for reorganizing the unit. That would make the budget narrative and its justifications all the more important. "Is Sergeant Johnston in?"

"Sure—just a minute."

Which was about how long it took before he heard the equally familiar voice, "Gabe! How's it going? Hey, what about the Gold? Six and one and a win over the Outlaws! That's playoffs, man!"

Things had not changed much at all, and Wager slipped into his familiar reply: "That's fine, Ed. It sure is."

"It really makes a difference to have a decent line, doesn't it? Gives the quarterback all day to throw."

"Right." Wager could still remember being called one of the front four, while Johnston spoke of himself as the quarterback. Sonnenberg, the unit commander, had been the coach. They were all supposed to go out and score against the bad guys. "What I called about, Ed—"

"And the running! Jesus, the running's really something this year!"

"Right, it's real good. Ed, do you have anything on a couple of kids named Sanchez? John and James. Brothers—late teens, early twenties, maybe. They work rodeo and probably do some ranching. Hired hands, most likely."

"Rodeo? I don't think we've got a thing on rodeo. What kind of ranch work do they do?"

"I'm not sure."

"Does it have to do with horses? Track betting? We got a Sanchez who's doing a little off-track action."

"What's his first name?"

"Emory. He's got a place out in Lakewood."

"That doesn't sound like it."

"Well, if I knew the crime category you wanted, I could look it up faster. That's how we reference our files now, by crime category: arson, embezzlement, extortion, fraud, gambling—"

"Try anything to do with horses and cows."

"Cows? They race cows now?"

"Ranches sell cow meat. Maybe there's something going on there."

"You usually find that with the processors, Gabe. We've got that listed under three headings: Fraud, Quality, and Weights and Measures."

"I'd appreciate a search, Ed."

"It's going to take a while. That's a lot of categories to cover. You have any other names? We can run the names through real quick."

"Just John and James Sanchez."

"Sanchez, John." Sergeant Johnston wrote it down. "Sanchez, James. I'll start with them. But like I say, it's going to take a while. We got budget hearing coming up and Suzy's all tied up in that."

"I understand."

"You're still over in Homicide?"

"Yes."

"I'll let you know what we find."

He thanked Johnston and thumbed his way through the directory of state offices. Ed was right—if the boys' names weren't on file somewhere, there was damned little to go on. DPD had the state's largest collection of contact cards, and he already knew they weren't there. And though there were ten million ways to reference and cross-reference material, an office only had time and space for a few methods, so that meant calling a lot of offices. The computer was supposed to improve on that, and it had in a few areas. But for some reason, Wager often found himself working outside those areas.

His eyes snagged on the number for the Animal Protection Office in the State Department of Agriculture. A woman answered, and when she heard what he wanted, the voice gained a note of bureaucratic worry over something that violated routine. "We're not allowed to divulge information like that over the telephone, Sergeant Wager. Any investigations we run or respondents we contact are treated as confidential."

"You can't tell me if a couple of rodeo cowboys have ever had problems with your office?"

"No, sir. Not without clearance from the director. I can connect you with him, if you wish."

"Not that important." And not what he wanted, either: a blizzard of request and approval forms that needed signatures from unit commanders and woke official curiosity about what in the hell Wager was doing. So much for the regulatory agencies. He pondered over whether or not to make the next call. In fact, if he hadn't promised Tommy, Wager wouldn't—he was beginning to feel more than a little foolish going around asking about the Sanchez kids. But like a lot of people, especially older ones, when Tom got a question in his head he'd fret and worry himself and everyone else until it was answered; and if Wager had to lie to him, he'd feel a lot worse than foolish.

"Juvenile Division, Sergeant Cole."

"Andy, this is Gabe Wager." He explained who he was looking for.

"Our files are sealed, Gabe. You know that."

"I don't want to see the files. I just want to know if the names are active."

A pause. "Sanchez. Jesus, we got so many Sanchezes. What about birthdates? You got that?"

"Just the approximate age. I can give you the father's name."

"Well, that'll eliminate half of them, anyway—the little bastards."

Wager told him as much as he knew.

"All right, hang on—I'll see what comes up."

In a couple minutes he came back with four names from the computer, but none of them matched Tommy's sons. "That's it, Gabe. That's all I got."

"OK, Andy. Thanks for the help."

Wager hung up, fingers lingering on the smooth plastic of the telephone. Then he swore and quickly hooked four numbers. "Jo Fabrizio, please."

"Officer Fabrizio, sir."

"You want to go out for a beer after work?"

"Am I supposed to know who this is?"

"Dammit, Jo, you know who it is. Yes or no, do you want to go out?"

"Are you sure you do?"

"I'm asking, aren't I?"

Maybe she figured that was the most she'd get by way of apology. At any rate, she said, "Might as well—it's the best offer I've had all day."

"I'll be by a little after four." Then he added in a quick mutter which she might not have heard. "And thanks."

. . .

My Brother's Bar had changed in a lot of ways: picture windows opening up one dark wall to bring in the light and curious glances from the street, another large room for rush-hour crowds, remodeled bathrooms that lost a lot of the aura which the dank, smelly stalls used to have. The last change didn't bother Wager, but the windows did; they even had potted plants hanging there, and next would come ferns. Then Wager would have to talk to Demetri—maybe take him out back and read state statute 18-4-507: Defacing Landmarks or Monuments. At least the barroom itself had not changed, and he led Jo to one of the small tables in a corner. He felt more at home with its dimness and the relaxed murmur of late-afternoon drinkers, and it was still his favorite place. No loud music, no tweedle and zap of electronic games, no television set. You could do what you came there for: sit and drink. And, if you wanted, you could talk.

"Hi, Gabe—the usual?"

He said yes and Jo nodded, and the waitress, sliding a clean ashtray on the table, went quickly to the pickup with the orders.

"Did you find out anything for Tommy?"

He shook his head. "I put out a few feelers. But nothing's turned up. I don't really expect it to."

"Why?"

"The lead's too vague—no specific crime, no names of associates. Unless there's a complaint record somewhere naming his sons, the chances are pretty bad for learning anything."

They talked about how disappointed Tom would be, and what other avenues Wager might try; they talked about the morning's homicides and about the officers they knew who would be competing in the International Police Olympics down in Arizona. They talked about anything except their argument, until finally, Wager, feeling his third beer loosen the taut muscles of neck and shoulders like a deep sigh, said he was sorry she'd thought he was serious last night.

"You were."

"Not really. Not at first, anyway."

"It sure sounded like it." Jo, still nursing her first beer, looked up. "What gets me is that you say you're fed up with women who hint around and never say what they mean. And then when I try to tell you something, you don't want to hear it."

"I'm willing to talk about whatever you want to. I just don't like guarding myself against being used."

"Vacation."

"Dammit—"

She laughed. "See? One word and your hackles are up."

"Well, that was the wrong word."

"Look, Wager, you don't want to be on your guard around me. Why should I have to be on my guard around you? Why shouldn't I be able to talk about whatever I want to with the person I care about? Why should part of my life be closed off because you close off part of your life? Don't you think I get fed up with men who get mad or hurt or sulk when I mention something they don't like?"

She was taking a lot of the things he felt and turning them around for use against him. Especially that part about not being able to bring up certain topics without someone getting hysterical. Lorraine had a whole encyclopedia of such topics, and now Jo was telling him that he did too. She should have been a lawyer.

"Well? Am I right or wrong?"

He took a deep drink and thought about that, and about what was the truthful answer. And when he decided, he felt something akin to a sense of freedom that surprised him—as if some internal fist which had been clenched around the dos and don'ts of his life had relaxed a bit and it wasn't so bad after all. "OK. I guess you're right. We should be able to talk about anything."

"You mean that?"

"Yeah, I do. So go ahead: talk."

She laughed again, more with those eyes than with her voice. "No, you start first. Or you'll say I'm manipulating you."

"All right. How'd you like to see a rodeo this weekend?"

CHAPTER 3

Jo thought it was a wonderful idea, and Wager learned something else about her: she knew a lot more about the sport than he did, especially girls' barrel racing.

"All girls go through a horsey stage, Gabe. Haven't you ever heard of *My Friend Flicka?*"

"Is that like *Lassie Come Home?*"

"Only if you've got a small horse or a big dog. I used to barrel race—Daddy bought a quarter horse for me named Doodles. She was quick—good speed and turning. But a lot of girls rode better than I did. I never made it past the Little Britches level."

"Why not?" Wager surged the Trans-Am up the wide lanes of I-70 toward Empire Junction and the Berthoud Pass turnoff. Ahead, still bearing large patches of snow on the gray-and-yellow rock above timberline, peaks rose sharply against the dark of high-altitude sky. Closer to the highway, the forested slopes showed streaks of talus slides and plunging streams from the spring runoff, which was heavy this year. A deep snow pack, a quick hot spring: the radio was talking about floods on both sides of the Divide, and already a couple of river rafters had drowned.

"I discovered boys. And cars. Daddy finally had to sell her. He sold the horse, the tack, the pickup truck and trailer, and he used to say if the barn had wheels, he'd have sold that, too."

"He didn't like horses?"

"He didn't like taking care of her. She was never ridden, so she acted up a lot. It was my job, and I didn't do it. Too busy having fun in high school."

The rodeo they headed for was a lesser one, like those sponsored by small towns all over Colorado. It was an amateur show, Jo explained, a pumpkin roller with small prizes and jackpots, and there wouldn't be any big-name cowboys from the Professional Rodeo Cowboys Association. "They won't waste a weekend on a show as small as this one." But they might see some of the association's permit holders, young cowboys trying to get enough experience and earn enough money to qualify for the big time. "A rider has to win a thousand dollars before he can get his PRCA card. So it just makes sense to go against people you think you can beat. It's sort of like minor-league baseball."

"I thought that's what college rodeo was for."

"That's another way of getting experience, and some good training, too, if the coaches are any good. Little Britches, High School Rodeo Association, Intercollegiate Rodeo, they're all good training. Most of the pros do it that way now."

"And for somebody who doesn't go that route, is this one of the ways?"

"About the only way. It's awfully hard, though, to come in green and compete against high school and college rodeo champions. There's a lot to learn, and a lot of the riders even at these small rodeos have been competing for five or ten years already."

Tommy had said the same thing when he telephoned Wager and told him that his sons were supposed to be at this rodeo. The stockman for the show had seen the names on the list of registrants and recognized them. "I don't know if you want to go over there, Gabe, but if so, it's on Saturday, near Winter Park."

"You want to come along?"

The telephone was silent, and Wager could imagine

Tommy sucking on a cigarette while he thought about it. "No, I guess not. They'd see me and wonder what the hell I was doing there. I got stock to look at, anyway."

"I haven't found any police record on either of the boys."

"I'm relieved to hear that. I did find out that John does some drinking at a place in Glenwood Springs—the Hanging Lake Lounge."

"Who gave you the information?"

"An old boy I used to travel with. He saw Johnny there three or four times, he said. John's working out that way, but he didn't know at what. I don't know if there's anything to it, but that's all I got."

"I'll check it out. If you hear any names, let me know."

"Will do, Gabe. *Adios.*"

And he had checked out the bar, with the same results: nothing official in police files, no contact card in the DPD computer.

They slowed behind a laboring tanker truck that jetted black smoke from its upright exhaust as the driver geared down on the long climb to the summit. When a passing lane opened, Wager swung out and floored the pedal, the Trans-Am settling against the pull of its engine to dodge quickly back in front of the truck.

"I'm glad the road's not icy." Jo looked over the edge of the unguarded highway where the tops of pine trees fell away toward a foamy streak glimmering far below. "It's a bad road in winter."

"You come up here skiing a lot?"

The question meant more than it asked, and Jo answered its full range of inquiry. "Not anymore."

That was the way they handled the inevitable questions about each other's past. First, Wager tried not to ask because it wasn't any of his business; and if on some impulse he did, he refused to pick at scabs. That had been another of Lorraine's specialties which surfaced through the cracks of their marriage: she just had to know—completely, precisely, absolutely. She had to know what he meant when he said anything and what he meant when he was silent. And if he had no intended meaning at all, she had to know what that meant, too. She would have, he'd often thought, done damn well in the old Interrogation Unit. "I never learned to ski."

"We'll have to try cross-country."

"Is it any easier than downhill?" Wager had seen a film of a hot-dogger bouncing down cliffs of humped snow, blond hair wild against an aura of glaring sun, knees almost as high as his black goggles while snow clods exploded from his skis. He'd be willing to try it. Even if it broke both his legs—and it probably would—Wager would try it. But he wasn't sure how much he'd enjoy it.

"Not necessarily. But we can go at our own pace. We won't try anything we're not ready for."

"All right," said Wager, relieved. "You got a date for next winter."

They crested Berthoud Pass, skirting a parking apron crowded with cars bearing a variety of out-of-state license plates. Beyond the heavy dark timbers of a restaurant, the towers of a cable car marched above stony tundra and snowfields toward the peak above. Across the highway, a closed chairlift disappeared among stunted pines. Ahead, flanked on the east by the wall of the Front Range, a gully dark with pines gradually widened into a broad valley that was patched here and there by the paler green of aspen stands. Far to the north, a band of ragged blue and snowy glimmer, was Rocky Mountain National Park.

"Sometimes I forget all this exists," murmured Jo.

Wager's eyes and mind were rested by it, too. It had been a long time—over a year?—since he had been away from the streets of Denver with their steady pulse of unnatural deaths and far from natural lives. He, too, had forgotten how clean a sky could be, how massively the earth could loom over the scratch of a highway down below, how far—when the walls and office towers and neon glare were gone—one could see. His hand touched hers resting on the seat between them. "It's peaceful."

Her hand turned up to welcome his.

Stretched across the highway that formed the main street, a red, white, and blue banner read "Welcome to Buckaroo Days." On the dozen or so lamp standards that marked a vague center to the string of buildings scattered down each side of the pavement, red, white, and blue ribbons spiraled up to a cluster of wind-tossed bows. A Saturday jam of pickup trucks and four-wheel-drive vehicles filled the lot of a large, modern grocery store advertising cold beer and picnic supplies. Car traffic moved slowly up and down the highway to nose in and out of the few side streets and to swing in sudden halt at various shops and motels and fast-food stores that filled the ground floors of timbered buildings whose cantilevered balconies thrust out over busy malls. Wager asked at a gas station for directions to the rodeo grounds and then followed the highway a mile or so until they saw the large sign and arrow pointing left: "Buckaroo Arena—Rodeo Today!"

He turned in behind an oversized pickup towing a horse trailer with two brown rumps jiggling against the sway of the dirt road. They lurched through the stately shade of an aspen grove and then into a stubbled field where teenagers wearing orange vests wagged their hands at the arriving cars and headed them into dusty parking rows. At the far end of the field where tires had mashed pale tracks in the mown grass, the arena's white paint glared in the sun, and they heard the quack of the announcer's voice introduce someone who mumbled something into the microphone and was answered by the sound of polite applause like a mild surf lifted on the wind.

"Do you want to look for them before we go into the stands?"

Wager nodded. "We can ask around, anyway." He wasn't sure what he would do if he found them. Check them over; see if they had two legs, two arms, one head, all regulation issue. Tell them hello from their dad, maybe. And perhaps admit to himself that they weren't the reason for this trip but the excuse—that it made Wager feel less guilty about sneaking out of Denver for a while.

He angled away from the line of people in boots and cowboy hats and jeans filing from the parking lot toward the grandstand gates. "Where are they likely to be?"

"Behind the chutes looking at the animals, I suppose. But we'll probably need a pass to get there."

They walked around the outside fencing, where officials and participants parked their cars. Here and there, cowboys unloaded gear from camper shells that weighed down the back of their pickup trucks; vans, their side doors and roof vents flung open for a breeze, showed other cowboys eating or smoking and working with ropes or leather rigging. Most were young, and near some stood nervous mothers and fathers asking if their son was sure he had this or that, or offering advice he already knew, or making him idly kick the dirt with red-faced embarrassment. Others, old enough to be free of parents, looked their way and grinned and turned to the more serious business of sizing up the girls. They flitted like butterflies through the cowboys' parking area and then resettled along the fence near the contestants' gate. There, number tags pinned to the backs of checkered shirts, young men filed in and out past a guard who looked like the others except for a cast on his leg and a badge on his shirt that said "Arena Policeman." Wager asked if he knew the Sanchez brothers.

"Not offhand. You got numbers for them?"

"No. But they're registered."

The guard called to one of the girls. "Teri, let me see that there program you got."

The girl, seventeen or eighteen and chewing gum behind lips that never closed, said sure and glanced carelessly at Wager in his city clothes and then eagerly back at a pair of cowboys wearing large shiny belt buckles.

"Yeah, here they are. Numbers thirty-seven and thirty-eight. They're in all five events, so they're probably over with the riding stock behind the chutes. They're holding the drawing now for the timed events," he explained. "Most of the boys like to be there. Sorry I can't let you in without a pass."

"Any place I can leave a message for them?"

From the stands came the steady clump of boots on

boards and a ripple of laughter at an exchange between a clown and the announcer.

"Arena secretary's office, I guess. It's over there." He pointed to a door leading to a small room tucked under the stands.

Wager thanked him and led Jo to the plank door. A hand-lettered sign said "Arena Secretary: If You Got Business Come In. If Not Keep Out." He opened the door.

It was a cramped room with a beat-up metal desk piled high with papers and folders and even a stack of black-and-white photographs of smiling cowboys. Thumbtacked to the unpainted board walls was a variety of lists and notices; half-buried on the desk, a portable radio reached its antenna up for air and a drawn-out voice sang, "I'm laying down my ace of hearts for you." A harried woman under a tangle of bleached hair looked up and tugged a cigarette off her lip. "You need something here?"

"I'd like to leave a message for James and John Sanchez. They're riders."

"Riders and ropers, too. Sure, stick it up on that wall there. But hurry up—I got about two minutes to get up to the booth and then this office closes." She turned back to the form and scratched at it with a pencil.

Wager tore a leaf from his green pocket notebook and scribbled a line, then found a free thumbtack and stuck it to the board under the messages sign. "If the office closes, how will they get this?"

"It's open at halftime for a little bit. It opens for payoffs as soon as the rodeo's over. If they win something, they'll sure as hell be here. If not, they might. You finished yet?"

"Yes ma'am."

Jo and Wager made their way into the bleachers to find a seat high in the open section. The covered seats, already full, were capped by a roofed box, and they could see the announcer in a white cowboy hat and fringed jacket lean out of the window with a microphone in his hand. On the raked dirt of the arena floor, a clown in baggy pants, red underwear, and fright wig was going through his routine with the announcer as he chased after a yapping dog.

Across the sandy oval, another tier of bleachers was filled
with restless movement, and beyond, gigantic and rising
like a ragged wall, the west side of the Front Range loomed
clear and sharp against the blue sky.

"What did you tell them?"

"I asked them to meet me by the contestants' gate after
the show."

"Are you looking for anything special?"

Wager shook his head. "I don't know if there's anything
to look for. But I promised I'd look, so I'll look."

Jo pointed at a flash of color and sparkle at the far end of
the arena. "They're getting set for the grand entry. I used
to love this part!"

"Did you do this?"

"Sure! I was on a girls' riding team, and we'd do the
county-fair rodeos around Denver—four or five every summer. Figure eights, cross-overs, in-and-outs—you name
it."

Wager couldn't name any of it. The most riding he'd ever
done was on a fenced track with a horse whose head came
up only when it faced the barn. Which was fine with
Wager. "Pretty exciting, was it?"

"The practices weren't, but the shows sure were. Everybody rode a lot faster then. And it can be dangerous, too, if
you tighten up the formations."

"But fun," he said, watching her eyes.

She nodded, a strand of dark hair blowing across her
forehead, and her smile light and quick with remembered
excitement. "Here they come!"

The announcer's voice rose until it was drowned out by
the frantic thump of the small band and finally by the
cheers of the crowd. From an opening in the fence at the
arena's far end, two columns of riders galloped hard, one
file led by the American flag, the other by the flag of Colorado. Standing in the stirrups and lashing their reins across
the horses' necks, the riders leaned forward, wind pushing
their hat brims back, and circled the grounds in two loops
that, still galloping at full speed, curved back to cross in the
center, then open to loop again. With the thud of hooves

and a spray of flying dirt, they circled once more at a gallop, the hoots and yelps of the crowd and the crash of the band driving them faster. Then they skidded to a halt in front of the announcer's booth, a long straight line of gasping horses and girls sitting at stiff attention. The flags snapped in the middle of the rank.

"Ladies and gentlemen, the Buckaroo Team Riders! And here comes the rodeo royalty, ladies and gentlemen, our Rodeo Queen, Miss Sharon Dingle, and her lovely court. . . ."

Quickly, the arena floor filled with winners, runners-up, and entrants to the local beauty contest; rodeo committee members; contestants, clowns, judges; and an assortment of Boy Scouts and service group representatives who helped make the show a success and who each deserved a big hand from the crowd. Following introductions and prizes awarded to winners of an earlier kids' rodeo came the National Anthem; and amid the cheers that covered the last few notes, Jo and Wager settled back for the first event, bareback bronc riding.

The Sanchez brothers' turns came near the end of the go-round, after a series of rides, some of which lasted the full eight seconds. But most ended with either the cowboy flying hard into the dirt or the horse choosing to run or twist rather than buck. James's name boomed out of the loudspeakers, and a second or two later the gate to chute two flew open and the horse and rider, plunging with jarring shocks, exploded onto the sand.

"It's a good ride," said Jo, and it was. Sanchez's left hand stayed high and clear of the horse and saddle, while his knees, pumping with the twisting leap of the horse, lifted to drive his spurs above the animal's shoulders. Writhing high, the unbridled horse twisted and tried to plunge its head down and heels skyward to rid itself of the flopping, clinging rider. But James, fist tight on the grip, hung on until the eight-second buzzer sounded and the pickup men galloped in to lift him off the bronc and guide the suddenly calm animal toward the exit. Vaulting across the pickup man's horse and into the churned dirt, James walked stiffly, head down, through the applause and cheers of the audience.

"The score on that fine ride for Jimmy Sanchez—the score on that one was . . . seventy-two points! That puts him in third place so far. Jimmy Sanchez riding Cottonmouth for seventy-two points and into the money, ladies and gentlemen!"

"Seventy points is a pretty good ride," said Jo. "The maximum's one-twenty, but no one ever gets that."

"Those are the judges?" Wager pointed toward two men standing near the chutes and scribbling something on their clipboards.

"Right. They give points to the horse and rider both, so the cowboys want to draw a horse that bucks really well."

"James looked like he did pretty well to me."

"His style wasn't as smooth as the first-place rider, especially when the horse was fishtailing."

The other brother, John, fired out of the next chute on a stocky, roman-nosed horse that hopped stiff-legged toward the far fence as one of the judges at the gate turned his back and held his clipboard down to his side. The announcer explained that the rider had a zero score for failing to have his spurs over the horse's shoulders when the animal made its first jump out of the chute. A pickup man raced to lift him off the animal, and he disgustedly grabbed his hat from the ground and knocked the dirt off as he trudged back through the applause.

Calf roping, steer wrestling, and saddle bronc riding came next, and both brothers failed to place in the money in any of the events. John completed his ride on the saddle bronc, but his score was low; James, almost flung from the pitching saddle, reached down with his free hand and touched leather, disqualifying himself. Finally, as the show reached halftime, Wager made his way through the crowd to the arena secretary's office to see if his note had been picked up. A man wearing a bolo tie and a hat shoved back to show his bald, freckled head sat behind the desk adding up figures on a creaky machine.

"Can I ask you a couple questions about the rodeo?"

The watery blue eyes glanced at Wager's slacks and city shoes, and the man nodded. "You a reporter, are you?"

"Just interested. Is this rodeo open to anybody, or do you have to have some kind of permit?"

"The only permit's a thirty-five-dollar entry fee for each event. Used to be twenty-five, but rodeo expenses go up about like everything else, don't they? Hope it don't go any higher—hard enough to fill up all the events as it is." His sandy eyebrows popped up beneath the hat's wide brim. "You want to enter? Too late for that—entries closed two days ago."

"It's not my line of work," said Wager. "Do a lot of cowboys enter more than one event?"

"Sure—at this kind of show. Fees aren't all that high. Not a hundred dollars or more, like at the big ones. This way they can afford to find out what they do best. Then they can specialize. When they go up to the bigger rodeos, they got two, maybe three specialties. If they're not trying for All Around Cowboy, they stick with one. Spread yourself too thin, you never make any money, not in the big shows. Too much competition."

"About how much can a cowboy win if he comes in, say, third in bronc riding, like Jimmy Sanchez?"

"Sanchez? I just divvied up the bareback pot now. He won, let's see, he won a hundred and twenty-five dollars. Third place is twenty percent, and we had a pot of six twenty-five for bareback, counting entry fees and prize money. Yep, a hundred and twenty-five."

"The progam says he's entered in five events. So his entry fees were a hundred and seventy-five, and so far he's won a hundred and twenty-five of it back?"

"It ain't no way to get rich, is it? 'Course if he came in first in a couple events, he'd be ahead. This here's a small rodeo—little better than jackpot, but not much. But they got to start somewhere; I don't know too many sports or businesses that give you good money to go out and learn your job, do you?" He paused to scratch at a hairy earlobe. "Government work, maybe. Run for office—good money there for beginners."

"What other expenses does a cowboy have besides entry fees?"

"Oh, travel's the big one. That costs a lot. Most of them sleep in their trucks, but they still got to pay for gas, and it's a long way between rodeos. And food. Never met a cowboy wasn't hungry. If you're a roper or dogger and you got your own horse, you pay for his travel and keep, too. And if you don't, you got to rent a horse. Most cowboys at this level, they rent for a percentage of the prize money. 'Course, if they don't win, they don't pay. Now, a man with a good horse to rent, he's going to pick up some extra money. You can make some money judging or working around the grounds, too, but most of them want to be out there in the competition. Injury—this here rodeo has a real good policy: we pay the emergency care and one follow-up visit. Anything else is up to the cowboy. No hospitalization—we can't afford that kind of insurance. If you're a PRCA member, you can get a group policy for that, but none of these boys got their cards. And if you're married, you got all those expenses, too. But, hell, these boys, none of them's fool enough to be in rodeo and be married, too." He laughed a single high-pitched note. "Don't tell the girls that, though. Everyone of them thinks they're going to get them a cowboy!"

"How many rodeos like this does a cowboy go to in a season?"

"Like this? Oh, thirty, maybe forty—there's jackpot rodeo every Wednesday up near Granby, and a lot of these boys ride in that. And county fairs. Some of them last three or five days, so you can win average money as well as day money. If a fella wants to rodeo, there's plenty around, especially during the summer. But there's not much money in it. You get in the professional circuits, now, and go to a hundred, a hundred and fifty rodeos a year, then you might make some money. Of course, your expenses are higher, too, and no guaranteed income. Cheyenne— Frontier Days—that comes later in June. And the National Western in Denver. That one's in January. That's your real big ones around here. You'll see the best stock and the best cowboys at them. Got some other ones, too—not as big, but they pay: the Coors Chute-Out Circuit. They got regionals and finals, too."

"Any of these cowboys ride in the big ones?"

"Well, maybe in time, if they're good enough. That Jimmy Sanchez boy you mentioned, he might make it in a couple years if he gets good enough. But he's got a lot to learn. And a lot of people to beat to get there."

"What's a good rider make when he's at the top?"

"Rider? A good rider, I'm talking about, he can make twenty, thirty thousand. If he's real good in two events, he can double that. If he wants to be Cowboy of the Year, he's going to have to win fifty or sixty thousand."

"That's a lot of money."

"And if you're on top of the heap long enough, you can get endorsements and advertising and even movie work. It's worth going after, all right. But damn few ever get there." He lifted his face to the roar of voices that spilled out of the stands. "Barrel racing's started. Don't want to miss that—my granddaughter's riding today."

Wager made his way back to Jo, stopping to pick up barbecue sandwiches and cups of beer and to balance them past knees and the brims of cowboy hats until he made it to his seat.

"This tastes great!" Jo dabbed at a smear of barbecue sauce that landed on her jeans. "Wears well, too."

On the arena floor, a ground man sprinted out to right a yellow barrel that had been knocked over and to rake smooth the churned path of the last rider. The announcer told the audience about the history of Buckaroo Days and how they grew out of the first local rodeo in 1897.

"Did you see them?"

"No, and the note was still there. Jimmy won a hundred and twenty-five dollars on the bareback ride."

"That's not bad. There were a dozen who didn't win anything."

"Right. Now he's only fifty dollars in the hole on entry fees. And John hasn't won anything yet."

Jo sipped at the beer, which left rings of foam inside her

plastic cup. "Are you trying to tell me something, mister detective?"

Money may not have been the root of all evil, but Wager believed it was way ahead of whatever was in second place. "I just wonder how they pay for it all." With rape or homicide, there were often other, less rational motives. But with many crimes, it was simply that someone was trying to get a little more a little quicker than the law allowed.

"They work all week and spend their pay on Saturday rodeos. A lot of amateur cowboys do that."

"I see."

The barrel righted, the announcer introduced the next rider, and she came galloping into the arena through the tunnel at the far end. Shouts and cheers and howls of "Go, Connie, go!" spurred horse and rider through tight loops around the barrels, and Jo provided a commentary of things Wager should look for. She had praise for the riders who stood lightly in the stirrups and leaned forward far enough to talk in the horse's ear; their ponies hunkered down and dug furiously with hind legs as they spun past one barrel and dashed for the next. Then, as each rider lapped the final barrel, the entire arena cheered her final sprint for the timing lights that stood on tripods just in front of the tunnel.

"I never could do that," said Jo. "You have to try for tenths and hundredths of a second, and I always leaned back going around the barrels. That slowed us down."

"Can they get hurt at this?"

"If a horse goes down, sure. And I saw a girl get a concussion when her horse ran into the tunnel wall crossing the finish line."

"But that wasn't why you quit."

"No—I guess I never was afraid. It goes too fast . . . it's too exciting to worry about that. I just lost interest because of all the work to do it well."

The final contest was bull riding, and Jo said that was the only event that scared her.

"The bulls go after the riders. They try to hook or step on them. I've even seen bulls try to roll on a rider."

"Isn't that what the clown is for?" asked Wager. "To distract the bull and give the rider a chance to get away when he's thrown?"

"I know that's what's supposed to happen. But it doesn't always work." Her long hair stirred in a sudden gust of wind that swirled around the stands, lifting loose scraps of papers and dust and chaff. "The horses try not to step on anyone, but a bull goes after anything it sees. They're killers."

The first bull, part Brahma, supported what Jo said. It lunged into the arena hooking hard at the rider clinging like a wart to the loose skin of its back. A quick spin and sudden reversal and the cowboy, hatless now, was flung aside like a chip. The bull, bell clanking wildly as it pulled the grip rope away from the animal's stomach, aimed a horn at the scrambling cowboy while one of the clowns, the bullfighter, slapped at it with his hat and danced away toward the barrel clown. Spearing first one way then another with its thick, blunted horns, the bull caught sight of the barrel and veered in supple motion to thud it solidly as the clown curled inside and howled with mock terror while the rubber-coated barrel wobbled toward the fence. A gate swung open, and the bull, calmer now without rider or bell, disappeared from the arena with a final kick of its heels at the gateman.

"Wow," said Jo. "You've got to be crazy to be a rodeo cowboy, and crazier still to get on one of those things."

Wager wasn't going to argue that. "It looks like the rider got hurt."

Hatless, the young man staggered toward the chutes with an arm dangling straight but oddly loose at his side. Even from this far away, Wager could see his lips stretched over the glimmer of gritted teeth and the sheen of heavy sweat on his forehead. A couple of cowboys hopped off the fence to walk with him as the loudspeakers announced no ride for the contestant and asked the crowd to give that cowboy a big hand for a real good try.

James once more finished out of the money on a bull that

wanted to run more than buck, but John came in fourth with one of the few rides that managed the full eight seconds. After the final contestant and the business of thanking the audience for attending and promising to see them all at next year's rodeo, the announcer said goodbye and happy trails, and Wager and Jo drifted with the crowd stepping down the bleacher seats to fill the aisles and the stairs outside. They angled out of the flow of people and made their way to the contestants' gate, where a small crowd waited for relatives or friends or just to glimpse their favorite riders. Jo and Wager worked their way to the rail fence and searched among the numbered shirts for James or Johnny.

"There's number thirty-four!" Jo pointed to a cowboy straining to heft a large red nylon bag through the gate. Wager caught his eye.

"You're James Sanchez?"

He was shorter than Wager and, except for a tightness at the corners of his mouth, looked even younger than his seventeen years. The dark curly hair and the eyes that were almost black reminded Wager of the way Tom had looked so many years ago. Lowering the heavy bag, he said, "Yeah. You the fella that put up that note?"

"Gabe Wager. This is Jo Fabrizio."

James touched his fingers to his hat brim. "Ma'am."

"Let me help you tote this." Wager hoisted one handle of the rigging bag and half-followed James as he wound through parked trucks and vans toward a dark green Dodge pickup with an aluminum camper mounted over the bed. Both were new and clean, and the Colorado license plates bore the three letters and numbers of the updated issue. Wager hadn't memorized the new plates, but he guessed that the USM prefix meant a Western Slope county. "Congratulations on your win."

"It was a rank horse. Anybody ought to ride good on a horse like that."

"A lot of riders didn't stay on at all," said Wager.

"Well, I'd of liked to done better."

"Is the stock a problem at these rodeos?"

"Yes, ma'am. It ain't very consistent. And the best ones go on up to the big rodeos pretty quick."

"I thought you should have had a reride on the bull."

"He had his mind set on running, didn't he?" He unlocked the camper door, and they shoved the bag into the truck. "But I should have rode better even at that."

"At least you didn't break your arm like that one rider," said Wager.

James gave a little laugh. "Yeah—third time, same arm, for him. He just got the cast off last week."

Wager glanced at the saddles and ropes lining one side of the truck bed. "All that equipment's yours? It looks pretty expensive."

"The rigging? Yeah, it's best to have your own. And it does cost, that's a fact." He folded up his shirt sleeve and began unwinding tape from his right arm. "Anything particular you wanted to see us about, Mr. Wager?"

"I'm a friend of your dad. I told him I was coming up here, and he asked me to say hello, that's all."

James carefully folded the elastic tape and reached down to unbuckle the straps that held his dull spurs on scarred and deeply creased boots. "Haven't heard much from him in a long time." He straightened, the rowel clinking against its stop, and looked at Wager with eyes that flatly masked any feeling. "In fact, I didn't even think he knew we were alive."

"He wanted to get up here," Wager lied. "But he had to go to Oklahoma for some stock."

"Yeah, right. Well, that's nothing new. He always did have something better to do."

"Who has something better to do, Jimmy?" A taller cowboy rounded the side of the truck. A couple of years older and heavier across the shoulders, he had the same dark hair and eyes. But the chin on this one was bonier and longer, and bore a thin white scar just above the jawline like an old knife wound. "You the one that left the note for us?"

James introduced them to John. "He says Daddy asked him to say hello."

"Oh?" John's mouth widened slightly in a polite smile. "Thanks. That nice of you. Nice of him to think about us."

"We enjoyed the rodeo," said Jo. "Do you have another one next weekend?"

John's eyes went up and down Jo's shirt and jeans with a practiced glance before he smiled. "Sure do. We'll be over in Utah. Week after, down in Walsenburg. Maybe we'll do a little better there—I sure hope so. That's a PRCA rodeo."

"Are you PRCA members?" she asked.

"I got my permit. Jimmy's got to wait until he's eighteen for his. If Ma signs for him."

Jo had told Wager about the certification rules: after a rider obtained his beginner's permit, he had three years to win a thousand dollars in PRCA-sanctioned rodeos in order to earn his full membership card. "If she won't," said Wager, "maybe your dad will."

"We don't need him to sign," said James. "We don't need him for nothing, now."

"Jimmy, these folks ain't interested in that. What line of work you in, Mr. Wager?"

"I work for the city of Denver. Do you rodeo all year round?"

"We aim to in time. I guess it runs in the family."

"Can you make a living at it?"

"Didn't look that way today, did it? Cost us some money today, didn't it, Jimmy?"

"Do you win enough to pay expenses?" asked Jo.

"Not yet. We work a ranch over in Ute County."

"Which one?" asked Wager.

John hesitated, eyeing Wager. Then he shrugged. "The T Bar M."

"They let you off every weekend to rodeo?"

"Well, yeah. I'm the ranch manager and I work it out so's we can rodeo."

"That's lucky."

"Right. Jimmy and me, we're real lucky." John gestured to his brother to take off the number pinned to the back of his shirt. Then he did the same for James. Behind them, three cowboys watched a long-legged blond stride through the parking lot. She saw them looking at her and spit a stream of brown juice their way. A worn circle marking a tobacco can rose and fell on the smooth, taut curve of her jeans. One of the cowboys punched the other on the shoulder and said, "Gawdamn, Hern, how'd you like to swap slobber with that one?"

"Just what kind of work do you do for the city of Denver, Mr. Wager?" asked John.

"Police."

"Police? Well, now." He tied a coiled rope with a thong and laid it carefully in the camper. "Wouldn't have thought Daddy'd have a policeman for a friend."

"We grew up in the same neighborhood. I've known him a long time."

"Can't say Jimmy or I have. But no hard feelings—a man does what he's got to do, right, Jimmy?"

"Right."

"Maybe you and Tom can be in the same rodeo sometime," said Wager. "I know he'd like that."

"Might work out that way. We'll see what happens." John touched a forefinger to his hat brim. "If you'll excuse us, ma'am. We got to turn in our numbers and then get on down the road."

They watched the two cowboys walk with their stiff-legged gait toward the arena secretary's office, the tailored yokes of their western shirts rolling slightly from side to side. James's hat bobbed with the strength of what he was saying, and John's Stetson wagged a brief negative as they turned out of sight.

"Did you ever notice," Wager asked Jo, "how friendly civilians are after you tell them you're a cop? It's almost as warm and cozy as saying you have herpes."

"You could tell them you have AIDS."

"That's not my kind of disease, kid."

"We've got a whole weekend to find out."

CHAPTER 4

A couple of days passed before Wager managed to get in touch with Tom Sanchez, and there wasn't much to tell him when he did.

"I've asked around and haven't come up with a thing, Tommy. I'm still waiting on information from a couple other sources, but I don't expect too much."

"All right, Gabe. I appreciate your trying." The telephone line crackled as if water had seeped into the cable. "Did you get a chance to see them last weekend?"

"Yes. James came in third on the barebacks, and John got fourth on the bulls."

"Well, that ain't too bad. That's a good little amateur rodeo over there, so that ain't bad at all." Tommy cleared his throat. "Did—ah—did they look OK, Gabe?"

"They looked fine. They said they planned to be in Walsenburg in a couple of weeks."

"The Walsenburg rodeo? I could maybe get over that way. . . . You told them I said hello?"

"I did."

"What'd they say?"

"They didn't sing halleluja."

"No, I don't reckon they would."

"But they didn't tell me to go to hell, either. I think they'd like it if you went to see them."

"Well, I'll think about it." There was something else on his mind, and finally he came out with it. "I've been doing some more asking around, and I can't come up with nothing to get my hands on neither. It's like the *viejos* used to say, there's an itch but no place to scratch."

"I can't do any more than I'm doing, Tommy."

"I know that, Gabe—I'm not asking you to. But you remember that place over in Glenwood? That bar I told you about?"

He didn't, but he said he did.

"Well, I found out that Johnny drinks with a fella named Jerry Latta there. I asked this old boy to find out who Johnny was drinking with, and he said it was this Jerry Latta."

Wager remembered now: the Hanging Lake Lounge, where someone had seen John spend some time. Wager sighed and wrote it down; he'd wanted some more names, and now the old cowboy had brought one. "I'll see what I can find out on him." Which would probably be nothing. How many people could a rodeo cowboy drink beer with? "Do you know anything about him? Is he in rodeo?"

"No. I checked that—he's not a PRCA member, anyways. I never heard of him before."

"All right. Do you know John's a ranch manager?"

"Manager? Ranch manager?"

"That's what he said."

"I'll be damned!"

"How old is John?"

"Nineteen, twenty. He's a couple years older than Jimmy. That's really something: ranch manager! What ranch is it?"

"The T Bar M. Ever heard of it?"

"No. Where's it at?"

"Ute County."

"I never heard of it. I don't get out there too much."

"Isn't he young to be a manager?"

"Well, yeah. But he's got a lot of experience—and somebody over there must know a good man when they see one. That really brightens my day!"

"How much does he get paid for that kind of work?"

"Depends on how big the ranch is. It could be twice as much as what they pay a regular hand. But even if it ain't, that's a real good start for somebody that young. Ranch manager!"

And it offered a happy alternative to John's wasting his life in rodeo. "James works there, too."

"Now that's good—that Johnny's looking after his brother. That speaks real good of him, don't it?"

Wager answered the muted plea in the man's voice. "Yes. If something turns up, I'll give you a call, Tom."

"Appreciate it, Gabe—*gracias, amigo.*"

But nothing came up that tour or the next, and after a few more, Tommy and his problems were buried under the steady drizzle of cases spawned by the heat that filled the city's streets and left them baking long after the shadows of the mountains brought relief from the cloudless sun. The heat forced people out of their apartments and houses to sit on dark front porches or stroll the sidewalks and try to find a puff of cool air. It sent others into the air-conditioned bars to swig beer and sweat and finally to get happy or careless or mean. It led women to open their windows when they went to bed in the hopes of trapping a stray breeze, or to leave the back door ajar with the screen locked in futile security. All these things that in earlier times would have been harmless relief from the heat now made people vulnerable to those who had been waiting.

Wager and Max finished the day shift and rotated to the night, a new schedule that ran from 7:00 p.m. to 3:00 a.m. It put two homicide officers on duty for an hour past the 2:00 a.m. closing time for bars, the period when most of the drunken trouble was pushed out onto the streets to either sober up or explode. The hours from 3:00 to 8:00 in the morning were supposed to be covered by a homicide officer who was on call. All that meant, of course, was an extra stretch of duty that helped cover the manpower shortage and was not registered on the work roster unless the officer responded to a homicide. It was the new administration's attempt to cut down on overtime that had to be compensated for, but it didn't work. When a case came in at 2:45, the duty watch couldn't shrug and say to hell with it, let the on-call handle it. Instead, they grabbed a radio-pack and took the elevator down to the stale-smelling basement where the official cars were parked in their shadowy stalls. Then they squealed their tires across town through empty red lights to the cluster of figures looming over the twisted shape on the sticky sidewalk in front of a bar's orange-and-green neon.

"What's this one?" asked Max.

The uniformed officer wagged his flashlight beam across the body. "Stabbing. The ME's already been here."

"He was found on his back like that?"

"No—his friends turned him over after he got cut."

The flash of strobe lights from the police photographer winked like heat lightning against the dark storefronts on each side of the bar. It was a quick record of the site and the corpse. The lab photographer's real work would come at the morgue while they undressed the victim. As each layer of clothes came off, pictures would establish the location of all wounds, the angles of penetration, the cause or causes of death. But that would wait for the day shift. The victim wasn't going anywhere, and it cut down on the overtime.

"What's that all over him?" asked Wager.

"Beer. His girlfriend poured a couple pitchers of beer on him trying to wake him up after he went down."

"Was she sober enough to tell you anything?"

"None of them's sober. But here's what I got so far."

Walking Max and Wager through the action, the officer—a young one whom Wager did not recognize—traced the fight that started as the bar closed. "The victim's name is Sam Walking Tall and the assailant's been identified as Robert Smith."

"Is he an Indian, too?"

"That's what Sam's girlfriend says. That's her over there in the doorway." He pointed to a figure sitting on a low step and propped against the brick entry. Her head rested heavily on folded arms, and long gray-and-black strings of hair hung across her knees and brightly patterned dress and skinny shanks. "Looks like she's out again."

"I hope she tells the same story when she's sober," said Max.

"She said Sam and this Robert Smith knew each other on the reservation up in South Dakota—the Rosebud Reservation. Anyway, they were arguing all night long, and when the bar closed, Sam and Molly White Horse—that's her name—came out of the bar and turned here."

"Facing south?"

"Facing south. They went about six steps and Robert Smith came out of that doorway there and stabbed him."

"Did he say anything? Did Sam fight or challenge him or anything?"

"Not according to Molly. He just stepped out and swung and Sam went down, and Robert Smith ran off in that direction, west, across the street and into that alley over there."

"Anybody go after him?"

"Hell, they could hardly stand up. Anyway, they turned him over and saw he'd been stabbed, and the bartender called the police. Meantime, Molly's got this pitcher of beer and she's crying and yelling for Sam to get up, and pouring it over him like this." The shadow of his arm dipped to the still figure. In the background, black uniforms not quite invisible in the pale of the street lamps, the man-and-wife team of the Cadaver Removal Service waited to be called foward. Behind them, a news photographer kneeled to take a long-range picture of the scene and the police; and Gargan, crime reporter for the *Post*, stepped over the fluorescent tape and aimed toward Wager.

"Stay outside, Gargan. You know the rules."

"It's good to see you, too, Wager. What happened?"

He took the reporter's arm and led him away from Max and the uniformed officer. "You basic barroom stabbing." At least the television people weren't here screwing up the scene by shoving and scuffling to get closest and to interview witnesses before the police got to them. Their crews went home at midnight, but Gargan made up for them.

"Now stand over here till we get through."

"What is he, an Indian?"

"That's right. We'll tell you all about it when we get our investigation completed."

"Sure you will, Wager. I've heard that one before. Hey, Max—what's the story?"

Max lifted a hand but stood where he was with the still-talking officer; Wager tapped Gargan's bony chest with a finger. "Stay out of the way. Period."

"'Period'? Jesus, Wager, you almost sound like you can read."

"Nobody can read your stuff." He turned back to Max, ignoring the drawn-out haa-haa that Gargan threw after him. Wager could not remember the beginnings of his feud with the reporter, and in fact the beginnings were no longer important; Gargan was simply a shit.

Max was asking the officer, "Is the bartender still around?"

"Yeah. Inside there cleaning up. He didn't see the stabbing, but he verified that Sam and Robert had been picking at each other earlier."

"He's sober?"

"About the only one."

"OK, thanks. Write up what you've got and we'll take statements from the witnesses."

They tried to, anyway. The bartender, in a practiced way, told them what he had seen and then asked if he could close up and go home. "The wife'll be worried. She don't sleep good until I get home."

They let him.

Molly said she didn't have a home now that Sam was dead, and she wished she was dead too, and that if Wager couldn't give her something to drink would he at least shut up and let her go to sleep.

"This Robert Smith, Molly, you want us to get him, don't you? Molly, do you hear me?"

"I hear you."

"You want us to get the guy that stabbed Sam, don't you? Where does Robert Smith live, Molly?"

"Don't know."

"What about friends? Do you know any of his friends? Molly?"

"She's out again, Gabe. Let's take her in to sleep it off. She can tell her story in the morning."

"Max—hey, Max, how about telling me what's going on? Is that a witness? Did she stab him? Come on, Max, good police relations with the fourth estate, right?"

It took almost half an hour to book Molly into the detention center with an isolation hold on her. The turnkey promised she'd have a bath and breakfast and be able—if not willing—to talk to the duty officers tomorrow. The rest of the paperwork, including the responding officers' reports, took another hour to finish, package up, and leave in the tray to be combined with the lab reports when they came down tomorrow. Max finally talked to Gargan while Wager finished the cover letter for the captain to read in the morning, and the two men wearily rode the elevators to the main floor and walked out into the thinning summer night. This was one of the worst times, when the coffee tasted like sour water, the long hours piled like stones on weary shoulders, and a vacation didn't sound so bad after all. Above them, gaining outline against the sky, office towers rose toward a coming dawn; at the buildings' feet, darkness still filled the streets and alleys and covered whatever hole Robert Smith had found to crawl into. Down those alleys cruised police cars, their lights probing the corners, and within a few hours the day shift would begin to gather the facts of Robert Smith's life: where he came from, what he was doing in Denver, where he lived and worked, who his friends were, and where he might have run. He would be found. Then the statements and paperwork and laboratory reports and testimony would all be pulled together for his day in court. And Wager and Max would log another couple of hours of unpaid overtime.

"Take it easy, Max."

"Good night, Gabe."

· · · · ·

"Did Tom get down to Walsenburg to see his sons?" Jo sipped a glass of white wine with her seafood; she had already put in her eight hours and was unwinding.

Wager, going on duty, washed his supper down with a cup of coffee. "I don't know. I talked to him a couple of weeks ago, but not since."

It was difficult to meet Jo; she was on a day schedule and getting ready for work while he slept behind the tightly drawn shades of his apartment. But they managed an occasional dinner in the two hours between their shifts. Now they sat at a corner table in a restaurant crowded with young office workers meeting friends for drinks or an early dinner while the afternoon rush hour passed them by.

"That was a good weekend." She smiled in that quiet, almost secret way that had become a sort of code between them.

It had indeed been a good weekend, and Wager answered her smile, admiring her slightly high cheekbones and the way they tilted the corners of her eyes to match that gentle smile. "Maybe we should do it again."

"Too bad you have to go to work tonight. We could reminisce."

That would be good, too. "I've been thinking of taking a vacation."

"You what? What was that word?"

He knew she'd give him some heat. "You heard me. If I don't take the time, I'll lose it. That's what you told me."

"Hey, that's not my fault. It's department policy."

"Right, well, I've been thinking about it." And Chief Doyle had left a memo on his desk reminding him that he had ninety days in which to apply for his vacation and compensatory time. After that date he would receive the gratitude of Denver's citizenry for his contribution and start again from zero. "How much time do you have coming?"

"Is that an invitation?"

"Well, sure. Do you think I'd go on one of those damned things alone?"

"Since it's the first I've heard of it, I don't know what to think."

"Look, you've been yelling about a vacation. I assumed it was because you wanted to take yours with me. Wasn't it?"

"I have not been yelling!"

"You sound like you want to now."

"You're damned right I do." Her fork stabbed a shrimp curled in the rice. "And with good reason."

"What are you getting mad at? It's what you wanted—a vacation. Now all of a sudden you don't want to go?"

"Look, Wager, in the first place, I did not yell at you about a vacation. If you want to take one, fine. If not, that's fine too. It's your decision. In the second place, you're taking it for granted that I plan my life around yours. I don't. I earn my own money, I pay my own way, I've got my own life. If you want me to do something with you, you can ask me. Maybe I will and maybe I won't—but that'll be my decision to make. Not yours. I used to let a man tell me what to do, and I'm not about to start that again."

"I'm not trying to tell you what to do. We talked about this earlier, and I thought it was something you wanted. So I assumed—and with good reason—that you wanted to go on a vacation with me. Now what—you want me to send you a written invitation?"

"Yes, I want an invitation. That's a lot better than being dragged along without being asked. But mostly I want you to take this vacation for your own sake. If you want it, take it. If not, don't take it for my sake—I don't want to be blamed for it."

"Is that what you think? That the vacation's some kind of sacrifice?"

"Isn't it? Isn't that what you've been feeling? That's what it sounds like." She mimicked him: "'If I don't take the time I'll lose it—that's what you told me.' 'You've been yelling about a vacation.'"

He considered that. "Well, a little, maybe. I wouldn't have wanted a vacation at all if you hadn't said something. But here's what you haven't thought about, Officer know-it-all Fabrizio: we had a good weekend. I really enjoyed being up in the mountains with you. And I'd like to do more of it. So I wanted to take our vacations together. And

I thought that was what you wanted. Now is it or isn't it?"

"Yes."

"Then what the hell is all this fuss about?"

Jo sighed and closed her eyes a moment. "It's about style, Gabe. Yours. Sometimes it's like you have blinders on. You're going to get from point A to point B no matter what it costs you or anyone else, and to hell with anything or anybody who gets in your way."

He believed he understood what she was saying, but it didn't sound all that bad to him. "Anybody who's not stubborn better not be a cop. I'm a cop."

"That phrase covers a multitude of sins."

"Gargan said that once."

"The reporter?"

"Yeah. Only he was talking about police shakedowns and payoffs. A very funny guy."

"Well, I'm talking about us. Sometimes I think we excuse things in ourselves by saying 'I'm a cop,' as if that explained it all."

This time he didn't understand. "What things?"

"A hardness, maybe. A cynicism. An aggressiveness. And an increasing isolation from the very thing we swear to serve and protect."

A cop could afford to talk that way if all she dealt with was records. But it was different on the street. There, a cop who was seen as soft caused more trouble than he prevented because people would try to get away with more. You didn't have to go out and beat on skulls twice a day; but unless it was clear you were willing to, there was no respect from the street. And the street never gave anybody anything for free. "My style with you is too cynical and aggressive? Is that what you're telling me?"

The glint of humor in those golden eyes. "There is some of that, Officer Wager; there certainly is." Then the humor went away. "But what I think I mean is how easily we can cut each other off. Both of us. We have our jobs and so we don't really need each other—or anyone else. When you think about it, that's a little frightening. It's like our world is distant from everyone else's, and within that world, we're each distant from the other."

Yes. As Wager had learned from age sixteen on, every man died alone. When you accepted that fact, a lot of others followed, including the knowledge that every man lived alone, too. And that was something else Lorraine had not been able to stand. "You want to walk a beat holding hands?"

"Now you're really trying to be cynical—and dense. You know that's not what I mean."

"Maybe, maybe not. What I do know is this, Jo: a man who puts on that uniform better not count on anybody to help him who's not in uniform. And a lot of times, you can't count on them, either. You'd better believe you're out there alone. You start believing you're not . . . well, that's when you get in trouble."

"I know that, Gabe. But that's the street, and this isn't. It's the carrying over of that attitude into our feelings for each other that's frightening. Two minutes ago you could easily have told me to go to hell and walked out, and I wouldn't have said a thing to stop you. Just like," she added, "the other night. For no reason we argued and then we split and it could have stayed that way. I didn't want it, but I was willing to let it happen."

"I didn't want it either. I called you up later, didn't I?"

She laughed. "And gave me an ultimatum: beer or fear. I really like you, Gabe. I have fun with you—when you let yourself have fun—and you're good to sleep with. No, don't start acting nervous and tough; I'm not looking for a husband. I don't even want to use the word 'love.' But I like you very much, and I wouldn't want to be without you. Yet these moments come when I could shrug you off, and that's what frightens me—I wonder if I'm becoming an isolated function instead of a person."

"And you think that's what's happened to me?"

"Sometimes, yes."

Maybe it had. God knew that sounded like what Lorraine used to say in one way or another, that Wager was a cop and nothing else—and she wanted something more. "You know, one of the reasons I don't like vacations is that when I get back, my timing's off. It takes a couple tours to feel like I fit in again—to be able to see things with my skin as well as my eyes. What I'm trying to say is, yes, I do feel like a function, and it doesn't bother me. What the hell, it's what I'm paid for; it's who I am. What I am is who I am. And when I function well, I feel good. Everything else comes second."

"Everything?"

He nodded, not really wanting to say the word, but not willing to lie, either. "Yes."

"We're a lot worse off than I thought."

"So we enjoy what we've got while we've got it."

It was her turn to nod as she stared at the unfinished plate on the red-and-white cloth. Then, with a shrug, she glanced at her watch. "It's almost seven. You'll be late."

"Right." Wager signaled for the check, trying to hide the relief he felt at seeing an end to this conversation, one that forced him to poke into areas of self that he preferred to leave sleeping.

In the parking lot, Wager held open the door to his Trans-Am for Jo. She hesitated before sliding in. "Are you sure you want to spend this vacation together? Are you sure it might not commit you to more than you're ready for?"

A touch of bitterness in that? Wager almost said he felt safe enough, but that sounded harsher than he meant. "We'll see what happens," he said. "You might decide you don't want a damn thing to do with me."

"I might."

.   .   .

The first person Wager saw in the echoing lobby of District One headquarters was Police Reporter Gargan. Wager pretended to be interested in a spot on the wall back by the elevators, but there weren't many places to hide as he crossed the expanse of brown tile floor, and Gargan called to him, trotting over from the desk sergeant's counter, a jingle of keys and coins in his pockets.

"Wager—wait a minute. I got some questions for you."

"I've got to be on duty in five minutes, Gargan."

"Won't take that long."

There was something different about the reporter, and it took Wager a couple of seconds to figure it out: no black turtleneck. Because of the heat, he had traded his usual uniform for a short-sleeved shirt open at the neck and bristling at the pocket with an array of ballpoint pens. It left him looking thinner and oddly nude and vulnerable, like seeing your father in his underwear.

"Remember the stabbing the other night? The Indian who got stabbed?"

"I do."

"What can you tell me about his assailant? Was he an Indian too?"

"That's what a witness said."

"Molly White Horse, right? And these two brought a feud down from the reservation, right?"

"I can't comment on that, Gargan. It's an ongoing case."

"Hey, I swear I'm not going to use any names. In fact, this isn't even a police story—my editor wants me to do a special on Native Americans in Denver. You know: what's happening to them, how they survive, how they don't. The sad passing of the old wild west. It's a big story."

Wager didn't give a damn what kind of story Gargan was working on; they had stepped on each other's toes too often in the past to kiss and make up now. "Talk to Chief Doyle in the morning."

"I got a deadline, Wager. And it's a bitch getting in to see Doyle!"

"A reporter's lot, Gargan, is not a happy one."

"Jesus H. Christ, a literary allusion from the world's only surviving Neanderthal. Thanks a lot, Wager. Maybe I can do you a favor sometime."

The new administration had put out a memo reminding officers of the importance of good public relations, so

Wager smiled and said thank you. The elevator closed on what sounded like a nasty word.

Max was already at his desk and shuffling papers when Wager turned in from the hallway that led to the homicide section of Crimes Against Persons. So far this year, each officer had twelve or thirteen folders in the open file to add to or check on or to just stare at and wonder when something else might turn up, something that could provide the legal evidence to nail a known killer or the clue that would point to an unknown one. Some of the files, usually the fattest, had been in the drawer for years, gradualy gaining this or that slip of paper, ocasionally reassigned from one detective to another as men transferred in and out of the unit. But they were never closed. The statute of limitations on homicides was forever, and these first couple of hours, particularly on the night shift, were usually spent consolidating the letters, reports, and memos that had arrived since the last tour of duty. The detectives placed the new information in the right folder, always with the vague hope that it might click something together; then they made telephone calls to those who had left home phone numbers, or to those other offices open, like this one, every day and every night.

At his desk, Axton yawned, the gap of his mouth half as large as Wager's head, and rubbed his thumbs into bloodshot eyes.

"You're off to a good start," said Wager.

"It's the Maestas case. I was in court all day."

"I thought that finished last month."

"Continuance—psychological evaluation. Now we're back in session and I'm still the advisory witness."

It wasn't unusual for the night shift to be up twenty-four hours; a lot of things couldn't get taken care of during their official work period when everyone else was asleep. But none of the extra chores was as wearing as sitting in a hot courtroom on a wooden bench and listening to lawyers. "It goes with the territory."

"Don't it, though."

They settled back into the stack of envelopes, routing sheets, and interoffice mailers. On the gray filing cabinet, the radio in its charging unit gave its familiar crackle of the night police business in District Two, one of the most active of the city's four districts. Occasionally a tone alert broke into Wager's concentration and he half-listened to the all-channels broadcast. So far they had been for ambulances or fire equipment; as yet no voice had called for Union 6, the designation that had been shifted from Rape to Homicide. The new administration reasoned that victims of sexual assault might be further offended by hearing an officer use "Union 69" to call Detective Nine from the rape team. It was one of those nice touches of public sensitivity that came from new blood in high administrative levels, and that brought a slight smile to Wager's cheek.

"I'll be damned."

Wager looked up at Max, who was reading through the thick packet of an autopsy report.

"You know what Sam Walking Tall died of?"

"Three and a half inches of steel," said Wager.

"That wasn't the immediate cause of death."

"What was?"

"He drowned."

"He what?"

"The beer. The guy drowned in beer. Molly White Horse poured the beer over him and it went through the hole in his chest into his lungs. He drowned."

Wager pushed back against the creak of his desk chair. "What the hell? We don't have a murder charge on Robert Smith?"

"He didn't murder him. Assault One, maybe. But the public defender's office will probably go for Assault Two as a misdemeanor—the bartender said Sam and Robert had been picking at each other all night, so they'll try to show provocation."

For which the maximum sentence could be two years and a five-thousand-dollar fine. But Robert wouldn't get that much. With time off for good behavior, he might serve six months in county jail. Moreover, the search for him would lose its intensity with other law enforcement agencies—you kept your eyes open for a murderer, but there were so many assault suspects that it became a matter of luck to catch one. And there was something else: "So now we have to pop Molly for killing him?"

"We can suggest a finding of accidental death."

"Sure we can. A guy gets stabbed in the chest, dies outside a bar in front of witnesses, and the DA calls it an accident. I can see what Gargan and some of those other assholes will put in the paper. There goes the policy of improving press relations." Wager's guess was that the prosecutor would charge Molly with negligent homicide, which was also a class one misdemeanor; but she could end up serving more time than Robert Smith, who had started all this crap.

"Well, the medical fact is that he drowned—old Robert got lucky and Molly didn't. Sam didn't have much luck either, come to think of it." Max yawned again. "But it's up to the DA to sort out now." He scribbled a note and clipped it to the file. "It looks like we just solved another homicide, partner, and Assault just got another case."

Wager should not have been surprised—he'd seen a lot of strange things happen in the continuing attempts to place the flow and chaos of human passions into the rigid boxes of legal definition and punishment. Criminally negligent homicide—the section that would apply to Molly—was defined by the Criminal Code simply as "conduct amounting to criminal negligence," and that gave the DA a lot of room to act. But it, too, was a box; it excluded Molly's drunken love for Sam, her intention to wake him up rather than drown the poor bastard, her total ignorance that she had been the one to kill him. All of that could be heard as mitigation for sentencing, but it didn't fit into the box of guilty or not guilty. She had done it, and they had her statement—which would have to be taken again after reading her the Miranda Warning—and the DA's policy was to lay the heaviest charge on perpetrators. "I guess we have to pick her up."

Max nodded and glanced at his watch. "Let's wait awhile—she's probably not hitting the bars yet. Besides, she might as well have one more good drunk before we haul her in."

"Yep." Law and justice were two different things. Sometimes they worked out together, and a lot of times they didn't. Wager was a servant of the law—justice was supposed to be found in the courts. He had to remember that. Sighing, he finished filling in an inquiry out of San Diego about any unsolved murders using barbed wire for bondage. Wager had inherited an old case that fit the m.o., and he forwarded copies of pertinent documents and requested San Diego to send what they had. The next slip of paper was a telephone message received at 8:05 a.m.: Please call Tom Sanchez. Very Important, with his ranch telephone number. Wager checked his watch and decided that 10:00 at night was still early enough, but a voice croaky with sleep answered.

"Tom? This is Gabe Wager. I just got your message—sorry to wake you up."

"Gabe? Hey, *no problema,* man; it's OK—I'm glad you called. Yeah, I—ah—I went over to see the boys at the Walsenburg rodeo."

"How'd they do?"

"Aw, fine. They had an open go-round, you know, for non-PRCA members, and damned if James didn't take first place on the broncs. That boy's got promise, Gabe. He's a hell of a lot better than I was, his age."

"Great. How'd John do?"

"He earned a little bit of money—a couple of fourths. That ain't bad; he had some real good competition over there. The Mountain Circuit's a tough circuit, and ain't none of them easy."

"That's good to hear, Tommy." Wager waited, wondering if this was the reason for the Very Important noted on the message.

"Listen, Gabe, why I wanted to talk with you . . . ah, what I asked you about, you remember?"

"Sure. But I haven't run across anything new yet."

"I see. Any idea how long it's gonna take to find out if there is anything?"

"It just takes time, Tommy. Why?"

"Well, I told them I'd come out and visit the ranch in a week or two. I sort of invited myself out, but they said OK. But I thought if you knew something I could talk to them about—you know, show them that I'm interested and all . . ."

"Have you said anything about it?"

"No, not yet. Hell's bells, it was enough just saying hello after all this time. But it went well. I mean, they really were glad to see their old man. So I figured I'd go out and visit the ranch. Look around and see what kind of setup Johnny's got for him and Jimmy."

"That sounds fine, Tom. Go ahead and do it."

"Right, I am. It's just that maybe there's something about the ranch—maybe you could find out if there's some information there, you know?"

"All right, Tom. I'll do what I can."

"Thanks, Gabe. And I just wanted to let you know that things look pretty good with me and the boys."

"I'm glad to hear that. And if anything comes up on Jerry Latta, I'll let you know."

"Right—yeah—I forgot all about him. OK, Gabe. Thanks again."

Wager hung up and wondered briefly if Tom's sons really had been that pleased to see their father. Tom himself seemed too eager to convince both of them it was so. But that part of the problem wasn't his, and in fact, if he had been Tom, he'd simply hire a lawyer from Ute County to go through public records and see what turned up about the ranch. But he wasn't Tommy, and the man probably didn't have that kind of money, anyway. That's why he had come to Wager. That, and the deep-seated feeling that if you had to deal with the law, it was best to seek out a cop who was a friend because there were a lot of them who weren't. He took a mouthful of coffee and dialed the WATS operator and told her what number he wanted.

"Ute County Sheriff's Office, Deputy Schrantz speaking."

"This is Detective Sergeant Wager, Denver Police. I'm trying to get some information about some people who live out your way."

"What kind of information, Sergeant Wager?"

"Any kind of contacts you've had with them. It's a problem of witness credibility."

It wasn't an unfamiliar request. "Who're you asking about?"

"Sanchez." Wager spelled it. "John or James."

"Got a Herman Sanchez who gets drunk and gives us some trouble now and then. Runs sheep up on the Uncompahgre."

"These two work on the T Bar M ranch."

The line was silent. "That's over near the Dolores, isn't it? In Old Woman Canyon?"

"I don't know."

"I haven't heard anything about them. What've you heard?"

"It's something that came up in an investigation. I'm just making a routine check."

"What kind of investigation? What are they supposed to be doing?"

"I'm not at liberty to discuss that, Deputy Schrantz."

"Well, now, Sergeant Wager—this here's our jurisdiction. If you got some kind of information bearing on our jurisdiction, we'd appreciate knowing about it."

"The names came up in relation to an occurrence here in Denver, Deputy. The men aren't suspects, and this is just a routine inquiry."

"Uh huh. Well, as far as I know neither one of them's in any criminal activity of any kind. You want me to investigate further, Sergeant?"

"No thanks."

Wager had lived up to his promise, and that was enough.

He hung up and finished his coffee and turned back to the paperwork that was his official worry.

"You ready to go arrest that vicious killer, Gabe?"

"Let's do it—let's get out of here." He stretched and lifted his coat off the hanger. "Denver will sleep safer tonight."

CHAPTER 5

Wager had just finished shaving and washing down a Marine Corps omelet with half a pitcher of orange juice and was checking the contents of his gym bag before his afternoon workout when the telephone rang. He flicked off the answering machine and said, "Hello."

"Gabe? This is Tom. Listen, can I see you right away, *amigo*? I'm in town, but I won't be here too long." An urgency made his voice tense.

"Where do you want to meet?"

"Same place as last time? That's where I am now. Thanks, Gabe."

Wager found him sitting behind a glass of beer near the doorway of the almost empty bar. Tom stretched the crease of his mouth into a smile. "Sorry to keep pestering you, Gabe. I know you got a hell of a lot better things to do than mess around with me."

"It's no problem," lied Wager. "Did you get over to the ranch to see the boys?"

"That's what I want to talk to you about, Gabe. I was wrong, flat-out. There's not a damn thing wrong up at that place."

"You looked the ranch over?"

"Yeah. It's a real big spread, and they run some cows and

have a kind of campsite for river rafters. It's a real good job for both of them."

"I'm glad to hear it. I guess you are, too."

"Yeah, I am. I mean, not that I thought the boys were in any real trouble, you know. But you hear these things and you start to worry. . . ."

"I can't blame you. They're your sons."

"Right—*familia*. I ain't been much of a father to them, but I damn well know one thing: family's about all a man's got in this world."

Some had one, some didn't; Wager nodded. In the rear of the bar, a heavy electronic pulse started up and a woman sang thinly, "And then there's your wife—"

Tom frowned at his beer. "You haven't come up with anything new, have you, Gabe? This Jerry Latta or anybody?"

"Not yet. From what you tell me, I don't expect to."

"'Not yet.' That means you're still looking?"

"Some other people are. I ask a few questions here and there, they ask a few, somebody else asks questions. After a while some answers might come back."

Tom gave a snorty kind of laugh. "Sounds like throwing rocks in a goddam pond—after a while the waves come back."

"That's a lot like it."

"Well, I'm sure now the boys aren't into anything. I think it was just a bunch of crap and somebody got the wrong information or something."

"That's probably what I'll find out. And that's good news."

"Yeah, it is. I appreciate your help and all, too. I didn't mean to put you and everybody else to all this damn trouble. I guess I was so worried that I just didn't give it much thought—you know, about you having to bring a lot of other people in on it."

Wager splashed more coffee into his cup from the little aluminum pot the waitress had set in front of him. "What are you after, Tom?"

"What's that mean?"

"I mean it sounds like you want to know how many people I talked to about the boys."

"Hey—Gabe—*amigo*—no! I just don't know how you police people work. I thought it was just between me and you, you know? I thought maybe you could just look in some papers or something. I didn't know I was causing so much damn trouble for so many people, that's all."

Wager studied the man's dark eyes, which were stretched with sincerity and perhaps a touch of fear or pleading or both. In this light it was hard to tell, and Tom's words made some sense, because he'd been embarrassed to ask for help in the first place. Besides, whatever was going on—if anything was going on—he wasn't going to tell Wager. "I asked a couple of people around here and I talked to the sheriff over in Ute County. Nobody's heard anything about your boys."

"Well, like I say, Gabe, they won't because there's nothing to hear. But I want to thank you for your trouble. I just didn't know how much I was stirring up, and I feel bad about making you and those other folks go to all that trouble for nothing." He lifted his glass. "I should have just gone on over there right at first . . . but I hadn't seen the boys in so long. . . . Say, did you know John has his permit now? You know, with a lot of luck and a lot of work, they just might make it! I swear I wouldn't give them a fart's chance in a whirlwind to make any money rodeoing, but they're doing all right. They want it, Gabe—they really want it, and that's half the fight right there."

They spent the next half hour talking rodeo and Tom's sons' chances of making good money at it. When the beer and coffee were drained, Tom won the argument for the check and apologized again to Wager for all the trouble he'd put him to. "I'll be seeing a lot more of the boys, now, Gabe. Maybe I can give them some tips about riding."

They shook hands, and Wager watched the blue-and-white pickup pull into the light traffic of Colfax. Then he checked his watch and drove across town to the gym. There was still time for a good workout before reporting for duty. And to tell the truth, he was relieved not to have to worry about Tom and his problems anymore.

. . .

It was one thing to agree with Jo about taking a vacation, but it was something else entirely to decide when, where, and how much.

"It's too hot to go to Mexico," she said. Jo sat in shorts and halter and slowly turned the pages of a *Sunset* magazine filled with bright and glossy pictures of beaches and hotels, golf courses and mountains, dude ranches and swimming pools.

Wager, admiring the long, smooth muscles of her tanned calves and thighs, nodded and sipped the iced tea that cooled his hand. In the branches of the locust tree above them, an occasional breeze made the lacy green tremble, but for the most part the day was still and the gray, cracking earth seemed to give off as much heat as the sun. One thing he did not need was hotter weather. "I don't like beaches, anyway. I swim like a cannonball."

"You don't like beaches. That takes care of Hawaii."

"And I don't like any place that looks like a jungle."

"Maybe it would be easier if you told me what you do like."

"Hey, it's not just me going on this thing. It's your vacation, too. It has to be someplace you like."

"I like mountains."

"So do I—and they're cool."

She turned a few more pages. "Glacier National Monument? Here's an ad."

"What do they do there?"

"Well, let's see. . . . There's horseback riding, hiking, fishing . . ."

"Fishing? I like to fish. I don't know about doing it for three weeks, though."

"We could go to Europe."

Wager blinked. "What the hell for?"

"To see it. London, Paris, Rome—I've never seen it, have you?"

"Never wanted to."

"But doesn't it sound exciting?"

"Jo, I don't even speak European."

"They speak English," she said, and showed him the page with the picture of the British flag and some guy in a red coat and weird hat who looked like he was advertising gin.

"What about something a little closer? Something we can drive to. Airplane trips, hotels . . . Jo, that just sounds like one big hassle."

She peeked at him over the open magazine, her dark hair arcing near one of those laughter-filled eyes before it swept up past her ear and into the ponytail behind. "You sound like you're afraid of hotels."

"Who in the hell can have a good time with all those forks and glasses and things? And some waiter standing around watching?"

"I'm sure you'd get the hang of it quickly."

"Yeah, well, I probably would. But that doesn't mean I'd enjoy it."

"Maybe France." The eyes were still on him. "We could take the culture tour: the Louvre, Versailles, and those galleries and museums. You'd love that."

"Jo—"

"You could come back and tell Max all about medieval cathedrals or Impressionist painting."

"Jo—"

The magazine slipped to reveal her wide grin.

Wager set his glass firmly on the table. "You want me to take you away from all this? Come on—we'll have a mini-vacation right now: carefree lounging in your private suite, soft music by the am/fm's, a stimulating exercise for muscle tone and complexion. Come on, we'll have a fine time."

"It's too hot!"

He tugged her hand. "We'll cool off with a refreshing dip in the shower."

One of the first questions he asked Max that evening was what his favorite vacation spots were.

"We like Cozumel. They have these family specials, and we can all go down there for about as cheap as anything around here."

"What's so good about it?"

"Everything, Gabe. Good seafood, tropical scenery—it's a great place to just sit and watch the ocean. The kids spend all day messing around on the beach. No television, none of the big touristy things, no rushing around. There's nowhere to go anyway—it's an island. The kids really like it."

"But what about just you and Francine? Where do the two of you go for vacations?"

Max thought a minute. "I don't know; I guess we don't anymore. We always take the kids. But I still think Cozumel would be a good place for two people. You like to scuba dive?"

"No."

"You ought to try it, Gabe. It's really fun. And down there, the water's warm and clear and they've got these coral reefs. . . ."

Wager heard about brain coral and fan coral, about barracudas and groupers and hundreds of different kinds of colored fish; about some reef that you had to take a boat out to and dive down about two hundred feet to see.

"I thought you just laid around on the beach and watched the ocean."

"Most of the time, sure. But this was really worth doing, Gabe. I took my oldest boy with me, and we had a great time. If you want to take a vacation, that's the one for you."

Wager nodded and smiled and moved some papers around on his desk as Max started telling him about the other side of the island, the one that wasn't as good for skin diving, but had empty beaches and surf that the kids liked to splash in and out of. To Wager, it sounded as if the place had everything he had nightmares about: ocean to drown in, tropic climate for funguses, jungle for snipers and other friendly natives. When the telephone rang, he was quick to answer it.

"Wager, this is Gargan. What's this I hear about you arresting Molly White Horse for knifing Sam Walking Tall?"

"For homicide, Gargan. Not for knifing him."

"Man, you know she didn't kill that guy!"

"What I don't know is what business it is of yours."

"I told you: I'm doing a series on Indians in Denver. And when she told me the bond she had to post for killing Sam . . . Wager, that's unbelievable. You got witnesses saying he was stabbed by the other guy, and you go pick her up. It's really unbelievable!"

"She wouldn't have been arrested without probable cause, Gargan."

"The only possible cause is that you can't find the guy who did it."

Wager took a deep breath and reminded himself of Doyle's memo about press relations. But even he heard the tinge of Spanish lilt that signaled his anger. "The case is with the DA. You'll have to contact the DA's office for further information. Nice talking with you, Gargan."

"By God, I will! One of the things I've turned up on this story is the casual attitude of the police toward crime among the minorities. And this little deal is one of the worst examples I've run across. You better believe I'll talk to the DA's office—I'll talk to them about half-assed police work by people who don't give a damn who they bust!"

Max, eyebrows raised, glanced across his desk. "Your neck's red, Gabe. Gargan doing another feature on you?"

"He's upset because Molly was arrested instead of Robert Smith."

"We haven't found Robert Smith to arrest. Hell, he's probably back on the reservation by now; and the FBI won't go after him just for an assault charge. Besides, what's it to him?"

"He thinks we grabbed the nearest Indian to close the case. He's doing a story on Indians, so now he thinks he's got to protect their civil rights."

The big man pushed back into the startled yelp of his chair and studied the ceiling. "I wonder how the First Amendment applies to pretrial publicity in favor of the defendant?"

That was the kind of theoretical question young assistant district attorneys liked to argue on coffee breaks, and Wager had heard detectives waste hours pretending to be lawyers. For him, it was no issue: "Gargan doesn't know his ass from his elbow."

"The real question is how equal the state's right is to an unprejudiced trial. Ideally, it should be the same as the defendant's, you know? But most of the rulings are in response to the defendant's request. Now, if Gargan goes on a crusade against the police before the case goes to trial, that could make it interesting for the DA."

Though most of the time he kept it hidden, Max had a college degree—sociology—and it tended to pop out when he got talkative. It wasn't as bad as some—Golding, for example, who had a theory for everything. There had been a few times, in fact, when Homicide Detective Golding's case of intellectual bullshit had come very close to being terminal. But Max was Wager's partner, and you gave your partner a little more slack than you might someone else. Wager turned back to the pending memos and notices, and whenever Max would ask "Don't you think so, Gabe?" he would grunt something between a yes and a no.

Far down the pile of papers was another routine notice, this one from the Colorado State Patrol, District Two, seeking information on a hit-and-run victim tentatively identified as Thomas Sanchez. Wager's eyes skimmed past the name and jumped back, a prickly feeling tightening the flesh across his shoulders. Slowly he read the terse description—male, Hispanic, approximately fifty years old—and then the one-line history: the victim had been found beside Chaffee County Road 5 apparently struck by a car. Any law enforcement agency with pertinent information was requested to call. The circular was dated two days ago and had already been initialed by the detectives on the day shift.

Wager dialed the number and in a while a female voice said, "Colorado State Patrol, Salida Office."

He identified himself. "I'm calling about a notice you sent out on a hit-run victim, possibly a Thomas Sanchez. Has he been positively identified yet?"

"No, sir. You're the first call we've had on him."

"Is he dead or alive?"

"He's alive but still unconscious. Do you know him well?"

"Not too well. Why?"

"The victim's features are sort of messed up. The person who gave a tentative i.d. didn't know him too well, either, and couldn't be sure it was him."

"Can you send up a photograph?"

"We took some. But he looks even worse that way. The swelling should go down in a week or so, but we'd like to know who he is as soon as possible."

There wasn't a thing that told Wager it was definitely Tommy. How many Sanchezes lived in that part of the state? A hundred? A thousand? "Does this man have a lot of old injuries? Broken bones and scars?"

"He has a lot of new ones, Detective Wager. I don't know about old ones."

"Did you try fingerprints?"

"No record for this man as a John Doe, and there are so many Sanchezes that it's like having nothing at all."

And if Tommy had no criminal record or military service, there wouldn't be any prints to match; he'd be just as hard to identify as his sons, who also had no record anywhere. "Where is he?"

"He's in the county wing of the hospital right now. They're pretty anxious to get a positive on him so they can locate the next of kin."

And find out where to send the bill.

"We'd like one, too. We're not so sure that it was a hit-and-run."

"What's that?"

She hesitated. "The doctor's not certain about the types of injury. And we found no evidence at the scene or in the victim's clothes or flesh of any vehicle. A man hit that hard, there should have been glass or paint or something."

"You think it was an assault?"

"It could have been. Possibly linked with robbery—his wallet's gone. But his watch and a big gold ring and a large silver belt buckle were still on him."

"A big belt buckle? A cowboy belt buckle?"

"Yes."

"I see. All right, I'll drive down this morning. What's your address there?"

.   .   .

Leaving as soon as the shift ended, Wager figured three hours down, an hour there, and then three back. It left enough time to get some sleep before the next tour of duty. Without the traffic in Denver and its broad suburbs, he made good time, and dawn began to redden the sky just after he crossed Kenosha Pass and tilted into the long descent leading to South Park. Its fifty miles of level, treeless meadow separated the Front Range from the mountains of the Great Divide; and the vastness and chill of altitude and the widely scattered, lonely specks of light brought the familiar sense of foreboding that Wager always had when he traveled this stretch of road. At this time of morning, he especially felt it, when the raw light began to outline the shadow of an occasional ranch house or gas station, and made the mark of man seem flimsy and huddled beneath the looming peaks and a wide sky that was both close and endlessly deep.

He had fished some of the meandering streams that cut trenches across the park's windswept floor: Fourmile, Agate, the South Platte. Now ranchers were selling their land off in ten-acre plots to Denverites and Texans who parked trailers across the land like scattered square pebbles. They fenced the approaches to the creeks as their own; they used them for a couple of weeks, maybe for the one chilly month of July or August, and the rest of the year the land lay empty as it was now. This early in summer, the occasional dirt access road had not yet been churned to mud by the knobby wheels of traffic, and uncut patches of snow glowed in shaded depressions on the range. Deeper drifts began only a couple hundred feet up the flanks of the surrounding mountains, and some of them seemed big enough to last until the next snowfall in September. But they wouldn't; a few days of sun and nights above freezing, and most of the snow would drain off in rivulets to swell the rivers that carved their way to the Mississippi a thousand miles away.

In the forty miles between Kenosha and Trout Creek passes, two vehicles whipped by him, both semis that left a tense whine in the cold air and a streak of black smoke fraying against the morning sky. It was warmer now, both because of the sun that cast the Trans-Am's shadow on the twisting pavement ahead and because Wager was gliding into the valley of the Arkansas River. Below, past piñon-dotted hills of red sand that reminded him of New Mexico, the trees bordering the river made a wandering line of dark green against the paler shade of sagebrush. Beside the river, the busier lanes of US 24 led south to Salida, and Wager, half an hour from his destination, stopped at the junction for what the waitress assumed was breakfast. Through the window beside his booth, he saw the white walls and copper-green roofs of the state reformatory at Buena Vista. The lush fields, broken here and there by wire security fences, were still empty of prisoners, and, as he dipped toast into egg, Wager idly tried to remember the names of those he'd sent there. Fifteen—perhaps only twelve left inside now. This morning, as every morning, they would be eating a gummy breakfast off a scratched tray and then counting the silverware in at the wash window. Wearing unironed coveralls clammy with this week's sweat because tomorrow was laundry day. Maybe they would live up to the institution's name and be reformed; probably they wouldn't. Probably they would come out thinking they were a hell of a lot slyer than when they went in, and then, when they finally killed somebody, they'd run across Wager again. And their next vacation at state expense would be hard time in the pen at Canon City.

Vacation.

Wager sighed and finished his coffee, shaking his head at the waitress who hovered with a steaming globe to offer a refill.

If it wasn't for his promise to Jo, he'd be satisfied with this drive to Salida and back. See some nice landscape—look at the reformatory. What else could a man ask? But she wanted a three-week trip somewhere, and he had agreed. They still had not decided where. The number of places to visit seem to grow and grow, and so did the places he didn't want to see. But even narrowing things down hadn't helped. When he left for work last night, she had been talking about Europe again, and this time she didn't seem to be kidding.

The final twenty-five miles went quickly despite the increasing traffic. Wager glanced at the directions given him and slowed as he saw the cluster of signs marking the town of Salida bordering the river ahead. The patrol office was a small new building surrounded by a graveled drive and set to watch over the highway's traffic. Parked beside the building was a white sedan with the familiar winged emblem on its doors.

"Can I help you, sir?" The female officer looked up from a corner desk crowded with papers and a radio charger unit. The clutter of charts and notices and the snap of the radio were familiar, and equally recognizable was the stale odor of coffee that had heated too long.

"I'm Detective Wager, Denver Police. I'm here to identify a hit-run victim."

"Oh, yes!" She stood and shook hands, a heavy-set woman whose brown hair was cut just at her shoulders. She wore no makeup, and her grip was strong. "I'm Trooper Ingalls. I didn't think you'd get here so soon."

He explained that his tour of duty ended at three. Hers

was over at eight, she said, and they talked a few minutes about their bureaucracies. Wager declined a cup of coffee, and finally she told him how to find the hospital. "My relief's not due for an hour. But you can go look at him. I'll call and tell the nurse to expect you."

The hospital was a sprawling one-level building whose parking lot surrounded a flagpole and was beginning to fill with cars. Inside the entry, a board full of names listed doctors and medical units, and beyond that glowed the reception desk. Wager stood around until a gray-haired woman came through a door behind the desk to smile and ask if he was the one Trooper Ingalls had called about.

"Yes ma'am."

"Follow me, please."

Her crepe soles squeaked on the hallway's wax, and breakfast odors, reflected like the streaks of glare from the overhead lights, drifted along the plain walls. Here and there, wide doors opened to glimpses of rumpled bedsheets or a robed figure leaning for support against a chairback.

"What's his condition?"

"It's not critical, but he's still in ICU."

The woman turned down a corridor guarded by two swinging doors and then into an open room with a row of five beds. Two had curtains drawn around them, and Wager could see the busy white shoes of nurses at work. Two were empty and waiting under their array of chrome hooks and tubing and electronic monitors. In the last bed of the intensive care unit lay a small mound of covers. Transparent hoses ran from the mound, some holding a clear liquid, another moving slow, elongated bubbles of air and red-brown clots from the victim's mouth and out of sight under the bed. Under the murmur of professionally cheerful voices from the curtained beds came the steady hiss of a suction machine.

"He's still in a coma?"

"Yes. I'll tell the duty nurse you're here."

Wager leaned over the waxy face to study it in the gray

light of the room's single distant window. Blood-crusted pinpricks of stitch marks closed red and swollen lines of sliced flesh across the shaved eyebrows, the mashed nose, and through the upper and lower lips. The man's eyes puffed out almost as far as his nose, and against the white bandage wrapping his skull, the squeezed lids looked oily and black. A growth of whiskers peppered his jaw with white fuzz, and the asymmetrical swelling of the left side of his face lifted one ear higher than the other. In this light, it was difficult to trace resemblance to the face Wager knew.

But he had no doubt who it was, and the difference between what Wager saw and what he remembered as Tommy Sanchez made his stomach churn sickly around his morning's coffee.

"You—what are you doing here? Speak: who are you?" It was a heavily accented voice—German, Wager decided—and belonged to a tall man who glared at him over a pointing finger. "Who let you in here?"

"I was asked to identify this man."

"That is irrelevant. This ward is off limits. You should not be here. Stand over by that wall."

Wager stared back at the blue eyes and did not move. "Are you the man's doctor?"

"I am the chief administrator of this hospital and I have asked you a question. Now answer!"

"I am Detective Wager, Denver Police Department."

"Please keep your voices down. Is something wrong here?"

"Nurse, what is this unauthorized person doing in here?"

The nurse, blond hair pulled back tightly under a cap, raised her eyebrows. "He's a policeman. Mrs. Koontz said he could identify number five."

"He should be accompanied by hospital staff at all times. He should not be left alone here to do Gott knows what." The administrator turned to Wager. "Well? Do you know the patient? Speak!"

Wager's voice gained its slight Spanish lilt. "Yes. I know him."

"Well? Who is he?"

Wager smiled. "Your manners—did you learn them in Auschwitz?"

"That is impertinent!"

"Both of you please leave the ward. You're disturbing my patients."

"There's no change in his condition?" Wager ignored the administrator.

The nurse shook her head.

"You—come with me!"

Wager took a business card from his wallet and handed it to her. "Can you ask his doctor to give me a call as soon as there's any change?"

"Did you hear me?"

She nodded, a worried glance at the administrator.

Wager smiled thanks and followed the tall man's stiff-kneed stride into the hallway and down toward the reception desk. The man aimed at a door marked Hospital Administrator; Wager turned toward the exit.

"Where do you think you are going?"

"Wherever I want to."

"You will come here! I will report you to your superiors!"

"*Amigo*, I have no superiors. And if you want to stop me, you'll have to put me under arrest." Wager's cheeks tightened into a wide grin. "And if you put me under arrest, you will want to get a very good lawyer for yourself. Because false arrest is a misdemeanor—and I will be very happy to see you spend a few months in jail."

"Are you threatening me?"

"You're goddam right I am. Try me and see if I'm lying." He waited a long minute to give the man a chance, but he only stared at Wager, his mouth a tight purse and his jaw chewing what he would like to say. "*Adios*."

In his car, Wager breathed away his anger and thanked whatever gods were left that the German had not tried to hold him physically. He would have resisted, of course, and the local cops would have come; and Wager, armed and outside his jurisdiction by more than a hundred miles, would have ended up with six weeks' paperwork to explain it all. And no vacation—which might not be so bad after all.

He pulled into the parking lot of the Highway Patrol office, pleased to see that Trooper Ingalls's car was one of the two cruisers sitting there.

"Did you know him?" She leaned over the desk pointing to something on a paper for her replacement, a wiry and dark-haired man who looked up and half smiled because Ingalls knew him.

"It's Thomas Sanchez. He has a ranch near Antonito." He fished around in his wallet for a slip of paper. "Here's the rural route and telephone number. I'm sure he lives alone down there."

Ingalls copied it down. "Any idea what he was doing here?"

"No. He has two sons, James and John. They're working on a ranch over in Ute County, the T Bar M. As far as I know, they're his only next of kin."

"That's probably in District Four." She made a note to herself.

"Will your office be in charge of the investigation?"

"If it's automobile-related. If not, we'll turn it over to the Chaffee County Sheriff's Office."

Wager nodded, understanding that sheriff's officers were as jealous of their jurisdictions as any other police agency, including Denver's. And that their detectives probably shared the same suspicion of the State Patrol's ability to investigate criminal acts. Chasing speeders was one thing; running an investigation into an assault or homicide was something else. But every now and then one of the Smokies would see himself as a one-man police force, and you had to guard against that. The same defensiveness would greet Wager if he tried to poke into the sheriff's business, and he had to remember that despite any feelings he might have at seeing Tommy lie there like a pound of ground meat, it wasn't his case. "Would you call me when Sanchez regains consciousness? Or if it turns out to be a beating?" He handed her one of his cards.

"Be glad to. And thanks for coming all the way down here."

. . .

When Wager reported in, the long drive seemed as insubstantial as a half-remembered dream. On the trip back, slower because of daytime traffic, his mind had dwelled on Tom's bloated, purple face and his stillness in the network of tubes and sensors. And he had turned over the obvious questions. If Tom was hit by a car, what was he doing that far north of Antonito on foot? If he was beaten, why? The first question had a dozen possible answers—looking at stock and ran out of gas, or drunk and hitchhiking. Whatever. The answer to the second question could fall into three areas: robbery, the results of general hell-raising, or maybe something to do with his sons. He had had no wallet when he was found, but other valuables, easily pawned or melted down, had been left. Still, robbery was a good bet, because like a lot of cowboys, Tom enjoyed the feel of a roll of cash, and he liked to carry that roll with him. Finding that much money, the robber might have left the other things. In other words, there was nothing at all so far to indicate that his sons were somehow involved. Except the meeting last week to ask Wager to butt out.

Re-creating the scene in the bar, Wager wondered now if the man's eyes hadn't been tense with the fear that Wager would keep poking around. Perhaps Tommy had started something he wanted desperately to stop? For his sons' sakes? For his own?

Those and other thoughts had followed Wager into the short and restless sleep he managed to drop into that afternoon. And they still drifted in and out of his mind as he woke to the buzz of his radio clock and scraped the whiskers off his chin and from around his mustache. Had fear been in Tom's voice when he called Wager earlier? There weren't many things on two legs or four that frightened the man. Certainly not the threat of a beating, even one this severe—Tommy had hurt himself as badly when he was rodeoing and, riding hurt, had gone out and gotten busted up again. The threat of a beating might make him grin, but it wouldn't scare him. The only thing that might frighten him would be danger to his sons. But they weren't the ones lying in the hospital.

He poured the shift's first cup of coffee and pushed the nagging thoughts to the back of his mind; today was the first day of the rest of his life, with its own fun and excitement, and that was all Wager was being paid to think about.

On top of the stack of papers lay a memo from Chief Doyle citing a citizen's complaint from one Wilhelm Strauss, chief administrator for Salida Community Hospital, and concluding in an angry scrawl, "What the hell is this about, Wager?"

He had rolled a sheet of paper into the squeaky typewriter when Max, smelling of fresh aftershave, peered over his shoulder.

"What you got there, Gabe, a dog bite?"

That's what they called Bulldog Doyle's memos, the ones that bore handwritten comments in red felt pen. "Nothing serious. Just more paperwork."

"That's serious." Max settled to his desk and its own pile of papers.

Wager was telling Doyle about answering a request from the Colorado State Patrol for identification of an assault victim, and about explaining the false-arrest statute to the hospital administrator, when, beneath the slow clack of his typewriter, he heard the telephone ring and Max's answer.

"Yes—just a minute please. Gabe, it's yours."

"Detective Wager."

"This is Detective Allen, Chaffee County Sheriff's Office. Trooper Ingalls said you were the one who identified Thomas Sanchez. Is that right?"

"Yes."

"Have you known Sanchez for a long time?"

"Off and on since I was a kid."

"All right. Do you have any idea what he might have been doing before we found him?"

"No. He wasn't a suspect or an informant for me, if that's what you're asking. He was a friend who I saw every now and then."

"All right. Well, we haven't been able to get in touch with his sons, and I'm trying to put together this picture of what he was doing up this way. Is there anything at all you can help us with?"

"He worked for a rodeo contractor. He might have been on business." Wager figured it was his turn to ask a question. "You've decided this wasn't an automobile accident?"

"Yeah. The autopsy showed injuries consistent with a beating instead of a car–pedestrian accident."

"Autopsy?"

The line was silent for a moment or two. "Sanchez died about four-oh-two this afternoon, Detective Wager. Didn't the hospital call you?"

"No . . . no, this— No, they didn't call."

"I'm sorry to be the one to tell you, Detective Wager. I understood from one of the nurses that she was going to call and tell you."

"I didn't know he was that critical."

"Well, the doc said he had other injuries—old concussions—I guess that contributed to the death. But the real cause was two blows to the head with a blunt instrument. He never regained consciousness. It's a homicide."

"I see."

"I called down to Conejos County Sheriff's Office and asked what they knew about him, but all they have is his address on a ranch outside Antonito."

"Yes . . . he told me he had a small place there."

"All right. But he lived alone, and apparently nobody knows much about him at all. And like I say, we haven't been able to get in touch with his sons. They went up to Montana rodeoing or something."

"He didn't see much of them after his divorce."

"All right. But you see, the Conejos SO found his truck

at the ranch. So I figure for some reason he went with somebody who drove him up this way. Unless he had another car. Do you know if he had a second vehicle?"

"I only saw him drive the truck—a blue pickup with a white camper shell."

"That's the one, registered to Thomas A. Sanchez."

"He probably had cash with him. Maybe a lot."

"Why's that?"

"He bought stock for the rodeo. And I guess most of that business is done in cash."

"All right, that fits him not having any wallet. I've been thinking it was a robbery."

"That seems like a long way to take someone just to rob him. What is it, a hundred, hundred and twenty-five miles?"

"Maybe they were scared to dump him near home. They got three or four days down the road before we even knew who he was, right?" The voice paused. "How does this sound to you? Somebody tells Sanchez he's got some stock he wants to sell and offers to drive him out to see it. Then he robs him and, because Sanchez knows who it is, beats him to death—or thinks he does—and then tries to make it look like a hit-run."

It was a bit early to draw conclusions, but Wager said what Allen wanted to hear: "That sounds like a good place to start."

"You got any other explanation?"

"No, Detective Allen, I don't." Not anything with substance, at least. And the sheriff's officer wouldn't find much time for Wager's vague suspicions. His interest lay, as it should, in digging for the facts surrounding the act itself—locating any witnesses who might have seen Tom with anyone on that day, any reports of a suspicious vehicle, or anyone seeing erratic behavior at the time of the beating. Allen was interested in evidence that would stand up in court, and his would be the slogging chores of interviewing potential witnesses, showing Tom's photograph to hundreds of people, tracing down any threads he came up with. "Do you want me to try and locate his sons?"

"All right, that would be nice, you being Sanchez's friend and all. Like I say, Trooper Ingalls called the ranch where you said they were working, but they hadn't got back yet from Culbertson, Montana. So far as they know, he's still alive."

"She called today?"

"Right. The guy she talked to said they were going to stop at the Leadville rodeo before coming back to the ranch."

"Leadville, Colorado?"

"That's right."

"I'll see what I can do," said Wager. He hung up, his hand resting heavily on the telephone.

"What's the matter, Gabe?"

Wager looked up, the old familiar weariness of death making the flesh on his bones heavy and lax. "A friend died."

"I'm sorry." Max's head shook slightly. They both knew how little could be said, and less done. "You want a cup of coffee, partner?"

"Yeah. Thanks."

Max probably took a long time; Wager didn't know. With a start, he noticed the full cup at his elbow and sipped at the already cool liquid. Tom was dead and that was it—all of the man's life and energy and guts, all the things that he had meant and that Wager had admired and seen again as he sat there—all that was gone. And it seemed as if part of his own past was gone, too.

CHAPTER 6

"The sheriff's office still hasn't gotten in touch with them?"

Jo's voice interrupted the silence that had filled the Trans-Am when they entered the crowded Eisenhower Tunnel, where the echoing grumble of car and truck exhausts trembled the closed windows. A flashing red sign warned "Steep Grade—7% Next Six Miles," and told trucks to use low gear. They then were back into the hot sunshine at almost two miles of altitude, and before them the valley opened to show a corner of distant Lake Dillon and the clusters of resort communities around its shores. On the horizon, a blunt monolith shouldering up beneath a tattered cap of snow, Buffalo Mountain marked the Tenmile Creek valley and the road up to Leadville. South of Buffalo Mountain, the serrated peaks of the Tenmile Range were hazily reflected in the blue of the lake, and almost out of sight they could make out the pale streaks of ski runs carved through the black pines coating the mountains' flanks.

"Not to tell them that he died, no. The Highway Patrol called about the accident, but he wasn't dead yet."

"It seems ironic, doesn't it? They had just really found each other."

Ironic or related. Or maybe the gods took over when

people hadn't punished each other enough—but it was Wager's bet that the gods didn't have all that much work to do. "Yes."

"Did Detective Allen tell you anything about the killing?"

"Just what I've told you. He thinks it was the result of a robbery."

"And you don't?"

"It could be—that explanation shouldn't be ruled out, anyway. But it could have something to do with the boys, too."

"What?"

"I don't know." Wager glided into the left lane to pass a slow truck whose exhaust crackled with the engine's back pressure. "Then, again, it could be something different. Right now there's not enough evidence for any motive."

She watched the semi-truck drift back past the window as Wager threaded the Trans-Am through the heavy traffic of late spring and past one of the startlingly steep truck escape ramps that marked the long descent. "Do they ever use those?"

Wager glanced at the narrow strip of soft sand rising like a ski jump between the trees. "Every now and then. It beats going off the other side." He nodded at the ravine that plunged out of sight beyond the eastbound lanes of I-70. The far mountain was marked by the bald and rock-littered scrapes of snowslide paths that had uprooted the pine and aspen below tree line.

"Now that would really scare me," said Jo. "Riding down this hill in a runaway truck with no brakes, and hoping to hit that little bitty ramp at seventy or eighty miles an hour!"

"I don't know anyone who does it for sport," said Wager. "Not yet, anyway. Not like riding bulls."

"That's about the same." She shook her head. "Give me something I can have a little control over, something with a steering wheel or reins."

"I enjoy riding you when you're out of control," said Wager.

"Well, thanks a hell of a lot, cowboy. You'd better enjoy it, because that's the only prize you're going to win." She added quickly, "And don't start describing your technique."

"'. . . out where a friend is a friend . . .'"

"You'll be a real hit at the rodeo."

The highway leveled off at Silverthorne and the traffic tangled as feeder lanes led north and south to the increasingly congested towns that dotted the valley. On the lake, moving slowly in the light breeze, white triangles of sailboats glided in front of the surrounding mountains; all around this end of the lake, like fragments of row houses, condominiums stepped up the lower slopes of the hills. The road stayed crowded as it circled past the dam and the Frisco turn and through the narrow gulch that led to Copper Junction. There the four-lane freeway banked past another large ski resort toward Vail, taking most of the cars and trucks with it, and Wager turned with relief onto the narrower state highway that led over Fremont Pass to Leadville. It was there, at another small rodeo, that he hoped to meet Tom's sons. Regardless of how close to or distant from their father they were, the man was dead now, and they had a right to hear that from someone who cared about him, instead of from an official voice on the telephone.

And besides, Wager had a question or two for them.

.   .   .

The rodeo arena was just west of town beyond the newer homes that had spread out during another mining boom. Unlike Leadville's old downtown with its scattering of false fronts and turreted stone buildings put up in the nineteenth century, this area could have been a suburb of Denver. It had curving streets and cul-de-sacs and split-level homes offering a choice of three basic designs. On almost every block, for-sale signs were hammered into the thin lawns, indications that the latest boom was over and another bust had come. First gold, then silver, and now molybdenum. The only outside money came from tourists, now, during the brief two months without snow, and a series of red-white-and-blue signs made sure that few escaped the route to the rodeo.

"That wind is cold!" Jo shrugged into her parka as they left the car and trailed after a family toward the ticket booth. Despite the sun that glinted off the snow on the fourteen-thousand-foot peaks, Wager's cheeks tightened and he had to blink against tears that the dry, icy wind stung from his eyes.

"I'd hate to be riding today," said Jo.

"Is it worse in the cold?"

She nodded. "It's easier to get hurt when your muscles are stiff. Men and animals both."

The stands were placed facing away from both the wind and the afternoon sunlight that glared against the freshly raked dirt. Wager led Jo to a sheltered corner down near the arena barrier where the wind could not be felt as much. In a few minutes they were unzipping their parkas as the sun baked the crowd and the wooden planks, and drew out the odors of old lumber and animals and tobacco that reminded Wager so much of the rodeos he'd gone to as a kid.

"John's number forty-eight. I can't find James listed." Jo's finger slid down the names of competitors mimeographed on a loose sheet of paper inserted into the middle of the program. "Didn't they say both of them would be here?"

"They" was a man's voice Wager had talked to this morning when he called the T Bar M and asked for Tom's sons.

"What about?"

"It's an emergency. Is James or John available?"

"No. If you're calling about their daddy being hurt, I already been told."

"The boys haven't called the ranch?"

"What for?"

Because a ranch manager might be interested in the place. But all Wager said was, "Do you know where they'll be staying in Leadville?"

"No."

It wasn't much of a conversation and even less help; the man's slow voice offered nothing more, and Wager, deciding it was none of the man's business, did not tell him about Tom's death. He just said thank you and hung up.

Jo looked up from the program as a small band with a big drum started thumping out music from somewhere at the far end of the bleachers. Around them swirled a steady stream of excited faces and a large number of straw cowboy hats. "Do you want to go to the arena office? They might be here by now."

Wager nodded, and they elbowed their way beneath the clatter of heels thudding on the planks above. A haze of dust sifted down, swirled up again on eddies of wind, and settled on their parkas. The announcer's voice filtered through the crowd to welcome everyone to the first rodeo of the Lake County Jamboree Days, and the band started building up to the music of the Grand Entry. The office was a small trailer resting on cinder blocks and partially fenced off by wire mesh. A gap in the fence let them through, and Wager, looking out of place without a cowboy hat, joined the line waiting to get into the small office.

"Heyo, Dobie! What the hell you doing at this thing?"

"Picking me up some beer money. You bull riding today?"

"Bulls and barebacks, both. You seen Hugh around?"

Wager's turn came to shuffle up the board steps into the cramped room, where a sweating man chewed an unlit cigar and wrote in tiny print on a yellow tablet. "What you need?" The man raised his voice against the sudden cheer from the crowd and his bloodshot eyes glanced curiously at Wager.

"I'd like to leave a message for John Sanchez."

"Sure—message board's over there. Next!"

Four or five contestants were peeking over shoulders trying to read the pieces of paper crowded on the small square of corkboard. Wager tore a leaf from his notebook and reached in to tack it up, then worked his way back out again.

Jo, waiting, caught his eye and pointed. "He's over there—behind the trailer."

Through the figures hurrying as the announcer's voice ran over the last notes of the National Anthem, Wager caught a number 48 armband as it began to wink out of sight behind the steel bars of a portable stock pen and the bulky, restless animals it held. "John—John Sanchez—wait a minute!"

The face turned, puzzled.

"Just a minute, John!"

Sanchez saw him and paused, then the face said something to someone out of sight, and then it came toward Wager.

He nodded hello, his eyes touching Jo and then settling back on Wager.

"Can we talk somewhere quiet?"

"What about?"

"Your father."

"What about him?"

"He's been in an accident. A bad one."

From beyond a wooden gate leading to the chutes a voice called, "Sanchez—hey, Johnny, you're up!" And on the other side of the stands a clatter of loud applause and stamping boots swelled with the band and the announcer's voice.

"All right—La Hacienda after the show. It's south of town a mile or two. I got to go now—they're calling my number."

Jo watched the man trot away in a stiff stride. "He didn't seem very upset."

"They weren't very close. You saw that when we talked to them before."

"Still, he didn't even ask how badly Tom was hurt."

It could have been because he had his mind on the rodeo and his ride coming up in a few minutes. Or perhaps because he figured Wager would tell him soon enough. Or maybe he already knew.

Every now and then Wager forgot the reason he was at

the rodeo and lost himself in the explosions of excitement and speed, but for the most part he was preoccupied. Later Jo admitted that she, too, had only partially enjoyed the show. "But I don't know what else we could expect—it's not the easiest thing, to tell someone his father's dead."

For most people that would be bad news; for these two Wager wasn't sure. He wrapped his hands around the heat of the heavy coffee mug and felt the warmth of the large, dimly lit barroom begin to ease the cold muscles of his stiff back. Halfway through the rodeo, the shade of the bleachers had crept over their seats, and without the sun, that wind that scoured the snowfields on the fourteeners west of town began to knife through their clothes. By the time the rodeo ended, many of the spectators had given up, and those who stayed, like Jo and Wager, huddled together against the cold. In the car, they turned the heater up full, and by the time they inched their way through the traffic on the town's single main street, they warmed up enough to stop shaking. "It wasn't much of a rodeo anyway," said Wager. "They had some pretty sorry-looking animals."

Jo sipped at her steaming drink. It was a mixture of a little coffee and a lot of rum and called a Miner's Breakfast. The waitress promised it would get rid of a cold one way or another. "A lot of these amateur rodeos don't have any regulations to protect the stock. The flank straps weren't even padded on most of those animals."

Flank straps were used to make the horses and bulls buck harder. In professionally sanctioned events, a heavy sheepskin cushioned the animal's belly. But these today were simply leather straps yanked tight, and more than once, Wager had seen the raw pink flesh of bleeding ulcers where leather had chewed into the animal. In a lot of ways, the rodeos on this end of the scale were like those sad little carnivals you could still see traveling the back roads between towns too small for the big shows. Maybe in time they would belly up; but they hung on for as long as they could, patching up what was broken, painting over what was rusted, and squeezing one more season out of equipment that should long ago have been scrapped. It was a kind of defiance, and Wager understood it. Perhaps he even admired it. But it was harder to understand or admire doing it at the expense of the animals, and Wager wondered how long the stock contractor would get away with using damaged animals. "What was the prize money?"

Jo folded the program open and tilted it to the faint light from the bar. From a speaker somewhere across the room a steel guitar quavered through an equally metallic voice that sang, "To forgive is divine and you're making a saint out of me."

"It's not listed. Not much, is my guess."

"Probably enough to cover expenses and a little extra." Wager sipped his coffee and felt the hot liquid slide through the fading chill in his stomach. "It makes you wonder why the Sanchez boys keep doing it."

"There's a lot of money at the top," said Jo. "I read where last year's champion saddle bronc rider won over ninety-seven thousand dollars. And that doesn't include money for endorsements and fees for appearances. Of course, that's rodeoing full-time in the big time. I think the article said there were five thousand members in the Professional Rodeo Cowboys Association, but only a third could afford to do it full-time."

"That's a pretty good salary."

"The all-round cowboy won over a hundred and fifty thousand."

And that was even better. But for those few in the big money, there were a lot in these half-assed pumpkin rollers where, even when you won, you barely broke even. And if you started out like the Sanchez brothers without the schooling and totally on your own, your chances of getting up there were—as Tom had said—about as good as getting an abortion in the Vatican. Yet John and James did not give up; instead, they spent their money to chase their dream every weekend and even times in between. And they did it in a new pickup truck, using their own gear, while working for a rancher who didn't seem to mind paying them for not working.

"Is that them?" Jo squinted through the dimness at a cluster of figures who had just come around the partition guarding the front door. The group stood a moment talking earnestly about something, and Wager saw one shake his head no. The two hatted figures turned to look over the room. Wager stood so they could see him, and the two in cowboy hats pulled away from the others, who picked their way through the chairs and tables of the half-empty room to settle in a far corner and glance at Wager.

"Mr. Wager—ma'am."

"My name's Jo. Won't you sit down?"

They did, chairs pulled away from the table far enough to allow them to sprawl their legs. Neither took off his hat, nor did Wager expect them to.

"Care for a drink?" he asked.

"I don't mind if Jimmy don't. Hell, it's your party."

Wager lifted a hand for the waitress, and she took their orders. Gradually, La Hacienda was filling with cowboys and tourists and with the rumble of male voices. Here and there a girl in western clothes laughed loudly, the high sound piercing the noise, and someone started another record that sent a voice moaning, "You always were the sweetest just before you said goodbye."

When the waitresses brought their beers and Wager's fresh cup of coffee, Jo said, "You had a good ride on the bull this afternoon."

John bobbed his head thanks. "Yeah, well, given the stock and all, it wasn't too bad. We'll see what I draw tomorrow."

Wager asked James, "You're not riding?"

"No. I pulled a muscle in my belly up in Culbertson. I'll ride next weekend."

"How'd that happen?" asked Jo.

"My spurs got hung up on a bull and I couldn't pull loose. I could have rode today, but John said not to."

"Next week's a bigger rodeo," John explained. "No sense him making that muscle any worse on a piddly-assed show like this one."

Wager wasn't yet willing to bring the talk around to their

father. "Do you think you'll have a good chance to make it on the professional circuit? I heard that most of the pros are college graduates now, with a lot of experience in intercollegiate rodeo."

John's hat brim dipped assent. "It ain't easy, that's for sure. But there's still room if you're good enough. I may not be, but I'm sure as hell going to give it a try. I tell you who is good enough—that's Jimmy, here. This old boy's a rider!"

"John's good enough. He just don't like to brag."

"Still," said Wager, "I remember Tom telling me it's not like it used to be. He was afraid you boys were going to waste half your lives getting nowhere."

"He's a hell of a one to talk."

"Hush up, Jimmy." John explained it to Wager. "They're setting up a three-level system, now—regional circuits, national, and a new one, Tournament Rodeo. The regionals are mostly weekenders—part-time riders can go to those, and they're not so spread all over hell and gone. That's what'll help us out until we go national. For instance, the Mountain Circuit's Colorado and Wyoming, and it has its own standings and its own finals up in Cheyenne in October. If we do good there, we'll by God try full-time; we'll go on the national circuit. That's where the real money is, but you got to ride in a hundred and fifty, maybe a hundred and seventy-five rodeos a year. And do good in most of them." He drank his beer and leaned back.

"That's a lot of entry fees." Around fifteen to eighteen thousand dollars a year for each event entered. "Plus your other expenses."

"We got it figured, Mr. Wager. And we don't intend to come away losers all the time." He angled his empty glass at Wager and wagged it as he talked. "The money's there for the best man to take, and we aim to get our share."

Jimmy nodded. "I don't care what Daddy told you, Mr. Wager. We're going to get there."

"Tournament Rodeo has teams and sponsors—they pay entry fees and some expenses, and you might even get matching money in addition to the prize money. When that gets going on television, it's going to be big! And now's the time to start after it."

Wager said stubbornly, "But it's going to cost you a lot of money even to try. You must spend every penny you've got now."

"We don't ask nothing from nobody—and by God it ain't money that's going to keep us from making it. It'll be us! If we can't do it, that's the only damned thing that'll keep us from making it!"

"Jimmy gets kind of excited about the whole thing, don't he, Mr. Wager?"

"Being ranch manager must pay a lot better than your daddy thought."

"We do all right," said John. "It's good enough pay."

"You have plenty of free time, too. I didn't think a ranch manager could take off so much."

"Depends on how good the help is, don't it? Besides, if it don't worry the owner, I don't see why it should worry you."

Jo asked, "Do you like the riding events best?"

Both had the wiry build of their father, though John was taller and heavier. The only event in rodeo where size helped was steer wrestling; for the rest it was balance and quickness and—on the bulls—the ability to cling like a tick.

"We do timed events, too," said John. "Calf and steer roping. But that's something that takes a longer time to build up, and we ain't got good horses of our own, yet."

"I'm going over to the Roy Cooper roping school next year," said James. "We'll have enough money for it by then."

"Did you make or lose money today?" asked Wager.

John shrugged. "Paid for gas is about all. But I still got a chance at the average—I get that and some more day money, and we'll break even on this one."

The younger brother drained his beer glass, and Wager called for another round, including one for himself now that he was thoroughly warm again. Then he drew a deep breath. "The reason I wanted to talk to you . . ."

"You said something about Daddy being hurt?"

There wasn't any easy way to say it. "Tom's dead. Your father died yesterday afternoon."

John's brows creased together, and he slowly pushed a finger against his beer glass. James sat still and eyed Wager.

"They tried to get in touch with you, but you'd already left the ranch. So I said I'd come up and tell you."

"Dead." John's glass slid slowly across the table to trail a film of water that dried quickly. "I sure didn't expect that. He didn't deserve that."

"He deserved it. He deserved it and he got it."

"Shut up, Jimmy. You didn't know him. I did."

"I ain't shutting up. And I ain't sorry he's dead, neither. I ain't!"

"Shut up, I said!" The words jabbed across the table like a swift punch. "He wasn't all bad," John said to Wager. "He left when Jimmy was so little that he don't remember him, that's all."

"I remember what he did to Mama."

"That's enough, Jimmy." This time the warning was quiet, almost weary. "We appreciate your telling us in person, Mr. Wager. I reckon they've got him in a funeral home down there?"

"The hospital can tell you which one."

John nodded and moved to get up.

"There's something else," said Wager. "It wasn't an accident."

Both young men stared at him.

"He was beaten to death. He was hit with a blunt weapon."

"How do you know it wasn't a car that hit him?" asked James.

Wager tried to read his eyes. "What makes you think it was a car?"

"You told me it was an accident," said John. "He was all the time driving, so we figured it was a car accident."

"It wasn't. The autopsy said it was murder."

"Murder. . . . You got any idea who did it?"

"I'm not on the case," said Wager. "It's the Chaffee County Sheriff's Office. They'll probably want to talk to you."

"What about?" asked James.

"Anything that might help them out."

John said, "That won't be much. We didn't see much of him."

"Can you think of any reason why he might be beaten up?"

"No."

Wager sipped his beer. At the table next to them a half-dozen cowboys had settled in and were laughing loudly at something and flirting with the waitress. She grinned and said, "Anytime, cowboy," and they laughed again. "He didn't say anything to you?"

"What about?"

"He told me he was going to visit the T Bar M."

"He might have visited us," said John. "But we didn't talk much. Just about the ranch and rodeo and such." He drank deeply. "I thought you weren't interested in this case."

"I said I'm not assigned to it. I am interested—he was a friend."

"Yeah, well, we appreciate that. But there's not a damn thing we can tell you about him."

"How long have you been working at the T Bar M?"

"Me? A couple years. Jimmy just signed on."

"That's over in Ute County? On the edge of Canyonlands?"

"Yeah. Why you asking?"

"I like that country. I was thinking about taking a vacation out that way."

"There's a lot of country out there." John stood, James scrambling up beside him. "We're grateful you told us about Daddy, Mr. Wager."

"You don't have any idea what he might have been doing up around Salida?"

"No. We were up in Wyoming then."

"He worried about you two. He wanted things to work out for you."

John looked down at his thick hands and picked at something under a thumbnail. "He lived the best he could, I guess. That's what we all do, ain't it?" He touched a finger to his hat brim. "Ma'am."

Wager and Jo watched them thread their way between tables toward the group they had come in with. A voice or two called from the noisy crowd, and John lifted an answering hand in their direction, but he kept walking. Pausing at the corner table, he bent to speak for a few seconds, and then the two brothers went out quickly.

Wager said, "Be back in a minute" and worked his way over to the jukebox near the table. Four men sat with their heads close together. As Wager stood in front of the glowing record player, one of them turned to stare his way. He had pale red hair whose rough fringes dangled down his forehead, and a mustache cut to arc around a thin upper lip. Perhaps late twenties, early thirties; nothing else distinguishing that Wager could see in this light. But the man was interested in Wager. He stared until he caught Wager's glance; then he turned quickly back to the now silent men.

Wager dropped a couple of quarters into the machine and randomly poked the buttons. A few seconds later a voice wailed, "I asked for her hand, but all I got was the finger."

· · ·

"What's this about a vacation near Canyonlands?"

"We've been looking for an interesting place to go."

"I was thinking of Europe."

"I said interesting."

"Europe is interesting!"

"Well, maybe. But why don't you look in one of those vacation magazines of yours and see what they have around Ute County."

They had finally gotten a seat in a restaurant and were looking over the menu, which was decorated with pictures of miners and a languid young blonde in Victorian dress. Beyond the plate-glass window that fronted the narrow, long dining room, automobile traffic jammed up between the two traffic lights of Leadville's main street, and a steady procession of faces moved back and forth along the crowded sidewalk. On the wall facing Wager, an enlarged photograph depicted the town during the height of silver mining, and the present downtown section didn't look all that different from the photograph. Beside it, the same blonde stared out over the room, and beneath her was a scrolled name, "Baby Doe."

"Mind telling me why Ute County?"

"That's where the T Bar M is."

"That much I've figured out. What I don't know is why you want to go there."

"Tom's sons weren't exactly honest with us."

"I wondered what was going on back there—those questions you kept asking." She closed the menu and stared at Wager. "You were interrogating those boys! Even while you were telling them their father was dead, you were interrogating them!"

Wager didn't see anything to get excited over. "It's a homicide. Somebody murdered Tom."

"But they were up in Montana, at a rodeo."

"Maybe. Maybe they gave themselves enough time to swing through Antonito before they went north—it's about a five-hour drive at most from Ute County to Antonito. That might explain why he went willingly with his killers and why the wallet was missing: the sheriff would need time to identify Tom, and by then they would be in Montana."

"Oh, Gabe! You're talking premeditated murder—those boys can't be that cold-blooded!"

"I'm talking opportunity. They might have come by to visit and things got out of hand."

"But why would they kill him?"

Wager shrugged. "Hatred, maybe. He was pretty well worked over before he died."

The waitress came and apologized for taking so long to get to them. "Have you decided yet?" She shoved a lock of damp brown hair off her forehead and wrote down their orders. "Be a little bit—we're really crowded today with the rodeo and all."

"Do you really think either of them hated their father enough to do that?"

"That's one of the things I want to find out."

"You believe the murder might have been accidental— that perhaps the killer only meant to beat him up?"

That was consistent with the type of bruises on Tom's face—a series of blows that were not meant to kill. But there were murders, and there were murderers, and there were some ill-fitting pieces, too: why Tom went with his killers, why his wallet was missing if it was supposed to look like a hit-run accident. Until better evidence showed up, nothing could be ruled out. Which is what he told Jo.

She sipped at her wine and poked around in her salad. "What would they lie about?"

He told her what had caused Tom to come to him in the first place.

"Just rumors? That doesn't sound like much to be suspicious over."

"You've done barrel racing; you've been around these people. How many times did one of them come up and tell you what you ought to do for your own good?"

"Well . . ."

"Not once. They mind their own business, and they're proud of it. And somebody like Tom—just like his friends—would get pissed at anybody offering advice that wasn't asked for. No matter how good or how deserved or how well-meant."

"They are independent. Or like to think so."

"Which means that a hint would be enough for whoever told him. But Tom listened, and he didn't tell that whoever to mind his own business. He took it seriously, and I should, too." Especially since he didn't at first, and now Tom was dead.

"Why you?"

"He was a friend."

"And you don't think the sheriff's office is doing enough?"

"They don't know what Tom told me."

"Why didn't you tell them?"

"They believe it was a robbery, and that's the way they're approaching it. Any other theory's going to need hard evidence to back it up." Wager too drank a bit of wine. "And they might be right."

"What did Tom tell you after he went out to the ranch?"

"That everything was OK. That I shouldn't go asking around about the boys anymore." He pushed his salad aside to make room for the dish the waitress brought, saying, "Careful, that's hot," as she set it on the table. "But it wasn't what he said as much as how he said it. He sounded worried, not relieved."

"So everything wasn't OK?"

"That's another thing to find out."

Jo studied the heaping mound of spaghetti and sauce that steamed on the plate in front of her. "Well, if that's the only way you'll take your vacation, I suppose it's worth it."

. . . .

The first thing he felt was a smothering pressure across his mouth and then the unfamiliar softness of a body next to his. The warmth of an almost silent whisper moistened his ear: "Gabe—wake up. Gabe!" His eyes stared into the alien black, and then he placed where he was: a motel in Leadville, and Jo lay tensely beside him with her hand over his mouth. "Somebody's trying to get in. Are you awake?"

He nodded, and the hand pulled away. Wager eased silently out of bed, recalling the room's layout—the dresser with its large mirror and the suitcase racks across from the foot of the bed. Bathroom to the left. To the right, a low table and chairs under the curtained window; right of the window, the door to the walkway, where he heard the stealthy scrape of a tool probe for the latch. What he could not recall was if he had set the security chain. Behind, Jo moved in a rustle of sheets, and from the table beside the bed came the loud tick of his wristwatch. Feeling through the dark, Wager brushed lightly against the chair back where his holster hung; his fingers slid down the strap to lift the heavy weapon from the cool, worn pocket of leather. Toes gliding across the carpet, he edged toward the window and peered through a tiny gap in the thick drapes. The light over the door was gone, and in the shadows he made out only the back of a head and a shoulder as a man leaned close to work the lock.

With a sharp click, the latch tongue sprang back, and the noise seemed to make even his wristwatch hold its sound. Then, after a long ten seconds, the pale glimmer of the door eased open and a silhouette hung listening at its crack. Wager, his pistol held steadily at the poised shape two feet away, breathed silently. The door moved again, testing for the snug jerk of the safety chain, but there was none, and the silhouette moved quickly to slip into the room.

Wager said, "Freeze," and for a split instant the shadow did, then something leaped out to thud wildly against Wager's head, and he grabbed for the swinging arm and slashed his pistol barrel like a whip into the paleness that was the man's face. A breath of garlic and beer and tobacco grunted something, and then the figure kneed at Wager, the sharp bone catching his thigh with a numbing gouge, and twisted away from his grip. Wager swung again, happy to feel the weapon rake against the taut flesh over a skull and the man cursed and swung something that swished thinly through the air just in front of Wager's eyes. Wager's pistol came down on bone once more, and the man, gasping loudly now, pulled away with the clatter of something dropped and sprinted down the walkway, a staggering checkered shirt that flickered under the last two doorway lights and disappeared through the hedges at the motel's corner. Wager started through the door.

"Don't, Gabe—don't go out there like that!"

He paused, nude, then pulled the door shut. "You're right. I don't have my badge."

In the sudden glare of the lamp that Jo switched on, he picked up an open switchblade and placed the chain firmly in its slot.

"Why didn't you shoot him?" Jo, breathing rapidly, poured them both a glass of icewater from the bedside pitcher and sighed deeply.

"I didn't know if he was armed. Besides"—he wiped the snag of flesh from his pistol muzzle—"think of all the paperwork."

"I'm glad you didn't. And I'm glad you didn't get hurt. I don't think I could have kept from shooting."

Wager studied the switchblade, then pressed the release with his thumb and folded the long, grooved blade back into its handle. It was a good one, well designed, not one of those sold across the Mexico line to high school kids who bought them for the chance to feel tough. This one had blood grooves and a small guard that sprang out to keep your hand from sliding down the blade if you struck bone; it had a checked handle which would mask any fingerprints and offer a better grip if it was slick with blood.

"Did you see him? Do you know who it was?"

"No."

"What do you think he wanted?"

"Money. Whatever he could find."

"Do you think he was just a thief?"

He looked at her, but it wasn't fear that brought the question; her eyes were stretched, but with excitement and interest. "What's your guess?"

"Well, we've been asking a lot of questions."

"It wasn't one of Tom's sons. This guy was too tall. And he was wearing sneakers, not cowboy boots. I think he was just a thief. They're bound to be up here with all the tourists."

"But why us? Why this room?"

"I think he was going down the row and found somebody dumb enough to leave the chain off."

"Oh." It made sense, and she liked it better than the

idea that the Sanchez brothers were somehow involved. "I guess I shouldn't have thought what I did—I think I'm getting paranoid."

"A little paranoia keeps a cop alive."

"Thanks . . . but I'm glad you're alive. That knife—he tried to use it, didn't he?"

"He didn't have a chance to." Wager grunted, bending his leg and rubbing the soreness as he climbed back in bed. "He wasn't too good with his knee, either."

Jo's eyebrows lifted. "He didn't!" She looked under the cover and then back at him. "Did he?"

"Only one way to find out."

"Sex and violence? Is that all you're interested in?" She laughed and pulled him to her. "I guess it's too late to call in a report anyway."

"Too late and too much trouble. Up here we're civilians, remember?" Her arm tightened across his chest as he turned out the light.

The slow stroke of fingers up and down his stomach stopped. "Do you really think it was a burglar?"

"Sure I do." But as he played over the brief struggle with its blurred images, a vague memory began to emerge—a man with a curving mustache and a long fringe of hair curling up on the back of his neck.

CHAPTER 7

Molly White Horse—or, as someone had named her, Molly Pitcher—sat with her lawyer at the oak table in front of the spectators' benches. Across the aisle at the second table sat Deputy District Attorney Kolagny rustling through his sheaf of papers. It was a preliminary hearing, so the jury box was empty except for a guard and three men in the dark jumpsuits of the Detention Center. They were waiting for their arraignments to come up, and their faces held the blankness of inmates paraded before the public. Kolagny, with his usual arrogance, had ordered Wager to be present at the hearing as his advisory witness or else. Wager came, less because he was ordered than because Kolagny always needed any help he could get. He sat on one of the blond wooden benches and tried to stifle the yawns that kept surfacing through the drowsy heat of the courtroom. Outside the wide-open windows, the rush and clatter of traffic below increased the stuffy feeling, and Wager found himself wishing he could have bottled the icy wind of Leadville and brought it down with him.

"All rise!"

A brisk swirl of black robes, and the judge entered through the door leading to his chambers. He sat, and the bailiff began the hear-ye's and then called Molly White Horse. Her public defender, a short and pockmarked man with a full mustache, answered, "The accused is here, your honor," and patted the small, rounded shoulder under the dark dress with its splashes of scarlet flowers. His name was Parry, and there were always jokes made about him parrying the prosecutor's thrusts. But even if the jokes weren't very good, Wager thought the man was; and Kolagny would have to outdo himself just to stay even.

"Would counsel approach the bench, please. Mr. Kolagny . . . Kolagny—aren't you a counsel?"

"Yessir, your honor, coming."

Wager heard only a buzz of muted voices from the three men peering at each other across the barrier of the judge's bench, but he had a good idea what was being said: the judge asking if there were any grounds for settling this quickly, and of course the defense counsel would say no. No one whose client was up for murder ever gave an inch. Wager guessed Kolagny didn't give anything, either, because the judge nodded curtly and adjusted his glasses and the two lawyers strode back to their tables.

Kolagny argued that the evidence was strong enough for second-degree murder and asked that the charge be upheld. In the middle of the presentation, Wager felt a hand pat him on the shoulder and looked back to see Fred Baird, the lab technician, settle down on the empty bench behind him.

"You here for Molly's case?" Fred's sour breath cut through the heavily perfumed odor of his chewing gum.

Wager nodded.

"You think there's enough for second-degree?" he whispered.

"Hell, no. She didn't know she was killing him—there's no way Kolagny can show that Molly knew she was killing him."

Baird nodded once; the fluorescent lights in the high ceiling glinted off the streaks of scalp that shone through his thinning hair. Wager had not noticed before how fast

Baird was losing his sandy hair, or how tired and gray the man looked, either, as if his vitality were being drained off somewhere to let his flesh slowly collapse.

Then Baird shifted on the bench and the shadows disappeared, taking with them the haggard look and the little tinge of mortality that Wager had felt: Baird's and his own. "Did you tell him that?"

"Once. He didn't want to hear it," said Wager.

"Yeah. I thought manslaughter would be the max. Well, what the hell, I didn't have much to do today. Not much more than three months' work, anyway."

"Jesus, the state is really after this vicious criminal!" Gargan slid along the shiny wood toward Wager. "Bringing out all the big guns—I'm surprised you're not asking for the death penalty."

"She's not my candidate for that," said Baird.

"Hello, Gargan," said Wager. "Goodbye, Gargan."

"It's a democracy, Wager. I know it tears you up to hear that. And if you really want to get pissed, think about the First Amendment."

Wager sighed. Kolagny in front of him, Gargan beside him, and over his shoulder the fragrance of Baird's breath.

The lab technician was called to testify to the cause of death. At the trial, the medical examiner would be the one to detail the technical facts, but at a preliminary it was cheaper and quicker to use the police technician's statement rather than pay for a doctor's time. Baird half shrugged as he came back to his seat. Kolagny reminded the court that self-induced intoxication was not a defense to this charge and returned to his desk. The defense counsel took his turn and asked that the judge rule the death accidental and that any and all charges be dropped entirely on the grounds that Molly White Horse had neither the intention to kill nor the knowledge that she was doing it—not because of self-induced intoxication but because she did not know the beer was entering the deceased's lungs. It was self-evident, Parry said, that this uneducated woman who lacked medical knowledge had no idea of the extent of the victim's wounds and therefore was not acting with intent, with criminal negligence, nor recklessly.

"You hear that, Wager? You people shouldn't have brought that poor woman to trial."

That wasn't what he was thinking. As sometimes happened in the heat and the drone of voices, Wager's tired mind had a tendency to drift to those areas of thought that usually stayed at the edge of sleep. Right now, he was comparing court procedure and rodeo, the way they both tried to place rules and assessments on the chaotic flow of violent behavior. Here, the rules of evidence and procedure were played out in front of a judge who would declare either Kolagny or Parry the winner; in the rodeo arena, the judges applied rules to the fight between rider and animal and then said who won the most points. In both shows the animal was an excuse for the performance as well as a participant, be it horse or cow or Molly sitting there with her hair twisted up into some kind of braid that looked far younger than the curve of her slumped back and the narrow slope of her shoulders.

When Parry finished, the judge called a recess. "Time for his midmorning piss," muttered Baird. "I'll see you later, Gabe. Maybe I still got some time to get something done today."

Kolagny turned and beckoned Wager to his table. "We're going to get a trial out of this. You going to be ready to go?"

Wager looked at the man. He had been testifying in court before Kolagny had even sweated his application to law school. "I'll be ready."

"She saw the knife in that other guy's—Robert Smith's—hands, right?"

"That's what she said."

Kolagny was convincing himself more than Wager; but like a lot of lawyers the man needed an audience for his thoughts, and Wager guessed that was the real reason he had to give up his morning's sleep. "The most you're going to get out of this is criminally negligent homicide."

"Who the hell asked you, Wager? Who in the hell's got the law degree around here? You just get the facts; I'll handle the cases—that OK with you?"

"I'm your advisory witness, Kolagny. That's my advice."

"You keep your fucking advice until I ask for it, you hear?"

"You need more than my advice anyway."

The bailiff signaled the end of recess, and the judge, wiping his mouth with a handkerchief, reentered as everyone stood and then sat back with the shuffle and rustle of papers.

"Well." The judge hunched forward and looked at Molly. "A man's been killed. That's a highly serious action, and the charges are serious too. The defendant is apparently the cause of that death. Do you understand that, Miss White Horse?"

The back of the head nodded.

"That being the case, I feel there has to be a careful and considered weighing of the state's evidence. A man's death is not something to be shrugged off lightly. Therefore, I am ruling sufficient cause for a trial." He beckoned to his aide, who bent over and murmured. "Trial is set for . . . September fourteenth. I remind the defendant that she is still under bond to appear in court." The gavel dropped, followed by a general scuffling of feet and shifting of positions as Kolagny and Parry gathered their papers and left the desks, and the next lawyers came forward for their cases. Wager glanced at his watch: 10:30, and Sam Walking Tall's ghost had just been told that he had more respect from the state when he was dead than when he was alive. Wager yawned more widely. With luck, he could be in bed by noon and get his other four hours' sleep before his next tour.

.   .   .

His apartment did not have air conditioning, and the morning's heat lingered in the rooms as he opened the sliding glass door to his balcony and cranked out the bedroom window to trap any stray breeze. Ten stories below, Downing Street was quiet after the noon rush of office workers speeding toward various restaurants, and Wager could even hear the pad-pad-pad of a jogger cross the shimmering pavement at the intersection and head back under the canopy of leaves. The quiet stillness meant no breeze, and Wager, still sweating from a workout on his rowing machine, dragged the cold bottle of Killian's across his forehead. The exercise stretched and loosened those muscles that had tightened while he sat in court and especially as he listened to Kolagny. The beer was supposed to do the same thing for his mind so he could get the rest of his sleep. But it didn't seem to be working.

He thumbed through his green notebook for the telephone number and poked the little tune that rang the Chaffee County's Sheriff's Office. It took a minute or so for Detective Allen to be called to the telephone.

"This is Detective Wager up in Denver. Did the Sanchez boys get down there to claim their father's body?"

"Yes, they did, Detective Wager."

"Did they say anything about a funeral? Where and when?"

"I didn't think to ask them. Here's the local mortuary number if you want it—maybe they know about it." He read it to Wager. "Say, I found out why the hospital didn't notify you about Sanchez's death—I guess you stepped in shit over there with the hospital administrator, or something. Anyway, the nurse was going to call you and he told her not to, at least that's what she says. What the hell happened?"

Wager told him a little of it.

"All right. I guess she didn't have much choice if he told her not to. He's a foreigner, you know; kind of an asshole sometimes."

Wager knew. "Did you find out anything more about Tom's death?"

"Not much more than we already have. His sons weren't much help—they hadn't seen him in years, they said."

"Did you get in touch with his employer?"

A note of caution came into his voice. Wager's question was moving beyond professional courtesy into jurisdiction. "Why?"

"For some lead as to what he was doing up that way without his truck."

"He didn't know, Detective Wager. Like I told you, we don't know much more than we did. But I am working on the case."

"Can you give me his employer's name?"

"What for?"

"In case Sanchez has some pay coming. His sons might want to know about it. Did you tell them who he worked for?"

"Well, no. I didn't think of that—I figured they'd know. Tell you the truth, though, they weren't too interested in him."

"I'll pass it on to them."

"All right." He spelled the name and address. It was in Sterling, Colorado, in the northeast corner of the state and about 125 miles from Denver. Wager thanked him and after hanging up the telephone drew little doodles around the name and address. This wasn't his case, and he had plenty of Denver's to worry about. It sure as hell wasn't his jurisdiction, either. But his personal time was his own, and Tom had been a friend.

. . . .

He left in midmorning of the next day, aiming the Trans-Am up the long, straight lanes of I-76 as it sliced through the rolling, yellow prairie. On the western horizon, the ragged blue shadows of mountains gradually dropped below the sunbaked earth to leave an unbroken circle of sky and treeless land whose early green was felt more than seen beneath last year's winter-killed grass. It reminded Wager of being at sea, except that the oil-streaked concrete lanes split the yellow-and-blue world into hemispheres where, occasionally, a distant farm with its glimmering buildings and huddled cluster of tiny trees swung past the car. Despite the official fifty-five-mile limit, what traffic there was cruised at seventy, and Wager—finding pleasure in the feel of motion—settled the car into the flow of semi-trucks and salesmen and the occasional tourist who preferred this route to the more scenic swing through the Black Hills.

Sterling was a farm and ranch community as well as county seat, and had a scattering of light industry and the various services that went with it. The ones located near the interchange where he turned off were the restaurants and gas stations that highway travelers wanted; farther in, he passed farm-equipment lots and grain elevators, shopping centers and meat-processing plants, before finding the major crosstown street he looked for. State Highway 14 led out again, west; and beyond a row of towering cottonwoods lining an irrigation ditch, he found County Road W, a straight line of gravel that led from one horizon to the next. Turning, he slowed at the occasional mailbox to read the names. Finally, on one of the mailboxes planted in a dirt-filled milk can that could be lifted on top of the winter snows, he saw the name D. W. Barstow, and a lettered board below it, Shorty Barstow Rodeo Company. He turned and clattered across a rusted cattle guard, balancing the Trans-Am on the dirt road's center ridge to keep its underside clear of the occasional rock.

The ranch road led up a shallow bowl of prairie that cupped Wager between the dry earth and the heat-paled blue of empty sky. It wasn't hard to imagine the sudden appearance, on one of the surrounding ridges, of a line of Pawnee horsemen, silent, ominous, as they studied the wide valley below. And Wager felt the tug of wonder that must have led the first Europeans across these grassy seas of rolling earth. The next ridge was right there: gentle and inviting in its incline, mysterious in what it masked from view. Even if you knew that when you got to the top you would see only another broad, treeless valley, you still wanted to go. Because beyond that shallow next trough, only a mile or two, would be another gentle ridge just as inviting, and who knew what might lie beyond that?

He took this thought with him as he slowly steered the Trans-Am up the ranch road to the rim of prairie and tilted over into the next valley. There, along a small twisting cut fringed with a ragged growth of cottonwood and hackberry, sprawled a scattering of ranch buildings and corrals. A windmill flickered slowly beside a large stock tank, and on a small rise behind the two-story farmhouse, Wager saw the ungainly antennas of radios and the broad dish of a television receiving station. As he neared the packed earth of the yard, a yellow dog padded slowly from beside an outbuilding to bark twice and then stand with its head sagging beneath the sun and its tail wagging slowly. By the time he pulled beside a flatbed truck parked near the screened porch, the dog had turned and plodded back to its shady sleep.

Wager stepped out of his car into the weight of the sun. He stood for a moment and listened to the small sounds around him: the distant lowing of cattle, the rhythmic squeal of the windmill beyond the house, a zinging hum from some hurrying insect, the slow tick of his cooling engine. They made the larger silence spread until it matched the breadth of prairie, and Wager let himself drift for a few moments into the widening silence. Then he turned and went up the porch steps, his heels clattering on the sun-faded boards and into the welcome shade of the porch.

A girl answered his knock—late teens or early twenties, with dark hair falling in loose curls to her shoulders. She wore Levi's and a plaid shirt and walked with the stiff knees of a horse rider. "Can I help you?"

"Is Mr. Barstow in? I'm Detective Wager. I called earlier to tell him I was coming."

"Oh, yes—come on into the office. I'll tell him you're here." She led Wager to a small room in the front of the house and showed him a cowhide chair. The other furniture was a metal desk and matching chair, a manual typewriter on a wheeled stand, and—on one wall—a console with a computer screen, keyboard, and printer. Against the other wall, surrounded by shelves of livestock reference books and file folders, was a radio set. Its ON light was a bright green, and Wager could smell a faint mixture of utilitarian odors in the quiet room: leather, tobacco and sliced apple, the slight chemical tang of warm electronic equipment. The girl keyed the microphone twice and then said, "Daddy? Daddy—this is Judy."

"Go ahead, Judy."

"That detective is here. The one from Denver."

"OK—tell him I'm on my way in. I'll be there in about ten minutes. And Judy, did you hear anything from Earl?"

"Not yet, Daddy."

"All right. See you in a bit."

Hooking the microphone on its bracket, she asked, "Would you like some ice tea? Glass of water?"

"Tea would be nice."

"I'll be back in a minute."

The house was one of those large frame structures that could still be seen on the few farms and ranches near Denver that had not yet been sold for development. Two stories high, one long axis formed the front with its wraparound porch; the other axis led off behind the house like the leg of a T. It held the kitchen and other work areas. Wager bet that tacked onto the kitchen was a glass-walled room with a cement floor, designed for the wife's potted plants and for the husband to kick off his mud-crusted boots when he came in from the farmyard. In the coolness he could hear the life of the house, a creak of someone moving around upstairs, the startled squawk of a chicken beyond the back porch. From the kitchen came the rattle of crockery. A radio or television noise flitted briefly and then faded, and the distant gurgle of water down a long pipe in the walls was followed by a door shutting and the murmur of voices. The girl came back with a large glass of iced tea. "I forgot to ask if you wanted lemon. We got some if you want it."

"This is fine. Thanks a lot."

She smiled and left.

Wager was halfway through the glass when he heard the creak of heavy springs and saw a pickup mounted with wooden cattle barriers lurch into the yard. A stocky man swung out of the cab and crossed the yard with the same stiff-kneed walk as his daughter. A moment later they were shaking hands. He was slightly shorter than Wager and had a chest that bulged against his shirt from his collar to his belt; his graying hair was cropped short and stiff beneath the Stetson that he placed carefully upside down on his desk.

"So Tom got killed. He was a good man, and a damn good wrangler. I'm mighty sorry to hear about it."

"Did the sheriff tell you how it happened?"

"Only that he got hit by a car. Damned hit-and-run." Barstow lifted the lid of a worn humidor and tamped a couple of pinches of tobacco into a pipe. "Have they been caught? The ones that did it?"

"He's a homicide victim, Mr. Barstow. He was beaten up and died of blows to the head."

The match paused above the pipe bowl. "Tom? Tom didn't fight. Not anymore, anyway. Hell, all he ever drank was beer."

"Did he work for you long?"

"Almost fifteen years. And he never got into any trouble in all that time." He shook out that match and lit another, the flame bobbing down toward the tiny hiss of the bowl.

"He was still working for you when he died?"

"Sure. He was one of my top livestock scouts. Harder'n hell anymore to find good bucking horses. I don't know how Tom did it, but he could come up with the rankest stock in the business. We had five of his picks go to the National Finals in the last four years—Mean Velvet and Velvet Whirlwind won Top Stock for saddle broncs." Barstow's head wagged. "I'm going to miss Tom. So is rodeo— he knew his horses."

"Was Tom on a scouting trip when he got killed?"

"I don't know about that. Down near Salida, was it?" The pipe was going now, and Barstow leaned back in his chair.

"Yes."

"Could've been. We don't get many horses from there, but he might've heard about one and gone over to look at it." He explained, "They turn up in the damnedest places."

"Is there a lot of money involved in rodeo stock?"

"A lot? Well, I'm a medium-sized outfit and I got fifteen, eighteen million tied up in livestock, equipment, and personnel. The big outfits, the ones that have their own arena crews and sound equipment and announcers and clowns and all . . . well, yeah, you can say there's some money in it."

"Did Tom carry a lot of money when he was buying horses?"

"Oh—I see what you're getting at. You think he was robbed and killed?"

"It's a possibility."

"Yeah, I reckon it is. Hell, that's nothing new out this way, is it? But if that's the case, they must've killed him before they robbed him, because Tom wasn't likely to just smile and hand over his money." The pipe stem emphasized the words. "He didn't like to fight—but he could."

"So he was carrying a lot of cash."

"I didn't say that. I don't know. But you're right, a lot of sellers do want to get paid in cash so they can beat the goddam IRS, and I don't blame them. Don't know how much longer that'll last, though. Now they're trying to make me fill out a goddam form on every damned head of livestock I transfer. But he wasn't buying for me."

"He wasn't?"

"Not unless he had a line on a really top horse. I got my strings filled for the rest of the season. Bulls are something else—we're always after bulls, because there's so many rides them. But I got my horses. Unless, like I say, he heard of a real champion. But he didn't tell me about it if he did."

"Was he scouting for anyone else?"

"He signed on with me."

"And you weren't buying."

"No. Tom would have to get the money from me to buy, and I didn't hear from him."

"What work did he do when he wasn't buying?"

"Driver. He was supposed to drive some bulls up to Belt, Montana, on the twentieth. That's about when it happened, wasn't it?"

"He was found the night of the eighteenth."

"Well, when he didn't show up, I have to admit I cussed him some." Barstow's voice dropped to a rumble. "Poor old Tom, and me calling him names you wouldn't believe. I should've known—it was the first time in fifteen years he didn't show up when he was supposed to. I should've known."

"When was the last time you saw him?"

"Tell you in a minute." He anchored the pipe in his teeth and reached for a desk calendar and wet his thumb on a grimy sponge sitting in a little glass cup. Then he flipped back through leaves that were filled with notations. "The fifteenth. He came in with some head I bought off Beutler and Son down in Elk City, Oklahoma. Unloaded and went on down to his place."

"He drove the semi down to his ranch?"

"No—took that back to town. That's where my depot is."

"Did he seem any different? Worried in any way?"

Barstow settled forward on his desk, his pale eyes narrowing, and he puffed and tried to remember. "He did have something on his mind, yeah. But he didn't say what it was. Tom wasn't the kind to bring his troubles to anybody if he didn't have to."

"Did he say anything at all? Can you remember what he said?"

"Let's see, now—he just said he had to get on down to his ranch. I told him he could stay over here in the bunkhouse—hell, he was going out again in four days—but he said he wanted to get on home."

"He didn't say why?"

"No."

"Is there anyone he might have spoken to? Anyone he was close to?"

Barstow's head wagged. "You can ask down at the depot, but I don't think so. Tom's like a lot of the boys—he went his own way."

"Did he ever speak of his family or his sons?"

"He did mention them. In fact, he went out to see them—out on the Western Slope, I think. He said they were into rodeoing. He was proud of it."

"This was before or after the trip to Oklahoma?"

"Before. He went out there for a couple days and then came back and had the run to Elk City, then went home."

"Did he say how his visit went?"

"No . . . come to think of it, he didn't say word one about the boys when he got back. Just made his run and went home."

"Did he ever mention the T Bar M ranch?"

"The T Bar M?" The man thought back, his broad thumb with its thick, ragged nail scratching at the bristles under his chin. "I can't place it. I don't think I ever heard of it. They deal in rodeo stock?"

"I don't know. It's the ranch his sons work on."

"Oh. No, I never heard of it."

Wager tried one more general question—did Barstow know of any reason why Tom might have been killed—and heard the answer he expected. He got the address of the company depot in Sterling and thanked Barstow for his time, then left the coolness of the large old home for the glaring heat of the prairie.

As he drove, Wager tried to pull some tentative conclusions out of what Barstow told him. One of the clearest was that Tom had not been relieved but worried by whatever he found at the T Bar M. A second one—still hazy—was that he had been killed by someone who promised him something or by someone he knew. Someone, anyway, who could talk him into the long drive from Sterling to Antonito, and then get him in a car and drive north to Salida. Maybe. There were still a lot of maybes, a lot of things he needed answers for, and he might as well start.

Wager caught sight of a public telephone in the corner of a cut-rate gas station and angled the Trans-Am out of the noisy truck traffic that followed the state highway through town. Punching in his travel and access codes, he added the number of the Chaffee County Sheriff's Office. Defensive or not, Allen was still a cop; he was supposed to want to put the bad guys behind bars. The telephone was picked up on the first ring, and Wager asked for Detective Allen. When the familiar voice answered, he said, "This is Detective Wager, DPD. I'm calling about the Sanchez homicide again."

"There's not a damn thing new since yesterday, Detective Wager."

"That's not exactly why I'm calling. I just talked to Sanchez's employer up here in Sterling."

"Oh?"

"He doesn't have much to add, but he did say that Tom was not on a buying trip for him. Any money he had would have been his own."

"All right. But that could still be enough for someone to rob him."

"He also said that Tom was worried about something before he went home on the fifteenth. But he didn't know what."

Somewhere on a neighboring line a tiny voice buzzed dimly. "Do you have any idea what it might have been?"

"I think he was worried about something his sons may have been involved in. But that's pure guesswork. I'd like to find out for sure."

"I don't remember asking for your help, Detective Wager."

"And I don't remember saying I could do a better job than you can. But maybe I can save you some time and legwork up at this end of things."

Like a mosquito, the blurred voice rose and fell. Allen was silent, and Wager could imagine a mental coin tumbling through the air. It came up heads. "Did Sanchez say anything to you about his sons?"

"Only that he was worried about them. He thought they might have been running around with the wrong bunch."

"When was this?"

"A couple weeks before he was killed."

"Why in hell didn't you tell me this before?"

"As far as I know, his sons are clean. I didn't find a thing when I checked them out. That's what I told him."

"And as far as I know, Wager, I've got a robbery-homicide by person or persons unknown. I don't need any half-assed, farfetched theory thrown in to screw things up!"

"The man was my friend, Allen. He asked me to help him and then he got killed. I'm not saying you're right or I'm right—all I'm saying is this is a possibility and I'm asking for some information from you so I can check it out." He added, "If I find anything, it's all yours—call it interdepartmental cooperation."

"What kind of information?"

"How about starting with the autopsy report?"

"All right. Is that all you want?"

"Did you go down and look at Sanchez's ranch?"

"No. The Conejos SO took care of it. I told you that."

Wager would have gone if it was his case. Any good cop would have gone. But he kept his voice carefully neutral. "Did they mention any signs of a fight or if the place was messed up or broken into?"

"No. I didn't ask them. But I reckon if it had been, they'd have told me."

"Do you know if Sanchez had a family lawyer, or if he left a will of any kind?"

"None's come forward, Wager. God damn it, you're looking at this thing like those boys wanted his insurance or something! I'm calling it a stranger-to-stranger: Sanchez got taken for a ride and beaten up and robbed. And in the process of the beating, he got killed. Now that's what happened, and in time I'm going to find a witness who saw something and in a little more time I'm going to have me the son of a bitch that did it."

"You're probably right, Allen. That's probably just the way it happened." But it didn't explain why Tom went willingly with his assailant. "You'll send that autopsy report along?"

"Yes, shit yes."

The next call was to Sergeant Johnston, who told Wager

that he hadn't gotten back to him because of the budget preparation. But just yesterday Susie had combed the files for information about the Sanchez boys and the ranch.

"Did she find anything?"

"No. No contacts at all."

"Will you look for a Jerry Latta?" Wager spelled it for him.

"All right, Gabe. I'll get back to you when I can—we're pretty busy with our own stuff, you know."

"I know that, Ed. I'm grateful for your help."

His next stop was the depot where the Barstow Rodeo Company parked its vehicles. It was a large compound of packed earth fronting a butler building that had three or four service bays for working on trucks. On the hardstand, a line of cattle trailers shimmered in the heat, their slatted aluminum sides bearing the initials BRC made to look like a cattle brand. Two tractors, bobtailed and nose-heavy without their trailers, were parked near a small cinder-block building that said "Office." Wager opened the door.

A middle-aged blonde whose makeup was carefully brushed on looked up from her paper-littered desk. "Hí— what you need?"

Wager showed her his badge. "I'm Detective Wager from Denver. I'm trying to find out some information about Tom Sanchez."

"Oh, wasn't that awful! And such a nice fella, too."

"Yes, ma'am. Were you here when he turned in his truck on the fifteenth?"

"Sure. That was the run to Elk City. Jason sent over for some Brahmas."

"Jason?"

"Mr. Barstow. Everybody calls him Jason. We had more bull riders register for the Strong City show than we expected, and he had to get some more stock in."

"Did you get a chance to talk with Sanchez before he went home that day?"

"We had a cup of coffee. The fellas always stop for a cup of coffee after a run." She pushed her fingers through the pile of stiffly curling hair that was equally pale down to the roots. "They tell me about the road conditions so I can pass the word on, or any equipment troubles they had on the run. That way I can schedule maintenance." The telephone rang, and she excused herself to talk to Norman about a generator. Wager glanced around the small office. A sagging leatherette couch shoved against one wall held a worn copy of the *Pro-Rodeo Sports News*. Filing cabinets and charts crowded the other walls. That and a small table with its dented coffee urn filled the room.

The woman hung up, and Wager asked, "Did Tom seem worried about anything when you talked to him?"

"Well, he was pretty quiet. But then Tom's usually pretty quiet unless he knows you real well. I remember Jason wanted him to stay over for his next run, but Tom said he had to get on home."

"He didn't say why?"

"No, but I figured he just didn't want to stay around. In fact, he did seem quieter than usual, and that would be like Tom: when something was bothering him, he'd be likely to go off by himself. A lot of the fellas when they have a problem, they'll tell me about it, you know? It sort of helps for them to tell somebody. But not Tom. He kept things pretty much to himself."

"Did he have any particular friends he might have talked to? Anybody he went around with?"

The blond pile shook slowly. "He had a couple drinking buddies, I guess—Larry Atchison and Tubby Tubman. I guess that would be the closest."

"Can you tell me where to find them?"

"Well, one of them should be up in Belt, Montana, right now; and the other one's probably somewhere between Hugo and Claremore, over in Oklahoma."

Wager thanked her for her time and asked if she'd give his card to the two men when they came back. "They can call me collect at this number."

The heavy makeup on her lips stretched into a smile. "Sure. You have a nice day, now."

. . .

Jo had asked if he wanted to have dinner after he returned from Sterling, and by the time he got to her house, she was well into a sauce for the broiled fish.

"Damn—I think I'm out of bay leaves—no, here it is! What did you find out?"

Wager stretched against the pull of muscles that had grown weary and tight on the long drive back down I-76. "All I really ended up with is more questions. But I managed to win friends and influence people."

"Who?"

He told her about his call to Detective Allen.

"Do you think he'll complain to Chief Doyle?"

"I haven't given him anything to complain about."

"It's his case and his jurisdiction."

"I'm sticking to my side of things."

"You're sticking your neck out, too."

It wouldn't be the first time, and there was no sense worrying about something that might never happen. Wager rummaged through the refrigerator and felt his dry mouth tighten at the sight of a frosty Killian's. But he picked up a soft drink instead. Despite what the long hot drive and his thirst told him, his working day was just beginning.

"I've got some news for you," said Jo. She peeked into the oven at the slabs of halibut beginning to sizzle in their juices.

"What's that?"

"I telephoned a girl I used to barrel race with. I thought I remembered that she and her husband went into ranching over in Ute County. I wasn't certain, but I called her parents, and it's the same girl."

"Well, that's certainly news, all right."

She pulled back from the oven door. "If you'll let me finish, wise-ass, you might think it is." She waited for him to make some comment. "So I called her, and they have a cabin they usually rent to hunters in the fall. It's not a dude ranch, but she says they'll be happy to let us rent it—they could use the cash. And they'll throw in a couple of horses as long as we care for them. She said they don't get enough exercise anyway."

"Horses? Jo, I don't know how to ride a horse!"

"It's easy," she said. "And you're the one who wanted a vacation in Ute County, remember?"

CHAPTER 8

Max asked the same thing Wager had asked himself. "You're going to ride a horse for three weeks?"

"I'll probably get off now and then to take a piss." It was Wager's turn to drive, and he had to stretch his legs to work the gas and brake pedals. The seat was shoved back against its stops so Max could fold himself into the car. It was almost 2:00 a.m., closing time for the bars, and they cruised past a small cluster of ill-lit corner taverns in the Chicano area near Hirshorn Park. On a weekend, you could count on a stabbing or shooting at one of the places, but weeknights, even hot ones like tonight, were usually quiet. Wager paused at Thirty-second Street and peered for a moment into the open door at the dark blue lights; a shadow or two moved across the dull glow, and a man came to the door and looked at the unmarked car. Then he pulled back out of sight. Wager finished his turn past the lesbian bar with its single yellow bulb lighting the front porch. It seemed no different from the small houses that filled the rest of the block, the only advertisement being a dirt parking lot that used to be a patch of lawn. A few expensive cars, Mercedeses and BMWs, were parked discreetly in the shadows of water-starved trees.

"Think you can handle all this excitement while I'm gone?"

"The excitement I can handle. Your friend Gargan is something else."

"Why?"

"You didn't see the article on Molly White Horse in this morning's paper? Gargan quotes some guy from the Native American Institute about the Denver police having a vendetta against Indians."

"What the hell for?"

"That he didn't say. But from there he goes into the Molly White Horse hearing. He makes it sound like you and I, old buddy, are Gestapo agents."

"Screw him."

"My sentiments. But money is that the Bulldog and everyone else up on the top floor will be very uneasy with this case. And when they feel uneasy, we feel downright uncomfortable. You're taking a vacation at the right time."

"It's in the DA's hands now—Kolagny's the one who pushed for murder."

"You know that. I know that. Even the Bulldog knows that. But nobody's explained it to Gargan."

Wager turned the car toward the Eighteenth Street viaduct and lower downtown. "Maybe I'd better stay. You might need some help with this one."

"You take off—you've covered for me enough times. Tell you the truth, Gabe, I'm glad to see you take a vacation."

"Why's that?"

"You need a change of pace. Everybody does. Recreation—you go out and get re-created."

"A part of me's going to get re-created on that horse. Have they told you who your new partner will be?"

"Golding. He comes on this weekend."

Golding. The guy with an opinion on everything, and all of them wrong.

"He's OK. A little full of himself sometimes, but he draws the same pay we do."

"Right. What's he into now?"

"Vegetarianism. He was telling me about his low-karma diet."

"What the hell is a low-karma diet?"

"Something he picked up from the Hare Krishnas."

"The hairy Krishnas? Does he hang around airports now?"

"No. They left some stuff on his doorknob—a bunch of propaganda and a vegetarian cookbook. He's been trying some of their recipes."

They crossed over the Valley Highway and followed dark and empty streets into the tangle of railway tracks and weeds that was the South Platte River bottom. "When I get back, you'll have your head shaved."

"It's not in my karma."

Wager drove cautiously, alert for any silent, gigantic shape looming out of the black and bearing down on them with only the slightest rumble of wheels. This was the time boxcars were switched farther down in the yards, and more than once he had almost been hit by one of the unlit, free-rolling cars. It was also the time when anybody down here shouldn't be here, and both he and Max glanced habitually out the open car windows into the shadows of the warm night.

"Jo's going with you, isn't she?"

"Yes."

"Better watch it, partner—you'll end up married one of these days."

"I've been there once. That's enough."

"Jo's a very nice girl. And very good-looking."

Wager knew that. But he was damned if he saw any necessary relationship between Max's statements. "I'm expecting an autopsy report up from Chaffee County in the next day or two. If it comes before I leave, will you give me a call?"

"Sure." Max frowned. "What case is that?"

"It's not ours. It's my friend who got killed—Sanchez."

They were silent as they worked their way back to the police garage, with side trips through one or another of the deserted and ill-lit corners of town where people went to do things they didn't want seen. They made a final pass through Little Juarez on Larimer Street, joining a small parade of blue-and-whites who also converged on that familiar trouble spot at about this time. Then Wager headed through the empty intersections toward District One headquarters.

On the way up in the musty-smelling elevator, Max finally got around to asking the question Wager knew he would ask. "Why do you want that autopsy?"

"A little light vacation reading."

They went through the familiar routine of checkout that Wager had followed so many times without even thinking about it: settling the radiopack into its desk charger unit, hooking the ring of car keys on the keyboard, a final look for messages. Wager spent a few minutes cleaning off the top of his desk and locking the loose junk in his drawer. Then he glanced around one more time.

Max grinned at him. "It's not that hard to let go, Gabe. Try."

"I feel like I'm forgetting something."

"Come on, partner—your vacation's started. Let's get out of here before somebody calls for a homicide detective."

Wager followed the man's wide back to the personnel board and moved his name to an unaccustomed slot: On Vacation. It looked odd over there, but it was too late now; and if he was lucky, maybe it wouldn't be a total waste of time. He and Max rode back down to the ground floor without speaking. In the parking lot, the big man gripped his hand. "Come on, Gabe, look happy—you're supposed to enjoy this. Believe me, there'll be plenty of homicides left when you get back."

Wager knew that. He knew that the department would survive even if he never came back. Cops were always coming and going—quitting, getting fired, transferring to other police agencies for better jobs—and the department managed no matter who went. Yet he felt the unease—not quite a threat—of his life shifting its points of reference. And as a part of that unease and foreboding, the pale orange light of the parking lot's sodium lamps brought something new to Axton's face; it was as if Wager were looking at it for the last time. "You watch yourself, Max."

"With Golding for a partner, I'll be wide awake every second." A massive hand gripped Wager's shoulder and gave it a squeeze. "Have fun—really! A little vacation's not going to kill you."

.   .   .

The cabin was better than Wager had expected, a long, low building made of thick notched logs with a rambling screened porch across two sides and an outhouse a hundred yards off. It had a rock fireplace for heat and a hand pump over a chipped sink for water. A propane-fed stove and a noisy refrigerator finished the kitchen appliances. Four single beds were lined up in one room, and the other was a combination dining and living area furnished with heavy wooden chairs and a large pine table. A sagging couch could also serve as a cot, and on the walls were racks and hooks and cabinets for guns and jackets and gear. The best part was the location—a half-mile away from the ranch house and out of sight on a narrow road that wound across juniper-covered hills.

Within a short walk, a small, rocky stream cut through the sandstone to join the nearby Dolores River. There were trout in the stream, Rusty Volker had told him, but the water was muddy now with spring runoff, and you had to use bait rather than flies.

"How much of the stream's on your land?" Wager asked. The two men had sat at the kitchen table in the ranch house groping for something to talk about while Jo and her old friend, Dee, giggled like schoolgirls and kept going from one corner of the house to another as they thought of something new to look at. Wager didn't talk horses or cows, and Rusty wasn't more than politely interested in the Denver Police Department. They were both relieved to find fishing.

"About a mile—it winds around a lot."

Through the wide glass behind the sink, Wager could see a distant level valley blue-green with sagebrush. But here, closer to the barn-red buildings of the ranch, the land was broken into low hills that showed ledges of red and yellow and orange sandstone. They were dotted with piñon and cedar and juniper that reached only a little higher than a horseman's head. It was like the caprock country down in New Mexico, and the land could fool you because it looked so level when you gazed across it toward the snowy peaks of the La Sals. In reality, it was cut by ravines and canyons that all tended to drift west toward the deeper cut of the Dolores River, and every now and then, from some sudden bluff, you realized that you were high up on a mesa's eroded surface and that the land stepped in vast ledges down and away toward Utah.

It seemed odd to have the sky open up in that direction. In Denver, the western horizon was blocked by the Rockies, and the palest skies were seen over Kansas, Here, the pale edge of the sky was in the southwest, over desert country; and beyond the horizon's curve the earth seemed void except for the occasional glimmer of distant, scattered mountain peaks. The whole world seemed to slope toward California. Which, he guessed, it did—if the Colorado River was any measure.

"Is it stocked?" Wager asked.

"The Forest Service stocks it upstream in the national forest." He grinned, drawing the skin tight around a long and bony jaw. "But some of them manage to get down this far."

"This looks like pretty thin grazing land."

"It is. You figure an average of forty acres a cow. And then they walk off a hell of a lot of weight going for water. But we could still make a go of it if it wasn't for the damned government. I swear those people back in Washington are doing their best to ruin as many ranchers as they can."

"Hard times?"

This was a subject that interested Rusty even more than fishing, and he leaned forward, the creases around his mouth coming back. "Damned hard. I just hope we can hang on till something changes for the better."

"Are the other ranchers having troubles, too?"

"I don't know anybody who isn't. The price of equipment, feed, fuel, medicines—hell, they've all gone up and up. And so have the damned imports. Now BLM wants to raise grazing fees, and we just can't get the beef prices to cover it all anymore. It's a wonder everybody just don't sell out and let them all become damned vegetarians."

"Help must be pretty expensive, too."

"Hell yes! When you can get it. And decent help you might as well forget about. Even the damned Mexicans are starting to ask minimum wage." He glanced at Wager. "Of course, I don't mind paying them—they know what a day's work is. But by God now the government wants me to start checking birth certificates or something. All I want to know is if a man can do the job. If he can, I'll hire him, and to hell with those people back in Washington."

"You don't have any hands working now?"

"Two. They're good boys, and I keep them on most of the year: old Henry and Joaquin. But come roundup, you take whatever you can get and you're happy to do it."

"Do most of the ranches do that? Hire a few hands full-time?"

Rusty nodded. "Unless they have enough family to do the work. Dee and I haven't got started in that line yet."

"How many ranches are around here?"

"Oh, six in this end of the valley. Another five up north. Not as many as there used to be."

"Is the T Bar M nearby?"

"Sure is. About twenty, twenty-five miles by the highway; a lot closer by horse. It's down on the Dolores below Rimrock. That's one of those that's give up and sold out."

"The ranch is sold?"

"A couple years ago. Somebody named Watkins bought it. Old Tyler McGraw, he just said to hell with it and sold out. Can't blame him. I'm not going to if I can help it, but I sure can't blame anybody who does."

"It's a cattle ranch?"

."Not much else to do with this land. Sure as hell can't grow anything on it. And with beef prices what they are . . ." He shook his head. "There's no way out—you hang on and starve or you give up." His eyes, too, went to the kitchen window and the open, empty land beyond. "I'm not giving up."

"But somebody bought McGraw's ranch."

"Yep. And I guess they're sweating and cussing with the rest of us now."

"Have you heard anything about the ranch since Watkins bought it?"

"Heard anything? Like what?"

Wager shrugged. "How they're doing. What they're doing."

"No. Never met Watkins. Dee and I drove over a month or so after we heard the ranch was sold—went over to introduce ourselves to the new neighbors. But the only one there was the cook. He said everybody else was out on the range. We left our telephone number, but they never called back. That doesn't seem very friendly, but with a new ranch and all, they were probably real busy." He sipped his coffee and eyed Wager. "You seem pretty interested in them."

"A friend of mine has a couple of sons working there. I thought I'd go by and say hello while I was over this way."

"Oh. Well, as far as I know, they're doing about as good as the rest of us. If you want to, you can take the horses over—makes a nice day's ride. You just cut over to White Creek Draw about ten miles north; it's a good trail."

Wager smiled. "That's worth thinking about."

Jo and Dee came in still laughing about someone they remembered from barrel-racing days. Dee was a short, blond woman whose face was starting to get taut and dry like her husband's; she still had an athletic body, and her hands always seemed to touch someone on the shoulder or arm or back. It had been obvious since they drove up how happy she was to see Jo, and that pleasure included Wager even if, on occasion, she didn't quite know what to say to a big-city detective.

In the moment of silence before she thought of something, a gust of hot wind from the Utah desert whistled emptily against the window screens. "Let me get you some linens and blankets." She patted Wager on the shoulder and disappeared again.

Jo, excited and happy, started talking with Rusty about which horses they could use. Wager half listened and nodded when he was supposed to and thought about the Sanchez boys and the autopsy report in the glove compartment of his car. Max had called yesterday evening to say it was in, and Wager picked it up on their way out of town this morning. Its form differed from the DPD style, but it gave him a clear picture of Tom's body and the cause of death: brain injury resulting from two blows at the back of the head, both of which fractured the skull and depressed it enough to indicate a cylindrical weapon about two inches in diameter—like a piece of pipe. A long list of scars and healed injuries was sketched in until the doctor got tired of detailing them and simply started saying "previous injury" and the general location. The most interesting part of the report to Wager was the indication of fresh scrapes and cuts along the knuckles and fingers: Tom had used his fists. There were new bruises on his forearms, too, which indicated defense wounds—the kind a man got when he fended off an attack with his bare hands. Additional abrasions on the elbows and shoulders and back indicated that he had been thrown or dragged across a rough surface like a road bed. Those last wounds still had dirt traces in them and probably came when he was shoved from the moving vehicle. Whether or not he was still fighting when he was thrown out, the autopsy couldn't say; but from the lack of grit and dirt in the cuts on his hands Wager guessed the man was already knocked out and no longer a threat to whoever was with him in the car. If they wanted to, they could have stopped and dumped him; but they didn't, and they got what they were after, a dead man.

The toxicology section showed no trace of alcohol, which wasn't surprising since he had been in a coma for days before he died. Nor was there much else in the report that seemed to be of help. What it boiled down to was that Tom went willingly with some people, then fought with them, then was clubbed unconscious, searched, and thrown from the moving vehicle. What was not indicated was a planned homicide—when a murderer plans the death of a victim, he doesn't give him the chance to fight back. It also indicated more than one person: a driver and one or more to thump on Tom. He was old, but he was tough and quick and wiry, and whoever he lit on had his hands full until he—or an accomplice—landed a couple of blows to the back of Tom's head. If the driver alone had done all that, the car would have been parked and Tom wouldn't have bounced and rolled off the pavement and onto the road's shoulder.

Dee came back with a stack of sheets and towels and blankets, handing them to Wager to take out to the Trans-Am. She also gave him instructions about how to turn on the gas at the propane tank and where the master switch was for the electricity.

"There's no TV down there, but we have a dish and the reception's real good. If you want to come up this evening and watch, we'll be real glad to have you."

Jo asked if they wanted the rent now, and Dee hesitated, then nodded firmly. Rusty looked away as Wager counted the bills into her hand. She shoved them quickly into the hip pocket of her jeans.

"I'll be down later to see how you're getting along," she said; and Wager eased the Trans-Am along the sandy ruts that wound out of sight between the knobby, tree-dotted hills.

It had taken them about an hour to unload groceries from the car and to stock the refrigerator and cupboards, Jo happy with the sense of domesticating the place and even Wager sharing the feeling that it was somehow theirs. They emptied their suitcases into the squeaky drawers of one of the old dressers, and Jo found a large blue coffeepot for heating and pumped up a stream of icy well water and filled it. Wager, nosing around the back of the cabin, followed a dim trail down to the creekside. A fringe of high weeds

lined the stream bank, and his approach scared a large
heron from a wide pool that formed against an overhanging
cliff of sandstone. He watched the bird rise swiftly and then
glide to gain speed and escape by skimming near the roil-
ing water. Then he climbed a low rise where the sparse
grass thinned to a crumbling shelf of wind-sculpted rock
that lifted higher than the piñons about it. From here he
could see the distant glimmer of snow on a bulge of mountains to the west—the La Sal range over in Utah. And to
the south a single mountain rose out of a level, hazy plain:
North Peak with its own coating of snow. Beyond that, by
fifty or a hundred miles, were the broken eruptions of the
San Juans, fourteeners whose snow showed the crumpled
blue of sheer faces and knifelike ridges. To the east, gradually rising to form a long, wavering line across the sky, timbered ridges and cliffs lifted into the snowfields of the
distant Uncompaghre Plateau; and closer lay a flat, treeless
valley where sagebrush darkened the gray soil in broad,
pale shadows. North, like sentinels facing each other over
miles of windy space, receding thrusts of mesas showed the
earth's old crust where the ancient river that was now the
Dolores had carved its way toward the Colorado. Over it all
was a cloudless blue sky as large as any Wager had ever
seen—as large and as empty, and it dwarfed even the wide
span of empty land that spread between the distant shining
peaks.

Between the high plateau of the east and the purple canyons where the Dolores and its feeder streams twisted out
of sight to the west were mesas and fingers of rocky earth
and sudden, thousand-foot-high escarpments of red-and-
yellow stone cut by gulches and draws and valleys. Covered with the piñon and juniper that grew wherever a root
could anchor itself against the wind, the draws and canyons
formed isolated worlds guarded by steep walls. It was down
into them that hunters went for desert sheep and deer, for
elk and turkey and bear. But that was a sport that no longer
interested Wager; he had not shot animals since he left the
Marine Corps. Nor did he want to, anymore.

A screen door slammed at the cabin, and Wager raised a hand to show Jo where he stood. She joined him and also gazed out across the wide sweep of ridges and valley and headlands of ancient caprock. "It's not the kind of scenery most tourists would like, is it?" she asked. "It has grandeur . . . but it's lonesome. Even the sunlight seems lonesome."

"So does your friend Dee."

"She says she's not." Jo shook her head. "But I think she is and doesn't know it. She keeps talking about having children."

"They don't want any yet?"

"They've tried, but I guess they can't. I didn't ask what the problem was."

Overhead, an eagle angled sharply across the blue toward a mesa's craggy face. There was so much earth and sky that the trees looked stunted, and every mark of humanity seemed limited and temporary as if it, too, could be swallowed. Carried on the wind like a distant moan, a cow's call drifted toward them.

Jo was right. It wasn't the kind of territory most tourists would flock to—no lakes or nearby mountains, no ski runs or plastic villages, no national monuments or striking rock formations. Without much tourism, with most of the mines long played out, only farming and ranching were left. If a man didn't make a living connected in some way with ranch life, he moved on. And from what Rusty said, even that was threatened.

"It's an empty country," said Wager. "I like it."

"So do I," said Jo. Then she poked his ribs with a thumb. "It's good horse country, too."

.   .   .

It took Wager a couple of days to begin riding with some of the ease and smoothness that Jo had. The new corral and barn behind the Volkers' ranch house were painted dull red and trimmed neatly in white, and the corral fences had been whitewashed to give the ranch a well-kept feeling.

A few carefully tended trees, fenced with chicken wire against the horses' teeth, were planted to bring shade for the next generation of Volkers, but for now the sun baked the sandy corral and horse droppings into a rich odor that nonetheless smelled clean. Sheltered against a wind-pocked ledge, two mobile homes rested on cinder blocks. One was empty; the other was shared by the two ranch hands: Henry with his silver hair and whiskey-red nose, and young Joaquin, who smiled whitely and spoke little English.

"Dee said we can use the old corral down near the cabin. Rusty's sending a couple bales of hay down tonight," Jo said. "That way we won't have to walk so far for the horses in the mornings."

Wager eyed one of the stubby brown animals, which cocked its ears at him. "I don't mind walking."

"Come on—I'll show you how to saddle one."

Jo and the horses liked each other, but Wager couldn't say the same for himself. It was, she said, because he wasn't familiar with the equipment and the animals—he was uneasy, and so they were. But down at the old corral and away from the amused glances of the hired hands, Wager learned to curry and wipe, to talk gently while he worked around the animals—"They like that"—to search the saddle blanket for burrs before lifting it over the horse's back, to free the blanket of any wrinkles that might chafe. He still had some trouble putting the bit into his horse's mouth in the mornings when the gelding was feisty and tossed his head, but Jo showed him how to run his thumb back along the animal's gum, and the mouth opened obediently.

"Don't get your thumb between his teeth."

"I'm not about to!"

Even on the first day's ride, a few hours out and back, Wager found himself easing into trust with the animal, and—with good advice from Jo—he learned how to adjust the rhythm of his body to that of the horse. At least on a walk or a gallop. With a trot, he still seemed to go down when the saddle came up, and more than once the jar knocked his straw cowboy hat down over his ears. He was careful not to push the horse to a trot when Henry or Joaquin was around.

Jo, of course, rode well; the happiness that showed in her face and voice was contagious, and he heard himself yelping as he galloped after her down one of the twisting trails that plunged through the scattered piñons. As Wager learned more, he gained appreciation for how good a horsewoman she was. It was a pleasure to watch her, on a morning ride after man and beast had warmed up a bit, as she clucked her horse into an easy gallop along one of the sandy tracks. Her weight moved forward over the withers and her head and back made a smooth, even line above the horse's bobbing torso. Wager, feeling his awkwardness in comparison, gave his horse its head and lumbered after, trying not to grab the pommel as the lunging weight between his legs swayed sharply this way and that over the rough ground in a futile effort to catch up.

"You did fine! You did great!" Jo reined to a short trot, then to a walk as the horses snorted and cooled in the wind along this ridge of high earth.

"Right," said Wager. His horse looked back at him, and in the large, moist eye Wager saw a touch of disgust. "But I don't think Old Paint believes you."

She leaned close to give him a kiss, the saddles creaking beneath them. "His name's Major. And he's not disgusted at all. He just likes to win—like someone else I know."

They followed the ridge out to a point of rock where the cliffs dropped away in steep, treeless shale and a tangle of fallen caprock. In the distance, a dark streak broken by foaming white patterns, the Dolores River made a tight bend against a five-hundred-foot wall of smoothly sheared sandstone. Beards of dark stain washed down the red wall where eons of seeping waters left mineral deposits, and from the top of the cliff, the piñon forest began again. In the arc of the river's bend lay a startlingly green triangle of growth, and Wager made out a mowing machine as it chewed its way across the level point and spit out tiny dots of hay bales. There weren't many places to grow fodder in this country; it was either too dry or too steep or both. Wager guessed that all the bottom land had been searched out and fenced off from the roving cattle so the precious winter feed could be harvested.

"Is that a town over there?" He pointed to a cluster of dark rectangles gathered around a froth of green. The thread of a highway bridge crossed the river, where the wink of sun on a windshield came like a distant, cold spark.

"That must be Rimrock. And that"—she pointed to the pale horizon downriver—"must be Utah, on the other side of that notch."

The glimpse through the wide V of the ancient river's course showed the mottled red and yellow of volcanic sands and the purple of distance.

"The T Bar M is upriver from Rimrock, isn't it?"

Jo glanced at him. "You still want to go over there?"

"That's the reason I came. One of the reasons," he added.

"I thought you enjoyed the last few days."

"I have. I didn't think I would, but I have. But I came up here to do more than fish or ride horses."

"I know that." She studied something far down in the valley.

Wager felt as if he had clumsily broken something, and he had a pretty good idea what it was. He had felt it too in the last few days, the sloughing off of the concern with death, a slow discovery of what it meant to have hours and even days without cleaning up someone else's mess. But Jo knew why he'd agreed to this trip. And she'd agreed to his reasons. "So what's the matter?"

"I'd hoped that . . . well, Denver's a long way off. I'd hoped that maybe for a little while you could forget you're a cop."

"Why?"

"So I could know some part of you that's not connected with the police—and maybe find some part of myself, too, that's not just cop."

Wager questioned her use of "just"; if, for him, these last

few days had been fine, they were still a vacation, an interruption of what he really did: police work. "We're only visiting here, Jo. The real world for us is back in Denver. That's the world we both go back to."

Beneath them the horses shifted, wanting to move on. "I was hoping we wouldn't bring it with us. Not so soon, anyway."

"I guess it's always with us."

"I guess it is."

She turned her horse and spurred it, startling it into a hard gallop back along the ridge. Wager's horse followed, and he half-consciously imitated Jo, leaning forward to clear the saddle. But an ill-focused anger at himself for shattering the moment so carelessly, and at her for being so vulnerable, loomed in his mind so that his legs worked by themselves to cushion the thrust of the grunting horse. Slowly the gap between them narrowed, and Wager, spitting sand from the hooves in front, found his anger tip into a kind of savage joy at the chase, and he lifted himself higher up the horse's shoulders. It responded with a greater lunge that suddenly matched Wager's rhythm, and he felt the lightness and ease and exhilaration that came with the wind and sound and motion and the knowledge that he and the horse were one.

Jo glanced back, surprised to see him so close behind her, and raised up in the saddle to let her horse slow when it would. Wager drew up beside her, his own horse dropping into a ragged gait that he couldn't figure out, and a few moments later both animals slowed to a hard-breathing walk.

"You said it before, Gabe: we should enjoy what we have."

"It beats crying over what we don't have."

"And after all, it's your vacation, too, isn't it?" Jo mopped at his face with her bandanna. "You've got dirt all over. I didn't think you'd be so close behind me."

"I didn't either. But I got the feel of it for a little while. It was . . ." He groped. "It was pretty exciting."

"Maybe there's hope for you yet."

. . .

The trail to the T Bar M was a dozen or so miles shorter than going by car, but it was still a long ride. Though they started early, by the time they wound their way down and up the steep walls of White Creek Draw, the horses were damp with late-morning sweat and swinging their tails irritably at the deerflies drawn to their matted flanks. At the top, Jo and Wager walked the animals to rest them, angling toward the tall skeleton of a windmill that marked a stock tank just beyond the low trees cresting the ridge. A tangle of cow trails converged on the large metal tub, and in the distance a scattering of white-faced Herefords looked their way with dull curiosity.

Jo watered the horses sparingly while Wager found the brake handle for the windmill. He locked it open as Rusty had asked them to. On the way back, they would close it again, to leave the tank filled with clean water and the green algae floated over the rim into the mud.

"The fence should be in another mile or so. Dee said the gate was at the foot of a cliff."

Wager finished his sandwich and rinsed his mouth from the canteen hanging on his saddle. Then, like his horse, he gave a little grunt as he swung into the stirrup.

The landscape grew noticeably drier in the miles they traveled from the mesa that sheltered the Rocking V ranch. Since passing the fence, they had seen no cattle at all, and Jo guessed they had wandered toward the draws and gullies where grass was heavier and the cliffs offered shade. Topping a sandy ridge, they saw the river below swing in a large curve between steep walls; the wind lifted from the canyon and brought a steady, faint rush from rapids that streaked the water white.

"I bet it's over where those trees are." Jo pointed to a swatch of paler green in a wide valley that slid toward the river, and they angled toward it. The piñons began to thin, and now the wide, sandy spaces between the gnarled trunks were patched with sagebrush and long weedy clumps of grass. Occasional thickets of hackberry and squawbush filled the narrow cracks where water collected from the high ground above, and in the open stream beds towered the scarred trunks of cottonwoods. They nudged the horses up the spongy sand and a few minutes later paused to look down at the scattered buildings of the ranch.

The main house sat in the deep shade of a row of cottonwoods, and another tree gave shelter to a long, single-story building that must have been the bunkhouse. The barn, its roof a patchwork of different-colored wooden shingles, stood near a network of weathered corral fencing, and a scattering of small buildings sagged emptily. Near the house were parked a couple of cars and a familiar truck, and on a small rise glinted the bowl of a television dish. As they approached, a large police dog began to bark loudly and ran toward them.

Wager and Jo reined in their nervous horses as the chained dog stopped to bark a steady stream.

"I've never seen a dog that big!"

It looked like a small donkey, its size made larger by the hair rising stiffly along its spine. A heavyset man came onto the porch. His voice reached Wager in a distant call: "Smokey—Smokey—get over here!"

The man hooked the dog's chain into a short leash and stood waiting as Jo and Wager clucked their horses forward. His face was a smudge of short beard, and he did not smile as they halted and said hello. Instead, he came slowly down one of the wooden steps and waited silently, his shadow a small pool under his feet.

"You're Mr. Watkins?"

"He's not here. I'm the cook."

"I'm Gabe Wager. We're staying over at the Volker place. Is John or James Sanchez around?"

He took another long moment to answer. "Yeah."

Wager kept his voice polite. "Can we talk to them?"

"Over there—the bunkhouse." He pointed to the low building that looked like a cinder-block motel. Most of the doors were closed, but one on the end stood open to the breeze. Wager and Jo said thanks and turned toward it.

"That's western hospitality?" Jo whispered.

"Western Transylvania, maybe."

"Don't say that. This place is spooky enough!"

Wager didn't know if "spooky" was the word, but he felt the man's eyes on their backs as they crossed the silent yard. The stillness was a contrast to the Volkers', where someone was always busy with some chore around the out-buildings—Henry fussing with a tool, his mouth busier than his hands; Joaquin coming in from or going out to one of the ranges in a rattling pickup. Something was always going on there. But there was no sound of a hammer or whine of an electric tool; a rooster crowed from one of the smaller sheds, but the only other sound was the wind. Glancing over his shoulder, he saw the cook still staring after them; the German shepherd, lying in the cool sand under the porch, watched them too.

Wager dismounted and dropped his reins over a saw-horse made into a roping dummy and sporting a two-by-four head and a pair of wide cowhorns. "John? John Sanchez?" He rapped on the doorframe, and in the answering silence a curl of white paint spiraled into the sand. "James?"

"Just a minute." The voice croaked with sleep, and they heard the rusty creak of springs. "Who is it?"

"Gabe Wager."

A rustle of cloth and the jingle of coins or keys in a pocket being jerked over knees. "Who?"

"Wager. We talked up in Leadville at the rodeo. I was a friend of your father's."

James came to the door still tucking his shirttail into the front of his jeans. He was barefoot and his black hair tangled stiffly at the back of his head. "What the hell are you doing here?" His eyes, no longer sleepy, stared at Wager. "Is something wrong? What's the matter?"

"Nothing's wrong. We're staying over at the Volkers' place. We wanted to come by and say hello."

He scratched at his face beneath the soft whiskers and stared at Wager. Then he blinked and looked at Jo for the first time. "Well, that's—ah—that's neighborly."

"Can we water our horses?" asked Jo.

"Oh—sure. I'll show you. Let me get my boots. We got

a trough around by the barn." He jammed sockless feet into his boots and led them around the bunkhouse toward the large building. "You rode over? Which way'd you come from?"

Wager pointed. "That way. Through your east gate. How's John?"

"He's fine. He's out riding fence today. I—ah—wasn't feeling too good, so John let me sleep in." The young man busied himself with the squeaking pump, and in a few seconds water splashed into the frayed wooden trough. The horses snorted thirstily and pushed closer. "Was it a long ride over? Did you come across the mesa or along the river?"

"The mesa," said Jo. "The east gate."

"That's right—you just said, didn't you?" He finished pumping, and the horses sucked noisily. "That's a hot ride. Nice day for it, though."

It was Wager's turn to nod. Behind James, the barn doors hung open to the shade. The building was of unpainted timber; the central portion of squared and notched logs rose about twenty feet to the peak of the sloping roof. Later additions had been framed to the sides with rough-cut boards. The only sound of life from the rambling structure was a flutter of sparrows that nested somewhere inside the gaping hayloft door. The dirt in front was unscarred by animal or tire tracks, and that was something Wager wondered about: where was the farm equipment—the tractors and haybalers, the rakes and carts, the machinery that, at the Volkers', was lined up for use or maintenance? "Do you run many cows here?"

"Enough, it seems like. I don't know how many for sure. Mr. Watkins wants to let the range build up some. And beef prices aren't all that good anyway."

"We didn't see any cattle at all coming over," said Jo.

"It's a big ranch. They're spread all over hell and gone."

Jo pulled the horses away from the water. "How big is it?"

"God, I don't know how many acres. It goes north along the river a long way. But most of it's not worth spit."

"You don't seem to have many hands for a place that big," said Wager.

"There's enough," said James. "Me and John. This time of year, we don't need any more than that."

Wager looked at the gaps on the barn roofing and at the ranch house with its white paint beginning to blister. "You have a cook, though."

"Yeah—Maynerd. He ain't much help. He ain't much of a cook, neither. But he keeps an eye on the place when nobody's around."

"How long has Watkins owned the ranch?"

"I guess a couple of years. I'm not sure."

"It belonged to McGraw before he bought it?"

"I don't know. I only been here a little while."

"Watkins must have a lot of money."

"Why's that?"

"To pay the taxes on this place—to keep it going."

"I don't know about that, Mr. Wager. Watkins meets his payroll. That's all I know."

"Are you and John going to a rodeo this weekend?" asked Jo.

"Yeah—there's one up in Grand Junction. Four go-rounds, so we might pick up some money."

"Is John riding well?"

"Yes ma'am, he is! Anymore, it's just like getting ground money when he enters."

"What's ground money?" asked Wager

"That's pay for working the rodeo grounds," answered Jo. "You don't have to win it, you just get it for doing the job—a sure thing."

"That's John, all right—a sure thing."

"How about you? How are you doing?"

"I'm hanging in there; I'll get my permit—at least John says so. He says I'm way ahead of where he was a couple years ago." He pumped up more water for the horses; Jo let them drink lightly again.

"Maybe we can see you there," she said. "I think Gabe's ready to look at some city lights."

"How long you been around here?" asked James.

"About a week." Wager smiled. "We're just getting to know the country."

James nodded, a tiny frown pulling his dark eyebrows together.

"I'm sorry I didn't get to your father's funeral," said Wager. "I didn't know where it was."

"What? Oh—yeah. Well, it wasn't nothing big. Family only, you know. And me and John was all the family he had."

Wager nodded. "As far as I know, the sheriff doesn't have any leads on who did it."

"I see."

"But your dad seemed to be worried about something just before he was killed."

"Like what?"

"I was hoping you might be able to tell me."

"I can't tell you what I don't know."

"I thought he might have said something to you when he came out here."

"No, he didn't. John's already told you, god damn it, we didn't talk about nothing. And what the hell are you doing poking your nose into this, anyway? It's no damn business of yours!"

"Take it easy, James. All I'm trying to do is find out who killed your father. Wouldn't you like us to find out?"

The youth took a deep breath, and underneath the silky black whiskers, Wager saw his mouth tighten around whatever he almost said. "Yeah. Sure I do. Even if he wasn't much of a father."

Wager said, "Some of the people your father worked with said he was worried. That was after he visited the ranch, and before he went home and was killed. I just wondered if he might have mentioned anything to you. That's all."

"He didn't say nothing to me. I don't know what he was worried about."

The shrill chatter of excited sparrows filled the silence of the barnyard. The horses, pulled away from the water again, sighed and stamped against the sting of flies.

"Did your father leave a will?"

"A will? Yeah—some lawyer sent John and me a letter about that. But there wasn't much. His truck and his place was all he had."

"And you and your brother get that?"

"Hell, no. The hospital put a lien on it. His insurance run out after a couple of days, and the hospital put a lien on the property to cover the bills. John told the damned lawyer to sell the place and pay them off so we wouldn't get stuck with the hospital bills."

"So you don't get anything."

"Between the doctors and the lawyers, I don't expect too damn much'll be left. If there is, John and me want to give it to Mama. We're doing all right—but she could use it. Hell, she earned it." He glanced at the sun. "I better get on to work. Appreciate your coming over to talk, Mr. Wager. I sure do."

They trailed after him toward the bunkhouse.

"I'd ask you to stay for dinner, but Cookie's kind of funny about people dropping by. He don't like it."

"I noticed," said Wager.

"Well, it's his kitchen."

Jo swung into the saddle. "Are you getting many rafters this year?"

"Rafters? Oh—you mean the river? Yeah, we got some. The sonsabitches camp anywhere they want on the property. Start fires, leave their crap behind."

"I thought Watkins set up a campground for them," said Wager.

"He did. But some of them don't want to pay to camp and they think they got a right to go any damn where they please. We spend four or five nights a week running them off." He looked at Wager. "Some people just don't have the sense to stay off other people's land."

CHAPTER 9

"ou almost threatened him."

"He took it that way, didn't he?" Wager ducked under the water and came up blowing hard from the cold.

They stood waist-deep in the creek behind their cabin, the shock of the water easing into comfort, and scrubbed off the dust and sweat of the long day's ride. On the shady side of the corral, the horses—rubbed with clean hay and fed an extra ration of oats—stood head to tail, wearily content to switch the flies off each other's face and to enjoy the dry breeze of a long evening. On the bank, reflecting the clear green of the sunless sky, two wineglasses and a bottle rested half submerged on a ledge of water-smoothed sandstone that the stream had carved into the stony bank.

"Turn around—I'll do your back." Jo squirted a palm full of biodegradable soap from a plastic bottle and scrubbed at Wager's tender muscles. He had expected his legs and bottom to be sore after the day's ride, but there didn't seem to be any reason why his back and neck should ache, too.

"OK—my turn."

He dipped under the current again, a wave of noisy bubbles over his head, and popped up. Jo handed him the bottle, and he massaged the thin foam across the smoothness of her back. Beneath his dark hands her shoulders looked pale and fragile, and the way she arced against his fingers' pressure made her flesh, despite her toughness, seem vulnerable to some pending but unknown threat. It was a note of vague sadness that seemed to drain some of the remaining light from the grass and earth that surrounded them, and to leave her pale form even more isolated against the coming darkness. Wager's hand slid down the wet softness of her body, and he rested against her as if to keep her anchored in the current that pulled ceaselessly at them both. He felt himself between the taut swell of her buttocks, and despite the cold water, his own flesh stirred. She, too, felt his throb and pressed back against him; then he reached to feel the flat suppleness of her stomach and the soft rise below that and finally the tangle of warmth that opened to him as she slowly leaned forward against the stony bank and reached to guide him gently into her.

Their sighs were no louder than the murmur of the creek, and overhead, the rustling, liquid sounds of the willows echoed their slow rhythm and rose in the wind and stilled into a crystalline moment that stretched like a high, tense, inaudible note; then they rustled again as the wind stirred to become alive, and the creek—its sound louder under the cooling sky—once more tugged at their flesh.

Their eyes said what neither would speak; silently, they gathered the glasses and bottle, the towels and sandals and soap, and picked their way over the stubbled trail to the cabin.

"I'm cold now." Her flesh drew into a shudder.

"Let's get warm again."

"Let's."

Later she murmured, "James didn't have any marks—you know, from up at Leadville."

Wager stretched against the hard pad of mattress and pulled her closer beneath the thin blanket. Above, the peaked ceiling flickered with shadows from the fireplace, where a piñon log flared its hot fragrance into the room. It was appropriate, Wager thought, to have the curiously mixed and deep moment—a moment of love and fear and union that had given him a glimpse into a new area of himself—bracketed by the questions and suspicions of police work. But this time he wasn't the one who brought it up. He smiled wryly. This time he did not try to bury whatever he had discovered, to hide it in the cushioning routine of his work. Yet it happened—Jo's comment hung in the air like a summons. And it unmoored that moment and nudged it into the flow of time and away from him toward memory. Its loss left him holding more tightly to her slender form.

"Gabe? What's wrong?"

He shook his head. "Nothing. Everything's perfect." Was perfect. "He's hiding something—he knows what Tom was worried about, but he doesn't want me to know."

"And you think it has something to do with the ranch?"

"It's the only thing that makes sense." But if pushed, he'd admit it was more feeling than sense, a feeling made stronger after seeing the place.

"There didn't seem to be anything wrong going on there. In fact, there didn't seem to be much of anything at all going on."

That was true. Wager guessed that none of the buildings had had any maintenance since Watkins bought the place. Why would a man give that much money to buy a ranch, spend more money on it for a couple of years, and let it begin to warp and rot in the sun? And pay three or four men to sit around and watch it happen? "Not even ranching. That's one of the things that bothers me."

Jo sat up and pulled the blanket to her chest and emptied the bottle into their glasses. "So you want to frighten him into doing something?"

"Into saying something. If he was scared about his own father, he might be scared about me."

"I don't like that."

"What's wrong?"

"Suppose they try something? You've already said they might have killed their own father. And there was that man up in Leadville."

Wager shook his head. "They won't. It would be like a

confession. Besides, I couldn't think of anything better to do."

Jo wasn't satisfied, but she only asked, "What next?"

"Police work, I guess."

.   .   .

Rusty had a series of topographical maps carefully taped together and pinned across the wall in one of the empty bedrooms that he used as an office. He and Wager, drinks in hand, stood in front of it, and Rusty traced the red pencil lines that sectioned off his ranch from those surrounding it. The aroma of slowly roasting beef carried through the house from the firepit outside, and from the living room, Wager could hear Jo and Dee talking. They had been at the ranch for one week, and the Volkers used that as an excuse for a party—"We don't have too many reasons, so we might as well make the most of what we got, Gabe"—and besides, Dee had added, she'd gone long enough without another woman to talk to, so you two come on up this evening and we'll have us a barbecue.

Earlier in the week, Joaquin and Henry cut out a steer and butchered it. Now they stood, awkwardly trying to be at home in the boss's office, clutching their cans of beer and glancing occasionally out the window at the bed of coals and the roasting meat.

"The T Bar M goes all the way up to here?" Wager's finger touched a dotted line that crossed the swirl of contour lines marking high ground along each side of the river.

"I believe so. Henry, you used to work for McGraw—is that his north boundary?"

The bandy-legged man squinted at the map. His bony skull pressed against the thin flesh of a face baked the color of a paper bag. Under his beaked red nose, he jiggled his upper plate with his tongue. "Naw, that's the powerline. Here's the ranch boundary over this way—it goes along Gypsum Ridge down to the river. East, let's see—I should know where, I rode the sonabitch enough times . . . here, here's Angel Butte, and it cuts southeast from there."

Wager studied the USGS map with its washes of green ink to indicate forested areas. Most of that color was on the right side of the map, and the section that held the T Bar M was predominantly the pale tan of open range. Here and there were the dotted lines of unimproved roads and a crossed pick and shovel indicating old mines or quarries. "The highway doesn't follow the river all the way through the ranch?"

"No—the terrain's too rough," Rusty said. "Cost a fortune to cut a roadbed through those cliffs. There's some jeep trails here and there leading down to the water, but mostly the cliffs come right to the highwater mark. Only way through that section's by boat."

Henry's teeth clicked. "Sometimes that ain't no way, either."

The writhing blue line of the river swung up and then angled more directly west as it crossed into Utah toward the upper Colorado. The dark brown contour lines, marking forty-foot elevations, bunched tightly all along the riverbed, darkening most at the outer bend of each twist where the stream had carved the rock into sheer faces. Scattered along both sides of the cut, the alleys of feeder streams spread the contour lines out in long Vs that indicated sloping bottomland or meadows. "Do either of you know the Sanchez brothers? They work over there now."

Henry shook his head, lank white hair combed back to swing just above his shirt collar. "Not me. I ain't been on that spread since before Tyler McGraw sold it. Don't want to, neither."

"Why's that?"

"Don't like the people he sold it to."

That was all the old man was going to say. Wager glanced at Joaquin, a Mexican national in his midtwenties whose smooth, hairless face had a lot of Indian in it. "Do you know them?"

"No, *señor*. They pretty much stay over there. I don't even see nobody when I ride fence."

Wager glanced at the map again and at the wide area

traced off by Henry's finger. "How many cows does he have to run to pay the overhead on that place?"

"That many acres? Hell, that's about three times my spread—four hundred, at least."

Henry sipped his beer and shook his head. "And that's cutting it damn close. Prices drop a few cents, and he'd lose money."

"Does he have any other cash crops?"

Snorting a laugh, Henry shoved his teeth back with his thumb. "Rafters—he gets a good crop of rafters every spring at that camp in Andy's Gulch."

"He might be raising fodder in the bottomlands off the river—the ones he can get machinery into." Rusty shook his head. "But there's not much money in that. McGraw had to buy hay when he owned the place. And he's not irrigating any cropland. We'd sure as hell know if anybody was irrigating any cropland."

Wager had some experience with water laws and jealousies during an earlier case; both groundwater and surface water needed a use permit, and everyone guarded his shares closely.

"Besides." Henry drained his beer and crushed the can. "This here's cow country."

"Why are you so wound up about that place, Gabe?"

"I'm just trying to make sense of why someone would spend all that money for nothing."

"I see. Well, I reckon making sense of things is your business. I only wish you could make sense of what those sonsabitches in Washington are trying to do."

Wager listened through that drink and one more about the squeeze put on ranchers by high interest rates and low market prices—compounded by trade restrictions and imports, an unfavorable dollar, price supports for the steel industry which pushed equipment sky-high, chicanery in the oil markets, and reduced federal support to agencies that still had to be supported by local tax dollars. Rusty had graduated from Colorado State University with a degree in agricultural economics. Wager had the feeling that he was still applying his classroom theories to the ranch—and when they didn't work there, to national policies. And even to political philosophy: "It's those arrogant bastards in Washington, Gabe—that's what happens when you let those people take as much tax money as they want. They start to think you're their goddam slave!"

Joaquin and Henry finished their second beers and excused themselves to go out and look at the meat; Wager figured they'd heard it all before. But he, guest and virgin ear, stood with drink in hand as Rusty spilled all the ideas that had built up over the long days of silent labor and the nights with a wife who must have learned by now to nod and answer without hearing. Because that's what Wager was already doing. When finally the iron clang of the dinner bell broke into Rusty's monologue, Wager—stomach growling with hunger—followed with relief as the younger man led him around to the flagstone patio.

The meal was worth waiting for. Henry had basted the meat with his own secret sauce splashed out of a large pickle jar—"it ain't so much a secret as a mystery"—and Dee presented a tray heaped with fresh vegetables as well as loaves of newly baked bread. Rusty kept pouring bourbon, surprised each time he found Wager's glass still full, and Joaquin's contribution came after the dishes had been cleared and rinsed by Jo and Dee and shoved into an oversized dishwasher. A couple of quiet words from Henry and some gentle urging from Dee—"*por favor, Joaquin, por favor*"—and the young Mexican came back with his guitar to self-consciously strum it into tune. Wager's role again was audience—the excuse for others to perform in front of someone new.

"That was wonderful." Jo, her arm around Wager's waist, matched her stride to his as they walked slowly down the moonlit dirt road to the cabin. The bulky shadows of piñons crowded the road and made ragged holes in a sky that glowed from the brilliance of a high half-moon and the clear, wide band of the Milky Way that swept from one horizon to another.

"It was good." Wager massaged her neck, and she stretched against his hand with pleasure.

"There goes one—a big one!"

They paused to watch the scratch of cold light streak down the eastern sky. Tiny fragments broke from the tail, sparked briefly, then died alone as the meteor kept falling. Then it, too, winked out into blackness, and Wager half expected a sonic boom to follow. But there was only silence, and on the steady, warm breeze that slid down from the high country behind the ranch came the distant wavering yip of a coyote.

"Could you understand Joaquin's songs?"

"Parts of them. The singing runs words together, so it's hard."

"He has a nice voice."

And a wife and two children living with his parents in Sinaloa; he saw them for three winter months out of the year, and spent the rest of the time working in the States to feed them. Eventually, he wanted to send his kids to school in America. Henry, born in Spearfish, South Dakota, had drifted from ranch to ranch "seeing new country" until one morning he woke up and was sixty years old, "more or less." Then he decided to settle in this valley—"close enough to the desert to be warm, close enough to the mountains to have some green. I like it. I plan to die here."

Where the road curved around the old corral, Jo tugged Wager over to the worn rails. From the darkness, a looming mass plodded toward them and snorted its quiet greeting. Jo held out her hand, and the soft lips nibbled at the sugar cube in her palm. "I don't know when I've felt so at peace," she said, as much to the horse and the night as to Wager.

He had to agree. In time—and perhaps he already felt the first abrasive edge of it—boredom would come. But Jo was right. It was peaceful, and as Wager let himself surrender to it, the last clutch of tight flesh drained from his neck and shoulders to leave his body with that satisfying looseness that follows good exercise.

Their boots thudded softly on the earth as they neared the boxy shadow of the cabin. Wager made a detour around

to the outhouse and came back toward the glow from small,
low windows. He found Jo standing by the fireplace, frowning across the hooded lamp at the empty room.

"What's the matter?"

"I think someone's been in here," she said.

Wager looked around. "Why?"

"The bed." She gestured at the two cots they had pushed
together and anchored with sheets and blankets to make a
double. "It's been messed up."

"We messed it up this afternoon."

"But I made it again. I remember. Somebody's lifted up
the mattresses."

Wager pulled open the dresser drawers and gazed at the
clothes folded there. A clumsy hand had gone through and
then tried to smooth out its traces. "Wait here."

He went out to his car and flipped on the dome light; the
glove compartment, unlocked, was filled with maps and papers and loose items tossed there in such a way that no one
could tell if it had been rifled. In the side pocket of his door
he found the extra clip for his Star PD and checked the
bullets; none were missing, and he dropped it into his
pocket. He tried the trunk, relieved to find it still locked.
Opening it, he felt under the deck lid for his weapon. His
fingers brushed the holster, and he debated whether to
bring it into the cabin; but if he had, it would have been
found—it was safer out here. He slid the extra clip into the
holster and closed the lid. Then he ran his fingertips over
the paint around the lock, checking for scratch marks.

"They went through the cupboards, too. They tried to
put things back the way they were, but they couldn't." She
stared at him, eyes large in the shadowy light of the lamp.
"It wasn't anyone from the ranch."

"Henry and Joaquin were out of sight at different times."

"Oh, Gabe, it's not them and you know it!"

He agreed with her; he was only fencing off the other
possibilities before saying what he really believed. "I guess
I worried him, all right."

"What was he after?"

"It wasn't money." He fished in one of the elastic pockets of his suitcase and held up his checkbook. The spare cash was still pinched between the covers.

"He couldn't have driven over. We'd have seen or heard him on the ranch road."

"He probably came the way we went over there—by horse."

She went to the door and gazed out at the night. "How did he know we wouldn't be here?" Then she answered her own question. "He didn't, did he? Gabe, what if we'd been here?"

"He wouldn't have come in. He's not after trouble. He's looking for something."

"But what?"

"I don't know. We don't have anything."

"He doesn't know that."

"He does now," said Wager. Though they had not gone through his pockets yet, not the way they went through Tom's. Perhaps that would come next.

"The one in Leadville was after something, too, wasn't he? But what?"

Neither could answer that. They gave a final look through the cabin to see if anything at all was missing, then lay together in the dark, aware that their sheets and blankets had been probed by alien hands, aware of the spread of darkness beyond the screened windows, aware of the steady rustling of leaves and of grass that grew close to the cabin walls.

·   ·   ·

Two signs heralded Rimrock, the first a sun-worn square of red and yellow that offered rafting trips on the colorful and historic Dolores River; the second was a bullet-pocked highway sign: Rimrock, Elev. 5,402. Which, Jo said, was about 5,300 more feet than people.

The other businesses strung along the highway were content to advertise on the buildings themselves, and at twenty-five miles an hour, there was plenty of time to see

them all: a gas station, Vern's Place, which sold hunting
and fishing gear, three restaurants with bars attached, a
liquor store, a new brick building that said "Post Office"
and held a sign for Adventure in the U.S. Army. Beyond
the cluster of businesses, a scattering of homes baked in the
sun or clung to ridges among piñons; and past the town, the
highway picked up speed once more and bit its way up the
bluff to disappear against the sky outlining the next mesa.

Wager turned the Trans-Am into the gravel lot of Hall's
Grocery, a large building with plate-glass windows bearing
the prices of today's specials. The curving roofline seemed
vaguely familiar, and then Wager recognized it as a supermarket design popular thirty years ago and probably a rem-
nant of the time when uranium mining brought populations
into the barren hills surrounding the town. The uranium
went and so did the chain store. Rusty brackets still marked
the supermarket's old sign, though the new owner's name,
once a bright blue, now hid the middle ones.

"Do you have the list?"

Wager nodded. The week's supplies filled a page in his
small notebook and included a few things for Dee, too. It
took them some time to find it all as they pushed a wob-
bling cart up and down the narrow aisles past shelves
jammed with a little bit of everything. One corner held
fishing tackle, and Wager loitered there while Jo went in
search of paper towels. Another red-and-yellow sign offered rafting trips, and a hand-drawn sketch showed tourists how to find the Foamy Rapids Rafting Company.

"I think that's it—anything more you can think of?"

"Not here," said Wager. "But I want to look around
town."

It didn't take long to walk both sides of the two-block
business district. Wager stopped at the small liquor store
whose shelves carried a wide range of beers and bourbons
and little of anything else, and he bought a quart of Wild
Turkey as a thank-you gift for Rusty. They hesitated before
the Bonnie Lass Dress Shoppe so Jo could look at a dress
pinned stiffly against some cardboard. On a dirt side street,
a large farm home had been converted into an office for a

doctor and a lawyer, and a little further down they found a cinder-block box set in the middle of a gravel turnaround and labeled "Sheriff's Office." Wager noted the white four-wheel-drive vehicle with its official star parked a quick step from the open door.

"Want to visit?" Jo smiled.

"I'm not homesick yet."

But he did turn in at a large, unpainted barn sheltered by broken-limbed cottonwoods and marked "Farrier." A short, stocky woman in Levi's and a leather apron came out briskly through the dusty gloom of a stall to nod hello. "You folks need something?"

"Just a little information, if you've got the time."

"I've got plenty of one—have to see about the other." She dragged an orange bandanna under her chin and glanced at Jo, at her hair and clothes and boots, and then back to Wager. "Hot enough for you?"

"Plenty. Do you know where the Watkins ranch is? The T Bar M?"

"The old McGraw place, sure. You go south on 141 for about seven miles. It's a mailbox on the east side—can't miss it. Seven miles, then three miles east on the ranch road. It takes you down near the river."

"Are you the farrier? Or your husband?"

"Me. I got tired of keeping men in shoes, so I turned to horses." She invited Jo to laugh with her. "And a horse is a lot cleaner animal, ain't it, honey?"

"Have you done much work for Watkins?"

"The new fella? No. I ain't been out there since he bought the place."

"That's a couple years ago?"

"About that. Tyler sold off two Octobers ago. He had his place up for a long time before Watkins bought it. I remember he came in here just as pleased, said a real estate agent over in Delta had a buyer for him, and it wasn't a week later Tyler came by to say goodbye. I think he was kind of sorry he sold out and was leaving, but it was too late then, of course."

"McGraw moved away?"

"California. Around San Fernando, I think. Somewhere in the valley. Took his money and run."

"Do you know any of the people who work for Watkins? John or James Sanchez?"

The cropped graying hair shook slowly. "No. Not by name. I heard he's got a crew, but I don't know what he needs one for."

"Why's that?"

"I don't think he's running any cows out there. Unless he's got his own farrier or he trucks one in from outside. I guess he could do that, but it's a fool thing to do."

"I don't understand," said Jo.

"Oh, honey, anybody running cows around here's got to use horses. And anybody who don't get me out to their place in a year and a half or so, well, they just ain't using their horses very much."

Wager thanked her, and she said, "Sure thing. Seven miles south, then east for three. Can't miss it."

The late-morning sun bounced back from the highway and from the short sections of cracked sidewalk in front of this or that building. Between them, trails were worn into the dirt and reminded Wager of the side streets of his old neighborhood where pavement was scarce and the sand would get hot enough to sting your bare feet.

"James said they had some cows," said Jo.

"It wouldn't be the first time he lied."

A car slowly cruised down the highway past Vern's Place; the driver lifted a hand as he went by, and Wager waved in reply.

"Can we make one more stop?" he asked Jo.

"It's your vacation, too."

They drove down one of the empty side streets that led toward the river until they saw the red-and-yellow sign for the Foamy Rapids Rafting Company. Wager pulled under the shade of a cottonwood, and they sat a moment looking at the river. Here the water ran almost unbroken, an even sweep of current fifty yards wide. Willow shrubs lined both banks, and the water had risen to sway them rhythmically against its swift flow. Only occasionally did a small wave splash or the steady liquid rustle rise above the sound of the cottonwood leaves overhead; instead, the water ran silent and quick, carrying an occasional branch or peeled timber in ominous haste.

The rafting company was a galvanized Quonset hut squatting a few yards back from the bank on a shelf of higher land. In an open shed protected by a roof of fiberglass panels, a dozen or so silver-colored inflated rafts were stored bottom up, and racks held lines of wooden oars and yellow life jackets. A path had been worn from the shed to a gap in the willows and led to a small pier that floated on drums a few feet out from shore. Firmly tied to iron stakes driven into the sand, two aluminum runabouts were pulled out of the water, motors cocked clear of the ground. Behind the shed was parked a trailer with a high framework of angle iron for ferrying rafts.

"How'd you like to do some white-water rafting?"

"On that?" She looked at the silent river. A tangle of roots from a submerged tree glided past without a ripple. "Do you know anything about rafting?"

"A little."

"It looks awfully fast."

"What's a vacation without a few thrills?"

They pushed open the door cut into the end of the Quonset hut. Sprawled at a desk and reading a Louis L'Amour paperback, a boy in his midteens looked up suddenly. "Wow—I didn't even hear you drive up!"

He was shirtless and wore khaki pants cut raggedly off at the knees. A pair of equally ragged tennis shoes swung from the littered desk, and he quickly shoved the book into a drawer. "Yes, sir—can I help you?"

Wager was interested in a trip for two people and the equipment he would need.

"The smallest we've got is a nine-footer, but you don't want one much smaller than that, anyway," he said. "Not the way the river is now."

"Is it very dangerous?" Jo asked.

"Well, up in the canyon it's pretty heavy. We got almost twelve thousand cfs right now, and it's still rising. It's a real good runoff this year. But, no ma'am, it's not too dangerous if you know what you're doing."

"The canyon's a lot farther upstream, isn't it?"

"Yessir. But we run trips all along the river. A lot of people go in above the canyon at Bedrock and come out at Slickrock. Or they can take another leg down to here. It's a real nice run."

"You don't seem too busy."

"Well, no sir, I guess most people do get out at Slickrock. But this is a real pretty stretch of river—it's not as exciting as the upper end, but you still have some class threes. And with the water this high, we might find some fours."

"What's that?" Jo asked.

"The degree of difficulty," said Wager. "They have five classes. But a lot depends on how much water's in the river."

"Yes ma'am. Sometimes a class goes down with more water, but most of the time it goes up. It depends on the volume and how wide the channel is, and the gradient. Right now with this runoff"—his head wagged once—"it can get pretty exciting even with a class three." He added, "At the end of summer, you can almost walk across here. The flow drops to about a thousand cfs, then. But look at it now. When they get that dam finished up at Cortez, I don't know what we'll have left. They say they want to keep the river open for rafting, but I don't know. It'll probably level off at five or six thousand, and that'll make things pretty tame."

Wager asked about renting a raft and guide for two or three days, and the boy quickly pulled a rate sheet out of the desk and started explaining options.

"This is the best deal, the three-day discount package. We provide everything except sleeping bags and personal gear. And if there's any special thing you want to drink—you know, fancy wines or something—you got to bring that. But we'll make room for it in the ice chest."

"We want to stay on this part of the river. Camp over at the T Bar M and just poke around."

"Yessir, we can do that. But it's not as exciting as the upper part of the river. You'd really like that. With a five-day package, you could do both."

Jo turned from studying a photograph that showed a raft plunging steeply into a maelstrom of foam and half-seen boulders that towered over the figures in the boat. In the bow, three riders, hair blowing back, stared fixedly at something just out of the photograph in front of them, and the oarsman, mouth a tense line, had lost one oar and was fighting to cling to the other. "I don't think I want that much excitement."

"That's not this river—that's Big Drop, over on the Colorado in Cataract Canyon." He touched one of the blurred figures. "That's me. The one with his eyes shut. I was just a kid, then."

Wager studied the strip map of the river tacked to a partition; he located the T Bar M campsite marked by a red pencil. "Suppose we stay here the first night, where would we have to put in?"

"We could go in anywhere along here. Most of the ranchers don't mind, if we get their permission first. Ron's pretty strict about that—that's the owner—he wants to keep on their good side."

"What about the T Bar M?"

"They're about the worst along this stretch—they don't want anybody anywhere on their property. But Ron talked them into putting in a campground, and it's worked out real well."

"Was it that way under McGraw?"

"No, not for us, anyway. But he did get pretty testy about some of the private parties. Some of them leave a real mess when they go ashore, and you can't blame the ranchers for getting mad. But we've got a good reputation with them, so they don't mind us."

Above and below the campground, dotted black lines indicated ranch boundaries meeting the river. If they put in where the boy indicated, they would cross about one-third of the ranch's property above the campground and the rest below. "How long does it take to go this far?" He traced the lower portion.

"Half a day in this flow. There's some good rapids in here where we put in, and some more down here. And there's rocks and bars all along this stretch, so it stays interesting. Down here, below the campground, is Boulder Field. That ought to be good in this much water. Maybe even class four."

"Can we pull out and look at the shoreline?"

"If the owners don't mind."

"What if they do mind?"

"Well, we shouldn't do it. But I guess they wouldn't mind if they didn't see us."

CHAPTER 10

The boy turned out to be their guide, and his name turned out to be Sidney. Wager was relieved when he stopped calling them sir and ma'am and started using their first names as he stowed their sleeping bags and personal gear into large rubber sacks. The morning chill hung in the air, and the sun had not yet cleared the high ground east of the river when Wager and Jo parked their car at the office. But Sidney was already there, the raft mounted on a trailer behind a large, worn truck. In the bed of the truck was a mound of gear—a number of large plastic buckets with tight lids, coolers, chests, lines, oars, life vests. Sidney greeted them with a sleep-stiff smile and a good morning, and gave them ditty bags to carry things they might need during the day's float. "You'll want to put your lip cream and suntan lotion in here—sunglasses, medicine, whatever you want during the day. I've got a waterproof box for cameras, too."

Jo busily rubbed lotion onto her legs before handing Wager the bottle. "You've thought of everything."

"There's no sense being uncomfortable—a raft trip's supposed to be fun. Do you have fishing gear? We've got some extra rods if you don't."

They decided to bring that along, too. Last night, when the Volkers heard about the trip, Rusty named a couple of good side streams for trout. "Somers Creek comes in about here—you'll get some good fishing there."

"Did they tell you what to wear? What you ought to bring?" Neither Dee nor Rusty had rafted the river; it was something they thought of trying if they ever found the time. But she'd heard it was a nice way to spend a few days.

Jo showed her the mimeographed list of what to wear and what to bring. "They furnish everything else. I'm really excited about it. I've never been on a river trip before, but Gabe has."

"Just a few small ones when I was a kid." And in some circles, splashing a two-man raft down the South Platte through the heart of Denver wouldn't count at all.

"Well, it makes me kind of nervous just to think about it—all that water and those big waterfalls."

"Hell, Dee, they haven't drowned more than a dozen people yet this year." Rusty opened his gift of bourbon and poured drinks for all, a generous shot over a single cube of ice in each glass. "Don't want to spoil the flavor."

"Oh, they haven't drowned anyone—don't let him worry you, Jo."

"I'm not worried. This end of the river's supposed to be gentle. Besides, Gabe'll look after me."

"The water's pretty high this year," said Rusty. "It's one of the biggest runoffs we've ever had. But you're right, it's not like upriver—the gradient's a lot steeper up at that end. Ah, that's smooth drinking!"

"Oh—Gabe—I almost forgot." Dee fished out a large brown envelope. "This came for you yesterday."

Inside were two items forwarded by Max. The first was from the Organized Crime Unit: a colored Xerox copy of an i.d. photograph and a brief rap sheet from the Imperial Beach, California, Police Department. Sergeant Johnston had identified Jerry Latta—he had one conviction for auto theft five years ago, and his name had surfaced in an investigation of an organized crime network based in Southern California about two years ago. The details weren't provided—"I can talk to you about it but I don't want to put anything in an open memo, Gabe"—but nothing had ever been proved. Wager studied the small set of photographs and tried to remember if the stiff face was the same one he had seen in that restaurant up in Leadville, the man who had come in with the Sanchez brothers and who later had studied Wager so carefully before trying to break into their room. It was hard to be certain, but a penciled-in mustache made him look familiar. If so, then Tom was right to worry about his sons.

The second item was a newspaper clipping with Max's writing across the top: "Have a good vacation, Gabe." The headline read "Justice Not Blind Toward Native Americans," and the byline was Gargan's. The story focused on three police cases involving Indians and their mistreatment by DPD. The one dealt with in most detail was Molly White Horse. "Miss White Horse, whose command of English is limited, told this reporter that she had been terrified by the manner of her arrest and questioning by homicide detectives, and that despite signing the Miranda Warning, she had not understood the procedures involved." The rest of the paragraph outlined the charges against her, stressing the fact that Miss White Horse had seen the victim stabbed and lying prone before she poured beer over him in a futile and tragic effort to revive him. Gargan stated that Miss White Horse singled out an officer who seemed particularly eager to lay blame on her, Detective Gabriel Wager, whose unorthodox methods and challenges to departmental procedures had brought him to the attention of the press in the past.

"That's a bunch of crap!" Jo, reading over his shoulder, looked up angrily. "You don't even bring the charges—that's the district attorney's job. Kolagny! Isn't that who it is? He's the one Gargan should be after."

"Fame is fleeting," said Wager. "By the time we get back, Gargan will be on another crusade." But Wager could imagine Bulldog Doyle reading the item, his cigar tilting slowly up as his jaw clenched tighter and no Gabe Wager to grab for. As a matter of fact, Wager didn't like it much, either; but considering who it came from he wasn't going to let it steam him. By God, he was on vacation—at Doyle's urging.

Sidney and Wager heaved the last bundles of equipment onto the truck bed and climbed into the cab. It took over three hours to reach the launch site, and another to stow and lash the gear. They had lurched carefully down the shelves of a five-hundred-foot bluff onto a fan of sand and wiry shrub that formed the point inside a large bend of the river. "This is Lewis Bend—that was the Lewis ranch we passed back there. Make yourselves comfortable—I'm going to pull the truck back onto higher ground in case the water comes up." He pointed to a tangle of dried weeds and twigs snagged waist-high in the surrounding brush. "That's the watermark from last year. Ron wouldn't be too happy if I let his truck get washed away."

Here, the river swung its current against the far bank, a dark red cliff that rose fifty or seventy-five feet straight up before angling back toward the next shelf of the larger bluff above. In close, the water swirled in a broad eddy that tugged gently at the beached raft; between the eddy and the current, a ripple of rough water built into a series of small, choppy waves that foamed and splashed. In the current itself, the swift water piled whitely against a line of house-sized boulders and sent its roaring echo off the flat wall toward the clear blue sky.

"That's a lot of water," said Jo. "It's scary."

It was more water than Wager had ever ridden, and the channels between rocks seemed narrow, too. But there was no sense warning her against everything—she'd be worried enough. "The water's only going about ten or eleven miles an hour."

"It sure looks a lot faster."

"That rough water over there is called an eddy fence. See how it fences the water and all the flotsam into the middle of the eddy?" This wasn't horses, and Wager felt a little satisfaction at being able to tell Jo something for a change.

"All right! You two ready to raft?" Sidney, face shaded by

a frayed straw hat, grinned broadly as he hopped from the spongy stern tube of the raft to the rowing frame strapped amidship. "Come on—the river's waiting!"

They had placed the equipment in slings mounted on narrow frames that crossed the boat from one thick side tube to the other. Lashed tightly in place, the bags and boxes formed an uneven deck suspended above the boat's rubberized floor. In the center, long oars dangling on each side of the rowing platform, Sidney would sit facing the bow. In slack water when he rowed the boat downstream, he would turn the craft around so it moved stern first. In rough water, he faced the bow downstream to see where it was going and pulled against the current in order to slow the craft and guide it through the chutes and rapids. Life jackets snugly on, oiled and creamed against the glare of sun from sky and water, Jo and Gabe were told once more how to float through rapids if they were tossed out, where to sit for the safest ride, to keep their life jackets on in any rough water, to move to the downstream side of the raft if they were about to collide with a boulder, never to get in the water between the raft and a rock, never to go in the water on the downstream side of the raft if possible, to swim sideways or dive down if sucked into a hole. And to have fun.

"OK—all set? You get to push us off, Gabe. Jo, you get right up there in the bow—OK, here we go—give it a shove, Gabe. All right, here we go!"

He pushed the heavy raft into the eddy and splashed through the mud to tumble over the sun-heated stern. Sidney motioned him forward with Jo, and the two of them settled on the thwart tube, Jo clutching tightly at the thin safety line that circled the raft. Underfoot, the cloth decking heaved and wobbled, nudging their canvas shoes with the river's life; and in front, an unbroken wall of foam and plunging water, the main current began to pinch between ragged boulders black with spray.

"Wow, feel that!" Jo lurched as the raft walked across the choppy surface of the eddy fence.

Wager watched her face, enjoying the excitement that

widened her eyes as the raft caught the main current and surged forward. Behind them, Sidney heaved back on the oars, braking against the current and jockeying to position the raft in the center of the tongue of water that drew in a wrinkled, glassy sheet between gigantic rocks.

"Here we go!"

His voice was barely heard above the roar of white water, and the raft lunged forward. Both Jo and Wager instinctively leaned back from the plunge down toward the foaming brown turbulence that tilted skyward to engulf them. The raft stabbed into the river and lurched upward, the bow scooping a cascade of icy brown water over them and knocking a shriek from Jo as she clung to the safety line with both hands. Then they saw only blue sky and the distant, calm rim of canyon walls as the bow swung upward and Sidney rowed hard. For a long, tense moment, the boat hung at a steep slant while he pushed on the oars. Then, sluggishly, the bow began to tilt down over the first foaming roller, faster and faster as the rest of the raft followed, until, with an elastic snap, it hit hard, jerking Wager off the thwart and almost over the bow before it surged up the next foam-crested mountain. Behind, he heard Sidney's high-pitched howl of joy, and beside him, Jo, eyes and mouth round, gasped with cold and excitement and caught his eye and laughed loudly, her voice thin against the roar of water.

The next roller was smaller, the boat gliding smoothly over in a flexible undulation, and the waves gradually lessened until the raft offered a ripple of short, quick bumps and they glided onto a calm, deep section of the river that seemed as still as a pond.

"You like that?"

"Yes!" Jo took a deep breath and laughed again. "That was great!"

"I thought you didn't like riding things you couldn't control."

"I didn't think I did—but that was great!"

Sidney spun the boat around to show them the rapids they had just bounced down. "Take a look upstream."

From this angle, the water stepped upward and showed the blurry dark shapes of rock that bulged the water into white tumult, the tongues of current knifing through gaps, the turbulent series of waves formed by the plummeting water. "That's what we call a haystack—a bunch of waves as big as haystacks." He pointed to the evenly spaced waves hovering below the main tongue they had ridden. "It's not Snaggle Tooth, but in regular water it's a good class-three rapids. In water this heavy, I bet it's a four, easy."

"Are there any more like that?" Jo asked.

"You want more already, do you?" said Wager.

"Yes!"

"Gabe, you got a real river rat there—I've had some people ask to get out right here. And some who got out back there when they didn't want to." He pointed to another tongue closer to the low bank of the stream. "We could have gone over there—that's the easier way. But I figured you guys wanted a little excitement. Was I wrong?"

"You were right," said Wager.

Sidney grinned. "Man versus the river—the ultimate challenge!" He lifted a white string sack from the deck behind him. "We got a lot of flat water now. Who wants to celebrate the first rapids with a beer or soda pop?"

"I'm too cold to drink anything."

"The sun'll warm you up. Another hour or so, it'll feel good to go swimming." He pointed out a pair of plastic bleach bottles with the tops cut out and tied by the handles to the raft. "Time to bail—all hands work on this voyage."

On this stretch, the only sounds were an occasional bird squawk from the shrubs on the banks and the steady, slow splash of water scooped and dumped from the forward well. Sidney tossed the sack of drinks over the stern to drag in the cold water, and stilled the oars a few inches below the surface. "The current's faster just below the top." Occasionally, he gently nudged the craft back into the main flow of water, but for the most part they drifted and gazed at the silent cliffs and he answered their questions about the raft and the river. The raft was made of a bond of nylon and

Hypalon, with about two pounds of air in each of several chambers—"That's one of the valves there, that little round thing." It was twelve by six feet—"We got some nine-footers, but that's pretty small for the river right now. Anything bigger, like a sixteener, and we'd have trouble getting through some of the gaps." And Sidney had been on this river for four years—"I started when I was thirteen, but last year was the first season I guided solo."

The river's name came from the Spanish explorers of the eighteenth century—"Escalante wandered all around this part of the county." Most of the rock was sandstone alternating with beds of conglomerate—"I'm going to study geology in college"—and you could see bands of differing color from various mineral traces—"The red, that's iron oxide, and the blue-green's copper." He also promised to show them some fossils in the cliffs down below. "We'll have to walk a little ways, but it's not bad."

"Do you make this run a lot?" asked Wager.

"I wish I could, but there's not that much business at this end. Ron handles the upper end—it's a lot more dangerous. But sometimes I go two or three times a week." He added, "Not often, though."

"Do a lot of people run this section?"

"Independents, you mean? Some. Not as many as upstream in the canyon, but enough to get the ranchers mad when they start fires and leave their garbage all over the shore." He hauled in the tow sack and opened an orange drink, offering it to Jo, who accepted this time. "They're supposed to pack everything out, including sewage, but some don't, and that causes trouble for everybody. Ron's got a lease with the T Bar M to use their campsite, so we stop there whenever we want to. They charge for it, but that's included in your price."

"Do they make much money off that?"

He shook his head. "A few hundred dollars in a season, maybe. The real reason they do it is to keep us off the rest of the ranch. They just plain don't like anybody landing anywhere else on their property."

"What happens if you do?"

"They chase you off. They've chased people off in the dark—come down and made them pack up and raft on down in the dark. But it's a lot better now with that campsite. I wish more of the ranchers would do that—it might help the tourist business around here."

"Are there any plans for state parks along the river?" asked Jo.

"I don't know. But that's a good idea; rafting's getting to be big business, and you need a state license and all now. Over in Utah along the Green and Yampa, they have campsites. Something's going to have to be done here, too."

Gradually the sand banks gave way to steeper and steeper rock; the water scoured all but the toughest shrubs from the tumbled boulders that began to face the stream. Wager could see highwater marks like smudged lines a few feet above the surface, and occasionally the ragged limbs of a submerged bush snagged the water into long streaks. Sidney rowed a little more often now, angling the craft across the current to the inside of curves and away from the rock cliffs that formed the outside banks. The current, he explained, was usually strongest on that side of a bend. It could bounce the raft against the wall, giving him no room for his oar and possibly wedging them under an overhang. "I saw that happen to some people two years ago right along here. Independents. One of them got a pretty bad head injury when he got caught between the raft and a hard place. All you have to do is stay on the inside, and you can eddy out whenever you want." The sun, higher, weighed on their shoulders and made the raft's skin sting with heat. Wager dipped a bandanna into the river and wrapped its coolness around his head under his hat; Jo rubbed another coat of zinc oxide on her nose. That and the pink smears of Labiosan already on her lips made her face glow in bright stripes.

"What are you laughing at?"

"Put a couple circles around your eyes and you could be a rodeo clown," said Wager.

Jo reached over and wiped two large streaks across his cheeks, and he grappled her wiry arms. He lifted her, squealing—"Don't—don't!"—and they bounced across the tubes and plunged into the cold water

His life jacket popped him up into a spray from Jo's hands as she splashed wildly at him. "You rat!"

Above them, Sidney laughed and kicked spray their way with an oar, and Wager and Jo, luxuriating in the coolness of the water, leaned back to float in their life jackets like two small satellites beside the gliding raft.

"You want to take it down the next rapids?" Sidney asked Wager. "They're a class two—give you some good practice."

They clambered in, the sun now feeling good on chilled, tight skin, and Wager traded seats with him. Sidney gave him a little instruction on how to row, and made Wager turn the raft this way and that using both oars. The craft moved sluggishly and it took him a while to anticipate its heavy reaction, but gradually he learned to guide it with a touch of the oars and to let the current do most of the work. When that happened, the raft seemed lighter and more responsive, and Wager found himself starting to read the water and to glide from one side of the current to the other as the river wound in tighter curves. Sidney, clinging to the tow sack line and drifting behind the boat, pulled himself over the stern and hauled the line in behind him.

"You want to get more to the inside so you can line up for the rapids—they're around the next bend."

Wager shoved the oars and the raft glided toward the slack, where an occasional deep boulder threw up a boil of smooth water and stole the power from his stroke.

"OK, Gabe, that's good. Give it some backwater; you don't want to get too far over. A little harder now . . . harder . . ."

The river swung past a prow of tall sandstone cliff that seemed narrow enough to topple over in the next wind, then it started to bend back on itself. The raft's bow caught in the main current and swung sharply downstream, threatening to spin them sideways as they neared the hiss and rattle of the rapids; Wager heaved on the starboard oar and angled the craft toward the wide tongue of foam that tumbled in a long chute between boulders kicking a ragged wall of water on each side.

"Straight—keep it straight on—you're doing good . . . keep it straight!"

With a surge, the raft had its own life, and Wager felt it join the river's force as if to tell him how useless the oars and his puny strength were now; it jumped forward into the chute, and Wager jabbed at the heaving surface to keep the bow aimed down the center of the tongue. They neared a large mound of slick water, and Sidney yelled "Right—go right!" and he twisted the craft against the shove of tons of water as they shot in a sudden dive past a gigantic boulder that lay invisible from upstream. The raft tilted sideways up a shelf of smooth, foamless wave, and shouldered across the crest just below a large horseshoe of white spume that spilled upstream against the plunging current. Then they slid safely down the back of the wave into a long series of gentle ripples.

"OK! All right! Whoooo!" Sidney grinned and gave him a thumbs-up. "Man, what a hole!"

"What's a hole?" asked Jo.

He pointed to the wide depression of water on the downstream side of the boulder. A standing wall of foaming brown spilled upriver to try to fill the vacuum. At its flickering edge where the hard-looking slick water dived beneath the foam, a shattered tree trunk tumbled and rolled, lunging to break free but pinned between the two forces. "Right there. Man, what a hole! I didn't think it'd be that big—we'd be stuck there until the river dried up!"

Wager took a deep breath and shoved on the oars. Ahead, the valley widened as a large canyon opened in the left-hand wall, a broad alley between palisades that disappeared in distant heat haze. It formed a wide ledge of tree-and-brush-covered sand, and the river eased into ripples as the current, baffled by the shoaling bottom, twisted and started this way and that. Wager aimed for the deepest trace he could see against the sun's glare. "I'd just as soon scout the next class two first."

"You did all right, Gabe—you got us through it."

To his mind, Sidney did it by telling Gabe how to approach the rapids. And then it was the raft all by itself, because there was no way he could pull against a current like that. But as he had told Jo earlier, what's a vacation without a little excitement?

.   .   .   .

Sidney took them through the next plunging swirl of water, dangerous not so much from the gradient but from the twisting passages between gigantic rocks that strained the river into half a dozen narrow channels. Then it was Jo's turn over a series of shelving steps that bumped and quivered the raft and scraped the cloth bottom with ominous humps. They landed for lunch and a half-mile walk up a narrowing gulch to a high, scooped-out cliff of pink sandstone. Halfway up, a band of darker red formed a stripe across the clean face, and above that, another two hundred feet of looming rock, they could see brush and piñon fringing the abrupt ledge.

"Look up there," said Sidney. "Over there by that little crack."

High in the smooth face of the rock, they made out faint Indian carvings, the clearest an eagle with wings outspread and each feather marked by a careful, precise, shallow chip.

"That's really beautiful," said Jo. "It's so lifelike."

"Not too many people know about this one. I don't even think the rancher knows about it. It's a box canyon—the only way in is a deer trail up at the far end, and even the deer are scared to use it."

Wager brushed at the flies that had homed in on them as soon as they left the water and started through the thick growth of willow and chokecherry. A few ragged cottonwoods gave a little shade, but the only escape from the airless heat was here at the foot of the cliff, in the rock's shadowed coolness. Except for the petroglyph, no sign of any other human marked the wavering lip of stone that arced around them on three sides, and in the silence, if he listened hard enough, he might hear the click of the Indian's stone tools still echoing. "Are there a lot of gulches like this along the river?"

"Sure, but most of them you can get into and out of from the mesa. The ranchers farm the big ones, if they can get water to them. I like these little ones, though. Some of them you can only see if you fly over."

"How do you think he climbed up there?" asked Jo.

"I figure the ground was higher then. Unless he stood on a slab that broke off and made that rubble there."

"Does anybody know what tribe it was?"

"They're just called the old ones—the Anasazi. They were long gone before the Utes or the Navajo came."

She gazed at the pale pattern on the rock's sheltered face. "And that's all that's left."

The cottonwood trees, a hundred years older than any of the three, rustled slightly as a stray breeze swirled down from the mesa, and Wager wondered how many generations of those trees had grown and died since the Anasazi stood here and decided—or was told by a spirit—to leave this mark of his people's passing. In a way, that small chiseled pattern seemed like a caress across the stone and spoke more deeply than any of the steel-and-concrete buildings of Denver that weighed faceless and cold above dwarfed pedestrians. Here, though he and Jo were tiny specks at the foot of a cliff that seemed to be perpetually falling over them, their domination was by a kind of calm absorption into earth and sky. In the city was no absorption, only conflict and finally erasure.

In silence, they wandered back to the beach to finish lunch and poke among the rocks and sandbars on this side of the river. Wager tried a few casts with the rod and reel, but Sidney said the only fish he was likely to catch in this stretch were cats, and he needed dough balls for that. "There's some trout, but with the water this high and dirty . . ."

It was time to go anyway. Already the sun was westering, and now the east walls of the canyon brought out their hues of pink and red. They drifted past corners and buttresses of stone that hinted of standing gods or half-formed faces, and gargoyles who looked blindly down on the tiny raft sliding past their feet. Long stretches of water settled into smooth drowsiness, and they were in and out of the raft as the heat sank into stone and began to breathe over the river. A pebbled cliff of crumbling rock marked a series of ancient riverbeds, and Sidney tied up to show them the fossilized shells imbedded in hardened sand between the rounded stones of the layers. Farther down, they stopped for a side trip up a small crack in the earth where a stream of icy water scoured across gray marl in a series of low waterfalls that formed pools of clear, icy water. By the time the shadows of the western bluffs covered the river and relieved them of the sun, they were nearing the campground.

"That's the start of T Bar M property." Sidney pointed to a freshly painted sign staked between two rocks above the highwater mark. It read "Private Property—Keep Off—Trespassers Will Be Prosecuted."

Ahead, the canyon walls widened only slightly to leave a tangle of growth and steep, rocky talus that offered no safe beach for the raft or level place to camp. Whenever the bluffs behind the river opened to indicate a feeder gulch or a pocket, a posted sign ordered people away. Finally, where the east wall turned back in a wide gap to meet another large canyon, a sign said "Camping." Sidney turned the raft around and rowed hard across the channel, drifting them in at an angle toward the sloping dirt.

The raft nudged ashore, and Wager splashed through the shallow water to anchor the line to a whitened tree trunk tossed high into the grass. Together, the three of them hauled the raft high up the bank and Sidney secured it with a second line—"The river might go up another foot overnight"—and they began unloading the rubber sacks and boxes. Sidney baited a couple of drop lines and flung them far out into the channel—"Fresh catfish for breakfast, guaranteed"—and Wager and Jo found a stunted piñon growing out of the soft sand and spread their groundcloth and dumped the sleeping bags. By the time twilight thickened into darkness, the breeze was heavy with the fragrance of roasting meat and Sidney was rummaging through the ice chest for the evening's salad. Half-buried under the coals, a mound of foil-wrapped potatoes slowly baked, and Wager and Jo had opened a bottle of wine and were leaning against a still-warm sandbank to watch the silent river sweep by. Its pale surface reflected the sky's final glow, and rings and noiseless boils and eddies and tiny flickering whirlpools spawned by the strong current etched black lines on the smooth water and glided swiftly past.

"Lord, that food smells good," said Jo. "I'm starving."

Wager's mouth felt wet with hunger, too, and wine didn't soften it as beer did. But the aroma of cooking wasn't what had been on his mind as he gazed at the flowing water. "It's been a good day, Jo. I've really enjoyed this day. I've enjoyed being with you."

A smile crinkled at the corner of her eyes. "Better than being a cop?"

"No. I like being a cop. So do you. Maybe I'm enjoying this more because I know we'll go back."

She turned to peer at him through the dusk and started to say something that had a laugh in it. Then stopped. Finally she said simply, "I've enjoyed it too."

"Hey—suppertime! Come and get it or I'll throw it out!"

Sidney's call interrupted their long kiss, and Wager gave a little groan.

"Was that your stomach or mine?" asked Jo.

"It was me. But it wasn't my stomach—I think that gave up an hour ago."

"Mine hasn't—come on, last one gets the smallest steak!"

They ate sitting around a fire of driftwood, the smoke rising out of the glare of flames to disappear against the wide strip of stars marking the canyon walls.

"Do you want some help with the tent?" asked Wager. "Or don't we need one?"

"We can rig a fly if it rains. But this time of year, the only thing's a few thunderstorms, and not many of them. They can be exciting—a lot of wind and lightning and it comes down like crazy for a little while. But we're not likely to be hit with one." He waved his arm at the surrounding darkness. "Sleep wherever you want—we're the only ones here tonight."

"What's that over there?" Jo pointed through the brush at a dim glow that rose and fell against a talus of large boulders.

"That must be one of the ranch hands. They come down to see who's camped and collect the landing fee."

The bobbing glow grew stronger, and in a few minutes they heard the grind of a vehicle geared low against the rutted trail leading up canyon. A pair of headlights swung from behind a shoulder of rock to rupture the night and bleach the tangle of limbs and shrubs as it mashed toward them. A moment later the lights and engine died and they heard the sound of boots crackle in the dry grass.

"Evening, Sid."

"Hello, John—how about a beer?"

"Sure." Sanchez moved into the firelight, his eyes lingering on Jo's bare legs before turning to Wager and blinking with surprise. "I didn't expect to see you here."

Wager smiled. "Just enjoying my vacation."

"Here you go." Sid tossed him a cold one from the ice chest. "Not too many people along the river today."

Sanchez twisted the Coors in his hand and flipped the tab up, a tiny spurt of foam hissing toward the fire. "There'll be plenty before summer's out. Looks like it's still rising."

They talked briefly about the river and what lay downstream, Sidney asking about Boulder Field especially. John's glance kept drifting toward Wager, his dark eyes masking any expression.

"It was running thirteen thousand this morning. It's probably about thirteen five, now."

"That much?" said John. "It might get as high as last year—wash all you river rats clean to Utah."

"Wait till that dam goes in. We'll be running the river all year round."

"I reckon I can wait."

"How'd you do up at Grand Junction?" asked Wager.

"OK. Jimmy got some money, anyway."

"Is your next rodeo around here? Maybe we'll be able to make it."

The light flickered his face into shadow, turning the dark hat brim a dull orange over his eyes. "We'll be in Denver next weekend. There's a Mountain States regional we'll be going to." He tipped the can against the sky. "How long you staying with the Volkers?"

Wager shrugged. "Another week or so. We're in no hurry. There's a lot of country we haven't seen yet."

"Jimmy told me you came by the ranch. Sorry to miss you."

"Right. Me too. Why don't you come to the Volkers' sometime? We're staying at their hunting cabin, the one on the creek below the ranch house. Know it?"

"Never been there."

"It's easy to find. Come on by—we'll have a drink for you."

"Maybe I will." He crushed the thin metal between his fingers and tossed it onto the sand beside the fire. "Thanks for the beer, Sid."

They watched the jeep back and turn, its brake light flashing brightly, then bouncing away into the darkness.

"You two know each other well, Gabe?"

"I knew his father. I've just met John and his brother."

"Jimmy's all right—he's a good guy. A good rodeo rider, too."

"What's wrong with John?"

"Wrong? Nothing, he's OK. He gets kind of hard-nosed, sometimes—likes to act like this big bad cowboy, especially when there's women in the party. But he's really OK when you get to know him."

"Do you see much of them?"

"Only along here. I guess they patrol every night. Either Jimmy or John comes by every time I bring a party through, anyway."

"Do they patrol the other canyons, too?"

"I guess if they saw a fire they'd take a look. But there's half a dozen landings, and it could take all night to check each one—you have to drive way around to get in and out of them. And some you can't drive to at all—the small ones." A grin flashed orange against the firelight. "I made dry camp in a couple of them. If you go after dark and don't light a fire, there's no way they're going to know you're there."

An all-night patrol would explain why Jimmy was sleeping when Jo and Wager had visited the ranch. And it naturally raised the question why: Why would anyone want to spend that much time and effort making certain that no one camped on his land? The obvious answer was that the owner was hiding something, and that brought Wager around to the question what.

"Hey—you still with us?" Jo tilted a final glass of wine from the bottle and handed it to him. "I thought you almost forgot about being a cop today. I did."

"Almost," said Wager.

"And then came Big Bad John."

He asked Sidney, "Can you walk to the other landings from here?"

"Some of them. It depends on the river. If it's low, sure. But most of the rafting's over by the time it gets that low. In water like this, you might make it, but there are some pretty steep cuts you have to cross." He started gathering the tin plates and utensils. They scraped the garbage into a watertight bucket and sealed the lid against animals. With river water heated over the fire in a five-gallon can, they washed the dishes, and then they hauled the raft another few feet up the bank and tightened the lines once more. "It may rise, it may not; but it sure would be embarrassing to wake up tomorrow without a raft." Then they secured the rest of the scattered gear against wind or rain, and Sidney, surrendering to his yawns, unrolled his groundcloth and sleeping bag.

Jo and Wager found theirs in the dark and spread them over the soft sand. They lay together feeling each other's warmth against the chilling night as the fire gradually died to embers. Above, the river of stars gleamed with the crispness of a moonless night; a hundred yards away, they could hear the almost silent whisper of the ceaseless water. Across the stream, high on the opposite bluff, an owl hooted its furry call, and from the canyon where John had driven came the brief high-pitched shriek of a rabbit caught by some feeding animal. Jo stirred briefly in his arms at the sound, and then her breathing became deep and regular again.

CHAPTER 11

Wager woke to the rhythmic clack of a hand pump and the smell of frying fish. They were still in shade, but across the canyon the uppermost ledge already caught the sun and turned yellow and orange and pale gray against the blue of morning. Sidney had built up the fire and hauled in the lines to skin the catfish and lay slabs of cornmeal-crusted meat in hot grease; now he straddled the bow of the raft and worked a hand pump hooked to one of the tubes. Beside Wager, Jo's tousled hair sprouted out of her sleeping bag, and she lay motionless. Wager shrugged into the cold air and tugged on his cut-off jeans and a sweatshirt still warm from his pillow sack; his tennis shoes were damp yet, but the cold wouldn't last more than a few seconds. After splashing his face with river water, he asked Sidney what he could do to help.

"Why don't you pump up the raft, and I'll get breakfast going. It must have got a lot colder than I thought last night—the raft went down some."

"How much air do you want?"

"Just make it firm, like that bow tube. When the sun gets on her, she'll tighten up good." He went to poke up the fire and flip the fish.

Wager finished the last section of the tube, and Jo, face a

healthy color from sun and a cold-water scrub, called him to breakfast. He had not realized how hungry he was until the first taste of hot and fragrant fish, and the others must have felt the same way, because breakfast—fresh pineapple, slabs of thick-crusted bread, strong coffee, and icy orange juice—lasted about ten minutes. "There's eggs if you want them, and sausage. I brought it along in case the fish didn't cooperate."

Jo patted her stomach. "Not a thing more! That was delicious."

"People like my cooking better out here than they do back home. So do I."

They packed up and strapped the waterproof bundles and chests securely to the raft's D-rings and frames. "We'll probably bounce against a few rocks today—Boulder Field's going to be exciting. We don't want to go through there without everything tight and secure."

"Will it be like the rapids yesterday? Those first ones?"

"It's not as sharp a drop, but it's a lot narrower. And it lasts a lot longer. We'll have to scout it out before we run it."

Wager asked how far down the river it was.

"About eight miles. There's a good put-in just above, so we can get a look at it."

"I'd like to spend some time along shore before we get there."

"Most of what we'll be going through is T Bar M land."

"I know."

Sidney looked at him curiously. "They really don't want trespassers."

"I thought they wouldn't mind if they didn't see us."

"Well, yessir, that's true enough. But they really don't like it. And Ron would get awfully upset if he knew I was antagonizing them."

"Is there some way you can put me ashore by myself and pick me up later?"

Sidney ran his hand under the sun-bleached hair that curled at the back of his neck. "Are you looking for something?"

The question was bound to come, and Wager wished he had a better answer. "I'm not sure what I'm looking for. I'm a cop—we both are. And we're interested in what's going on at that ranch."

"You're a cop, too?"

Jo nodded.

"Man, I didn't think . . . I mean, he kind of looks like a cop, but you sure don't."

"You should see me in uniform."

He glanced from Jo to Wager. "What do you think's going on at the ranch?"

"I'm not sure anything is. That's what I want to find out."

"Why can't you just go there and make them let you look the place over?"

"It's their property. I can't do that without a warrant." He couldn't do it with a warrant, either, because it wasn't his jurisdiction. But there was no need to confuse the boy. "And I can't get a warrant without probable cause—without a good idea that something is going on."

Sidney chewed his lip. "Undercover? Is that what you guys are?"

"I'd appreciate it if you didn't say anything about it."

"Wow. It sounds like something from a book or movie or something." He nosed the spatula at some burned grease in the large iron frying pan. "It's kind of exciting."

"What I want to do is look around some of these side canyons, and do it without being seen."

"A recon mission?"

"You got it."

"Landing from rubber boats in enemy territory . . ."

It wouldn't be all that dramatic—Wager hoped it wouldn't be all that dramatic. But it wouldn't hurt if Sidney got caught up in the moment. "Just like that."

"Wow." He pointed downstream. "The next landing on this side's about half a mile down; you can walk there—the beach goes along to it. We can come down in an hour and tie up on the other side and fish some. You signal us when you're ready and we'll come across and pick you up."

It was as good a plan as any. Wager took off briskly, staying as close to the water's edge as the chaos of fallen rock would allow. Occasionally he found a deer trail that etched a faint shelf across the steep faces, and he followed that through the stiff grass and clumps of wiry brush. But most often he had to scramble around shoulders of shattered rock that led up to the mesa hundreds of feet above. After a good half hour of climbing up and down like an ant across the giant boulders, he saw a small V in the walls where a stream once cut its way down to the river.

He studied the notch. The steep cut led away from the main canyon, a tangle of willow and hackberry forming a thick screen along the river. Even the morning cries of birds had ceased by now, and the only sound was the water, a steady echo against the rock like a ceaseless wind. Keeping away from the scattered patches of sand that would leave footprints, Wager worked down spines of rock to the floor of the gulch and past a sign warning, "Posted— Keep Out." An animal trail tunneled through the bushes, and Wager, bending low, picked his way along the narrow path and up a shelf into a rocky field dotted with cottonwoods. Somewhere up the cliffs a crow squawked sharply, alerted to his movements, and in the heat Wager began to sweat and feel the sting of scratches on his arms and shins. But he saw nothing. He wandered several hundred yards to where the gulch began to close into a long slope of cactus-dotted soil leading up to the next bench of stone, but the only human or animal sign was a scattering of long-dried cow dung.

The raft was waiting across the channel when he got back; Sidney had tied to a spur of rock, and he and Jo made lazy casts downstream toward a large eddy. When they saw Wager on a boulder at the river's edge, Sidney pulled hard across the current. The raft was carried below Wager, and he scrambled across the jagged, slippery rock to the closest landing; Sidney, with a heave on the bending oars, nudged the craft against a sloping shelf of stone, and Wager tumbled aboard as he pushed off quickly into the main current.

"Find anything?"

Wager shook his head. "A bunch of horseflies."

"Man, those things smart, don't they?" Sidney was a little disappointed, but there were a dozen or so other places downriver.

"We didn't catch anything, either," said Jo. "But I had a strike."

"Hop over and wash off the sweat—it'll make those horsefly bites feel better. Put your life jacket on first, though."

The next landing was across the river where a tongue of stony soil tumbled down to disappear into the water. The raft touched briefly above, and then Sidney rowed hard toward the steep cut of the opposite bank. Wager scrambled up past the inevitable Keep Out sign to a shelf of level earth that formed the floor of the side canyon. Working his way across the sunbaked flat, he followed a dry wash beyond a line of heavy brush. Carved into the clearest section of the canyon floor, a small plowed field stubbled from last year's harvest wavered in the heat. A handful of birds scattered to fly up the canyon walls, and across the hundred yards of open field, a deer froze, staring at him, its black stump of tail twitching nervously. Beyond, where the field ended, an eroded rut of road curved away toward the mesa.

"Anything there?"

Wager, pulling himself over the side after his swim for the raft, grunted no. "An old field—corn, I think. Do ranchers grow many different crops in these canyons?"

"Mostly hay for the cattle. I didn't know you were in the homicide department."

Jo handed him a cold beer from the tow sack. "We've been talking police work."

"I am," said Wager, tilting the beer down his dusty throat.

"Did John or James kill somebody?"

"I don't think so. But I hope you don't talk it up too much. Undercover means secret—ours and yours."

"Oh no, I'm not going to tell anybody. God, if I did that—told Ron about letting you ashore along the T Bar M—man, he'd have my butt! He doesn't want any trouble with the ranchers along the river. They tried to close the river down a few years back and Ron had to get a lawyer and everything." He added, "And if anybody sees you, tell them you swam ashore to go to the bathroom or something."

"I won't tell Ron if you don't. How's that?"

The third time wasn't the charm; it was the fourth, and even then there wasn't much to see. The largest of the side canyons they had passed so far was masked for a quarter mile above and below by a wide lip of brushy earth rising a few feet above the river. Wager found a black plastic pipe trenched into the bank and leading under the loose soil past the river growth. About a hundred yards inland and fenced against cattle and deer, a wide field of earth was ridged into furrows where young plants made evenly spaced green dots in the sunlight. The siphon pipe carried the river water up to a gas pump and dumped it into an earthen reservoir about ten yards across. Lying flat like strands of spaghetti over one shoulder of the dam, a series of white plastic irrigation hoses led to each of the furrows. Looking closely, he saw that every other plant was marked by a popsicle stick, and looking even closer, he had the answer: marijuana. It was a marijuana farm, with about two thousand seedlings carefully set in and irrigated from the newly built pond.

He wasn't certain of the crop's exact value—it had been a long time since he worked in the Organized Crime Unit and he didn't have the latest street figures. But this much care and investment meant high-quality stuff, sensimilla plants, probably, and there would be a lot of profit at stake. If several other fields were scattered in these isolated gulches and canyons, it added up to enough money to kill someone for. Even your own father.

He wanted to take one of the plants, but each popsicle stick had a number inked on it. Given their value, they were accounted for and probably mapped on a chart kept for each field. Tended with individual care, they would be checked regularly, and any missing would raise questions. He took a last quick look at the field and the high canyon walls protecting it, then he made his way back to the beach, careful not to leave a trail in the soft sand.

"Any luck this time?"

Wager pushed the raft away from shore and glanced back. The screen of brush and low trees was unchanged, and from here this canyon looked no different from any other that sliced its way to the river. "Yep."

"Yeah? What did you find?"

"Come on, Gabe." Jo nudged his shoulder with her fishing rod. "Give."

"They're running a pot farm. A big one."

"Pot? Marijuana?" Sidney looked back at the silent canyon that glided out of sight around a bend in the stream. "I read about some guy over in Delta County growing marijuana in the middle of his cornfield. But I never thought . . ."

"Did you see the plants?"

"They've mixed them in with some other kind of plant, probably in case a plane flies over. But the real crop's happy weed."

"Well, man, that explains why they get so uptight about people landing on their property!"

It also explained a lot of things about the ranch and about Tom's worry over his sons. It explained how they could afford the time and money to rodeo so much. And if it didn't explain the whos and hows of Tom's death, it sure as hell offered a clear motive.

"What's the setup?" asked Jo.

"They pump water out of the river to a small reservoir— a little pond probably lined with plastic so it won't leak. My guess is they add fertilizers to the pond and then run the mix down the rows with a gravity-feed irrigation system."

"Sure," said Sidney. "You see those rigs all over—the farmers have these metal tubes they set in irrigation ditches and they hook up these plastic hoses to run downhill from the ditch."

Wager nodded. "That's what this looked like."

"Is it a big field?" asked Jo.

"About a hundred yards across—big for a pot farm. I think there's around two thousand plants. They went to a lot of trouble to dig the pond and set up a fence and the irrigation system. They're expecting a big payoff."

"Two thousand!"

"What's that worth? That many plants?"

"Depends on the street value. But probably between one and two million dollars."

Sidney stopped rowing and stared at Wager. "How much?"

He told him again.

"My God."

"Do you think they have plots in all these canyons?"

Wager didn't think so; not all of them were suitable for irrigation. But they would have other fields where they could—they would want to grow as much as possible in a season to make the investment pay quickly. And it didn't take much space or water to raise twenty or thirty plants here and there. They could have tiny plots wherever a spring seeped out of the sandstone cliffs or a hose could snake down to the river. In all, the operation could harvest tens of millions of dollars every fall.

"Man, that does beat raising cows!"

"The overhead can get pretty expensive," said Jo. "Even if the growers don't go to jail, they're going to lose that ranch."

One crop would pay for that ranch a couple times over, and Wager suspected this wasn't the first harvest. But Jo was right—the feds would confiscate anything used to grow marijuana, including the land, and that might explain why the owner wasn't too worried about keeping the place up. It was a write-off.

Sidney whistled a low, long note. "That much money!" Then he looked at Wager. "What do we do now? Do we go to the feds? The sheriff? What?"

That part was no problem—an anonymous telephone call to the Drug Enforcement Agency or a word to Sergeant Johnston, and a helicopter would hover over each draw and gully to study the land with binoculars. Those plants weren't going anywhere before autumn. But Tom's killers were something else. In addition to his suspicions, Wager had a motive now; but he knew damned well how much weight that would have when DEA got their noses filled with the scent of a marijuana farm. "I'd like to think about that for a little while. There's another case involved, and I'm not sure yet what's the best way to go."

"That's right—you're with Homicide!" Sidney's eyes widened as he stared at Wager and he put a few things together. "Somebody was killed because he knew about this place!"

"That's a possibility."

"And now we know about it—I know about it." The taut young flesh of his neck rose and fell as his Adam's apple bobbed.

"But they don't know you know. And I'm not going to tell them. Are you?"

"No way! I'm not saying anything to anybody!"

"And if anyone asks, you can honestly say you never set a foot on shore except at the campground, right?"

"That's right—that's the truth!"

Wager hauled the tow sack toward the raft and fished out a couple more cold beers. "Then let's forget all about this for now and enjoy the trip." He winked at Jo. "It's your vacation too, right?"

.   .   .

It took a while. Despite his promise to say nothing about it, Sidney kept coming back to the ranch and the marijuana. But gradually the fact of the river took over, and as they cleared the last of the T Bar M property, his conversation turned to the coming Boulder Field.

"We've got a good class-three rapids just above the Field, but we don't have to scout that one—in water this high, we'll get a lot of bouncing, but that's about all."

"Is Boulder Field dangerous?"

"It can be. But I've been through it enough times, in

higher water, too. If you know the approaches, you can stay away from most of the trouble."

They had broken down the fishing gear and stowed it in its tubing and secured it to the frame with elastic cords. Sidney tugged at the cargo ties and checked the security of the spare oars clipped tightly along each side tube. He told them to put their life jackets on and look around for any loose gear.

"Remember, if you go over, float feet first downstream so you can push off any rocks. Keep your feet high so they don't get hung up on the bottom, and you'll be all right. When you're past the rapids, you can eddy out just like we've been doing with the raft."

"Do you think we'll get thrown out?"

"It's happened. But we'll do all right."

The raft was moving faster now, the canyon walls closing in on both sides and rising in straighter sheets of vertical red that tilted the head back and back as they gazed upward. It reminded Wager of approaching an aircraft carrier in a small boat, and how the massiveness of the ship's overhanging steel suddenly dwarfed the tiny figures peering over the edge of the flight deck so far above.

"Those rocks look cold!"

Sidney nodded at Jo. "You notice that too? It always looks kind of dark and cold in this part of the canyon. Most rapids, I don't even see the shore. But here, I can't help it."

Still silent, the water deepened into a fast, smooth alley that frothed slightly at the shoreline. There, sharp boulders sent noisy, sucking whirlpools reaching out toward the raft, and the only growth was a few stubborn threads of grass caught in tiny crevices.

"The first rapids are around this bend—we'll hear it in a minute."

He pulled hard upstream to keep the raft on the inside of the sweeping arc, but because of the steep cliffs there was no slack water; it all sped faster around the bend, and suddenly they saw the tumult of spray and foam below them falling away in terraces of white water. The roar of the rapids, pent between faces of bare rock, bounced and doubled and almost drowned Jo's voice: "Oh my gosh—oh my gosh!"

"Man, she's running high—hang on and let her rip! Yeeeeha!"

Wager felt Jo tense as the raft leaped out over the first step and smacked hard against the water, washing spray across the tubes to plunge in an icy wave over their legs.

"Bail—bail it out—she's getting heavy!"

Gripping the lifeline with one hand, Wager scooped with the other, losing to the surge of water that poured in as the raft pounded down again, the solid shock quivering the whole craft and seeming to hold it for a moment fixed amid the plummeting white world around them until, with a sluggish waggle, it lifted again and lunged for the next level.

Oars flailing, Sidney half stood to shove the heavy craft toward a spume-filled eddy that spun in a gigantic, lazy circle against a strip of sandless gravel. The raft dragged awkwardly across the current, more water spilling over the stern, and then it began to turn backward, drawn stern-first toward the narrow chute closest to the shore. Sidney heaved on the oars, the choppy, broken water twisting the raft, and suddenly they were in the backflow of the eddy. The raft rocked from the turbulence of the rapids and the weight of the water sloshing back and forth over their feet, but the stream was calm in this spot, and Sidney gently guided the craft toward shore. Jo bailed steadily as Wager readied a landing line and hopped onto the steep beach when Sidney held the raft momentarily still against the pull of the eddy.

He turned the line around a flake of rock, and Sidney, hauling a longer line, clambered ashore to make fast the stern to another boulder.

"How about that? Wasn't that fun?"

"Fun and wet." They had to shout to be heard above the river; Jo beckoned to Wager. "Come on—let's take a look at Boulder Field."

The trail skirted a vertical face of orange rock that rose

out of sight above the maze of fallen stone choking the narrow canyon. They picked their way across house-sized boulders whose shattered ledges gave slight hand and toe holds. Gradually they climbed higher above the river and its noise and could look down at the long series of rapids and chutes and tortured water that plunged between the gigantic rocks in narrow, spray-filled channels.

"That thing looks like it's half a mile long."

"A little longer, I think. In low water, it really stretches out; in high water it gets shorter and faster and meaner."

"Look—there goes a log," said Jo. "Look at it!"

The tree trunk bobbed and plunged heavily through the black water and then suddenly reared to thud into a rock face. It swung in the high wave rebounding from the rock and lurched into a chute, disappearing in the foam to reappear a moment later end-first and shooting high out of a standing wall of white water to plummet hard into the river and be sucked down under a blanket of foam.

"What if something like that hits the raft?" she asked.

Sidney grinned. "That's what prayers are for." He added, "Don't worry—there's not many of them, even in rising water. And we'll be going faster than they do. We'll just make sure there's none coming down before we start out."

They spent a good hour scouting the rapids. Sidney pointed out the most likely tongues to aim for and the worst holes to avoid. Their route started on the far side under an outcropping of water-darkened wall, and stayed over there until about a third of the way through. Then it was best to try to cross and aim for the larger chutes that opened up on this side. "We always hit some rocks. Remember, when I yell 'Jump to' that means move to the side closest to the rock. It can be scary, but hang in there—we want to keep the raft's unweighted side upstream so we don't fill with water and get wrapped around a rock. I've done it—it's a real headache to get it off again."

"This looks bigger than the first rapids we went over yesterday," said Wager.

"It's not as steep a drop. But it's tricky because of all the boulders—some places there's almost no room to work the oars."

Just before the end of the rapids, they would have to pull hard back toward the middle of the river. "There's a big suck hole on this side—you can't really see it too well from here, but it's there. That's probably where that log is we saw go through. I saw a raft hung up in that thing a year ago and it took eleven of us to pull it loose. And the water was a lot lower then."

They worked their way back to the raft, Sidney reminding them what "Jump to" meant and what they should do if they went over. "It's really safer to go through in your life vest than in a raft because you've got a lot more leeway. Just don't hang your feet down and don't panic, that's all."

"If it's so much safer," asked Jo, "why do you keep telling us how to be careful?"

"Hey, that's part of the tour. You don't want this to be like sitting in your bathtub, do you?" He gave the raft's lines and straps a final tug for looseness and fray, tucking away loose coils and ends of line. Then he pressed his weight on each of the air compartments, testing their tautness. The rear half of the port tube felt soft, and he groped for the pump tied inside the bow. "We must have scraped something yesterday—this is the one we pumped up this morning, isn't it?"

Wager nodded.

"Not to worry. That's what this little jewel is for. And the other chambers are good and tight, so even if one went down we'd be all right. Still, we don't want to take Boulder Field with a soft raft if we can help it. Not the way it is today."

Wager glanced at Jo staring at the river. "Worried?"

"A little, yes. But it's exciting—I like it."

"Sidney's been through here a lot of times."

"He said this is almost the highest he's ever seen the water."

"It's the highest I've seen it, too."

"You've never seen it before!"

"All right—you two set for the big run? Everybody know what they're supposed to do?"

Sidney used the oars to hold the raft steady as Wager cast off the lines and jumped over the bobbing tube. Using the eddy's current to gain speed, he followed it upriver along shore and out toward the main current. At the top of the arc, he pulled hard on the oars to back across the eddy fence and thrust the raft into the current. A heavy shove on the oars to spin the craft, and they were neatly lined up for the approach to the first chute.

Swiftly, the raft neared the line of boulders, whose size kept growing until they seemed to tower even higher than the canyon walls on each side. Black and wet and creased with old seams and angles, they pushed a heavy wave back against the river to make the water confused and angry. The raft, tilting up on the wave, slid sideways, and Sidney grunted as he pushed the port oar against the heave of current. It angled to the chute and tilted bow down on the slick water and shot forward, hitting with a wrenching twist into the white foam that closed over the tongue of clear water.

"Here we go!" Sidney's voice sounded like a weak bird call through the tumult, and Wager saw Jo's lips say "Oh my gosh!" when the raft jetted forward fast enough to throw them back against the rowing frame. For an instant, all they saw was sky—a distant, uncaring, narrow strip pale with heat and touched here and there with thin, high-altitude clouds. Then they faced the prow of a giant triangular boulder like a fang knifing up through the foam, and the raft careened wildly up the wave at its base.

"Jump to! Jump to!"

Wager threw his weight on the downstream tube, leaning away from the boulder whose wet, sharp blade seemed to reach for him. The raft mashed against the rock and hung at a steep angle, and Wager had a vision of it flipping over on top of Jo and him and pinning them between its weight and the scarred, cutting face of the rock. Then it rebounded away, spinning off as Sidney heaved on the oars to pull free of the hole on the downstream side. He tried frantically to turn the raft bow-first before they were pulled into the next chute.

"Did you feel how cold that was?" Jo had to shout to be heard. "That rock—it just breathed cold air!"

Wager glanced back at Sidney as they jockeyed for the next chute; the young man pulled back with all his lean strength against the arcing shaft of the oars. But he wasn't looking downstream. Instead he gazed with surprise at something just behind him. Wager saw it too: a deep wrinkle in the left stern tube that, even as he watched, creased more deeply under the force of the current.

Sidney caught his eye and shook his head, the surprise giving way to worry. He was pulling too hard at the oars to say anything. And anything he said would be useless anyway.

They angled into the next chute, the water piling up on each side and rebounding to make a solid wall of white across the glassy surface flow. The raft hit and lurched upward, and Wager felt something thud into the air chambers, something akin to a club or a heavy punch that quivered the rubber skin beneath his hands. The tube he pressed suddenly slacked and wrinkles fanned out from his spread fingers, and he saw the hole which appeared like a sudden drop of black ink from the sky, silent under the roaring tumult of water. It was small, slightly larger than a pencil, perfectly round with a tiny fray at the edge as air rushed out, and he knew it was a bullet hole. Somebody on the rim above was shooting holes in the raft.

The port side buried as water poured over the soft tube, pulling them down and back into the current and making Sidney's mouth twist and pull with the strain of rowing. Jo grabbed Wager's arm and stared at him, her color drained to leave her eyes large and silently pleading. Wager had a quick, blind glimpse of the stony rims etched against the sky and started to shout "Feet first!" when a splash of foam drenched them. An instant later the raft was hit again. The solid thud jarred the frame, and he felt someting final tear away somewhere deep inside the craft.

Like a giant hand closing, the raft bent under from the rear as tons of water shoved violently against its canvas. Sidney, eyebrows pinched with interest as he studied the collapsing raft, looked as if he worked a new and challenging puzzle and seemed oblivious to the swirl of the river leaping above his waist. With a jolting snag, the raft caught and spun, another tube ripping open to broach them against the tumbling current and splinter the spare oars. The remaining tubes flipped high and dumped them into the raging water; Wager caught the glint of an orange life jacket as Jo swept over and past him, her arms and legs skyward, and then he was fighting for breath in a roaring whiteness that choked and blinded and terrified.

He tried to swing his feet high and downstream, but he was carried like a chip through warring currents and didn't know which was downstream. Something hard raked his arm and shoulder and stung for an instant along his ribs, and he suddenly found himself popping up in clear water long enough to gulp a lungful of air. Facing him, pulled into a deep hole where a tumbling cliff of white water endlessly fought against the sucking flow of the current, Jo, mouth agape for air, reached out for anything. Wager lunged against the river to grab for her but was thrown aside, glimpsing another orange speck—Sidney—flailing toward the struggling girl. Then something sharp snagged Wager's trailing leg and held it, the current pushing down and over him as he fought to yank his foot free of the cleft but was held and pinned by the icy rush of blackness. Yanking frantically, his foot slipped free of its tennis shoe and raked itself clear, the river tumbling him and bouncing him against boulders until he pulled a fiery breath of water and gagged, the choking, frantic convulsions filling consciousness and making him oblivious to the jerking and pummeling currents that smashed him from rock to rock and finally, with a careless toss, pounded him into numb oblivion.

CHAPTER 12

The first thing he felt was the cold. It was black added to blackness and wanted to finish overwhelming the last sentient fragment somewhere at the base of his skull. That final speck of resisting warmth was pinched between his arced neck and his tight, clenched shoulders, and if he could hold on to it long enough, the cold would stop pushing. But even as he grew aware of that struggle, he felt a searing convulsion in his chest, and by themselves his lungs clenched hotly against whatever tortured them and he felt his body twitch as he retched and rolled to his side and vomited a burning spray of liquid.

"Take it easy—you'll be OK. Don't fight it, man, just let it go."

He was wrapped in something soft and warm and somebody was holding his shoulders up and away so he wouldn't spew back into his own lungs.

His leg hurt. And his elbow. And ribs all along the right side. And now he could feel his muscles, pulled like cold rubber, begin to ache, and despite himself he groaned through the retching and tried to suck a clear breath deep into his still-burning lungs.

A spate of shivering began, starting somewhere deep in

his back and shaking his whole body with a snap that made the ache in his forehead rise into pain.

"He's shivering," said another voice. "That's good. It means he's fighting the hypothermia."

Wager squinted through the ache of his head and the heavy shakes that seemed to jam his very bones together with a dry, grating rub. In a narrow range of vision that seemed curiously dark at the edges, he made out a soggy orange life vest a couple of feet away flung against a beached rubber raft.

"Jo?"

"What?"

"Jo—where's Jo?"

A bearded face hung down to gaze at him. The man's tongue wiped across the smear of pink lip balm, and he finally said, "I'm afraid he's drowned."

Wager tried to shake his head, but the spasms of his flesh and the tightly clenched muscles of his neck and back wouldn't let him. "Not him. Not him—her. Josephine."

"Who?"

"Josephine. Fabrizio. A woman."

There was a long silence, and Wager fought to twist his stiff neck up so he could see the four quiet figures tall and lean and dark against the glare of sky.

"We only found one. I'm sorry."

.   .   .

The sheriff met him at the Rimrock clinic, where a nurse messed around and tried to act cheerful until the doctor could make it the hundred or so miles across the county. Despite its small size and lack of equipment, the clinic reminded Wager of the hospital where he had last seen Tom. He remembered the man telling him once that he hated hospitals. Despite all his broken bones and sprains and assorted abrasions, he said he only stayed overnight in a hospital once—"That's where you go to die, Gabe. Damned if I'll let them tote me to some place where you go to die."

Tom was right, it turned out; but hospitals weren't the only places to die. You could do that anywhere.

Wearily, he pushed that thought somewhere into the back of his mind. They had searched, Wager and the others, back up through the rapids, along the cliffs and snarls of tortured rock, downriver as they rowed the burdened craft. She was dead, and that was a fact as solid and cold and unmoving as one of those boulders ripping the river. She was dead, and that's all there was to it, and now a police officer stood waiting to fill out his report on another death. That's what happened when you died before you were supposed to—you made paperwork for cops.

This one was a short man who wore a heavy, cropped mustache to give his narrow face some weight. Beneath an equally narrow chest, his stomach swelled out in a tiny pot that reminded Wager vaguely of an ant's abdomen. But there was nothing antlike about his attitude—no darting hurry, no busywork, no nervous fiddling with his hands. Instead he sat calm and unmoving on the end of the next examining table while the doctor, still tight-lipped with hurry from his last case, aimed his little light into Wager's pupils and peered this way and that.

"I've notified Sidney's parents, Mr. Wager. You don't have to talk to them if you're not up to it."

"I can't tell them much."

"I know. But for some reason, folks seem to want to know everything about what happened." He paused. "I guess you've run across that in your line of work."

"Yes."

The nurse took a syringe and a tiny bottle of clear liquid from one of the steel-and-glass cabinets that crowded the room.

"We're going to give you a tetanus shot just in case, Mr. Wager," said the doctor. "It's a good idea when you've been in water where cattle are. Those are some pretty deep cuts along your leg." He pushed the needle into the neck of the bottle and gradually filled the syringe. "This won't be anything like what you've been through." He smiled and pinched the skin at the back of his arm and a moment later said, "There."

"Ron Honeycutt wants to talk to you, too. He owns the raft company—he wants to find out what happened."

"All right."

"We'll be out in the lobby. Take your time."

The doctor, stethoscope folded into the side pocket of his white jacket, smiled again. "You're healthy. No concussion, but you're going to be sore for a while. I'll write a prescription for something to fight any infection in those cuts. They should heal all right without stitches, but if they pull loose again, you might check with your own doctor when you get home." He scribbled something on a tablet and pulled the leaf off and handed it to Wager. "Take a couple of aspirin and get some sleep. Take it easy for a few days, too—you want to give your system time to get over the shock, OK?"

"Right."

He closed the door after him, leaving Wager to change from the medical gown to his clothes. He tugged on the jeans that a wet-eyed Dee Volker had brought earlier, and winced as he bent to pull his boots over his sore foot.

The rafting party that had found him, face up and floating like the rest of the river's scraps in a large eddy below Boulder Field, had found Sidney, too. Except that he wasn't face up. Jo's body, one of them finally said, was probably wedged under something on the bottom. There wasn't anything anybody could do now. But later, maybe, when the river went down . . .

They put him in the raft, still shaking and gagging occasionally as a breath stung something in his lungs, and rowed hard downriver. Sidney, deep cuts and scrapes seeming even fiercer in his bloodless flesh, was covered with a sleeping bag and tied to the after thwart.

It was a silent crew that took turns on the oars, the joy and excitement gone from their trip, and they didn't hide their relief when they spotted a riverside ranch and could beach and call the sheriff. Two hours later, Wager was rolled into the examining room in a wheelchair; the sheriff, efficient on the telephone, had called everyone concerned. Now they sat in the clinic's small waiting room.

Mrs. Hennon perched on one of the Naugahyde chairs, her husband on one side and a tall man in jeans and a khaki shirt on the other. Wager guessed that was Ron, Sidney's boss. Sheriff Akridge's mustache lifted and fell briefly. "You look a lot better, Mr. Wager."

"Thanks." He shook hands with the others, trying not to read the accusation in the woman's eyes.

"Mr. and Mrs. Hennon—Sidney's folks. Can you tell them anything about what happened?"

Wager told most of what he remembered, stressing that Sidney had done everything he could and had even tried to rescue Jo after the raft went under.

"But why him? Why couldn't you reach her?" The boy's mother stared at him with hot eyes. "Why him? Why Sidney?"

"I did try," said Wager.

"Sharon, it's not Mr. Wager's fault. It's nobody's fault— it's the river."

"It is somebody's fault! It has to be somebody's fault! It's just not fair!"

The sheriff glanced an apology at Wager, and Ron Honeycutt stood silent and face down waiting for her to turn on him.

"He was so young—he was going to college. . . ." The last word in a high whine that turned into a stifled wail, and Mr. Hennon, his arm around her shaking shoulders, guided her toward the twilight outside.

Wager and the others stood in uncomfortable silence until finally the sheriff cleared his throat. "We—uh—we got to hold an investigation into the accident, Mr. Wager. You know, get the facts and all. It's best to do it as soon after as possible. You want to do it here or would you like to come down to the office?"

"I want to get the hell out of here."

On the drive over to the small white box of an office,

Akridge said, "She don't really blame you, Mr. Wager. Nobody does. You know how women are—if they lose something, somebody stole it; if they have bad luck, somebody caused it."

The sheriff's words buzzed somewhere at the edge of understanding, held back by another surge of icy blackness even deeper and colder than those before: Jo was dead. She was dead. Dead.

"Women just can't help it. You know what I mean, Mr. Wager?"

"Right."

In the office, the sheriff took a few minutes to look over some paperwork and radio a message to Bob about serving papers. When Honeycutt arrived, he reached into a bottom drawer of the scarred wooden desk and pulled out a bottle of Canadian Club. Without asking, he set three glasses on a heavy corner and poured stiff drinks. The whiskey burned a cough out of Wager, but for the first time since he waked to the cold at the side of the river, he felt warmth begin to glow and loosen the sore muscles clenched around the center of his torso. And, at the heart of that more profound cold in his mind, he felt, too, the first tiny stir of rage.

Akridge poured another one for him; Ron Honeycutt shook his head no and the bottle tipped briefly over the sheriff's glass.

"Better than anything the clinic's got."

"Yeah."

"I'll have to arrest myself for practicing medicine without a license." He corked the bottle and shoved it into the drawer and leaned back and sighed heavily. It was time for business. "You say the raft had a slow leak in it?"

Wager took a deep breath and hauled his mind back from where it had been. "That's what Sidney said. I pumped it up this morning." This morning. The words didn't seem real. There was something wrong with them. This morning he and Jo had been sleeping together and waking slowly to the early sunlight on the cliffs across the calm ripple of the river. This morning they had the whole clean day ahead of them. A whole lifetime. That had been this morning.

"Mr. Wager? I was asking if you noticed anything else wrong with the raft."

"No. Except for losing a little air, it was in good shape. Sidney wouldn't have tried the rapids if he thought something was wrong with it."

"I know he wouldn't!" Honeycutt spoke for the first time. "He was careful and he knew the river—he wouldn't take chances, dammit."

Taking chances was a relative term. Sometimes chance and accident took what they would. And sometimes chance had help.

"Did—uh—did Sidney drink anything before? You know, a beer or some such?"

"Only soft drinks. Jo and I had a couple of beers, but he didn't have any."

"Ron? You said you had some questions."

Honeycutt fished in his shirt pocket for a package of cigarettes and stuck one in the corner of his mouth. Frowning, he lit it with a match scraped alight by a thumbnail. "I just don't understand why the raft behaved that way. I've never—never!—heard of a raft popping its seams like that. Even if one chamber went down, Sidney would have been able to steer it through."

"How did the raft act when it went down, Mr. Wager?"

"The whole rear end folded under in a couple of seconds. It broke both spare oars."

Honeycutt shook his head, tangled brown hair catching in the light of the desk lamp. "And you say it felt like something tearing underneath?"

"That's right."

"Did you see any logs coming down? Anything that could rip her open?"

"No. There was one log, but it cleared the rapids before we started."

The cigarette crackled. "It just doesn't make a bit of sense. I don't know, Sheriff, I guess the river does some weird things, but this just doesn't make any sense at all."

The sheriff wet his lips with his glass. "There's not much chance of finding that raft." It wasn't a question.

"Not till the river goes down, and then maybe never. We might find pieces of it, but . . ." Honeycutt trailed off in an awkward silence.

"Yeah," said the sheriff quickly. He jotted something in a notebook. "No broken oars or anything like that before you had the trouble?"

"No. Sidney was looking at the tube just before we swamped. So did I—it was wrinkling. Then the whole stern folded under." He saw it again. "We hit a rock and something ripped—I felt it in the tube I was leaning on— the port tube. It went, and then we were over." And Jo reached out for him but he wasn't there.

"I just plain don't understand it," said Honeycutt.

Wager offered nothing.

"The only reason any raft would act that way is if it was cut."

Leaning forward, the sheriff studied Wager. "You think that might have happened?"

"I don't know. We hit a lot of times before it sank. Some of the rocks were pretty sharp. I guess they could have cut it."

Honeycutt shook his head. "Rocks wouldn't have cut all the tubes at one time like that. I mean if somebody had cut the raft on purpose, she'd act just like that. But Jesus, Sheriff, that'd be murder! Sid and Miss Fabrizio . . . that'd be murder!"

"Don't go jumping all over some conclusions, now, Ron. We don't know what happened to that raft."

"But it's the only explanation why it went down! My rafts are in good condition—I check them out every week and after every trip. None of my rafts would go down like that unless somebody tampered with it." Honeycutt stood and took a last hard drag on his cigarette and jabbed it out in the sheriff's ashtray. "That raft had six individual flotation chambers, four in the tubes and two in the thwarts. And a twenty-four-ounce laminated skin. There's no way on earth the rocks could make all those tubes pop unless somebody monkeyed with them." He looked at Wager. "But who?"

"It wasn't anybody on the raft."

"It wasn't anybody at all that we know of," said Akridge.

"But if we can find that raft," said Honeycutt. "Maybe if we can find that raft . . ."

"It'll be harder'n hell to find and harder than that to tell the difference between a cut and a tear. But we'll look for it—along with looking for Miss Fabrizio, Mr. Wager. But" —his head wagged—"it might not be until September that the water's low enough to find anything." He turned to Honeycutt. "Meanwhile, Ron, I want you to keep quiet about the raft. For one thing, we don't have any reason to think that's what happened."

"It's the only thing that explains it, Sheriff!"

"And for another thing, you'd just get Mrs. Hennon even more upset. You saw her—you know what I mean. For a third thing, if somebody did cut that raft, I don't want them getting scared and running out of the county. I hope that's all right with you, Ron."

"Yes."

"Good. I'll be starting the search first thing in the morning. I reckon you want to go along—be here at seven-thirty. Now you go on—I got a few more questions to ask Mr. Wager."

Honeycutt paused at the doorway. "Mr. Wager, you signed a release, you know—you and Miss Fabrizio, both."

"I know."

"It's a legal document. A full release in case something like this happened."

"He knows, Ron. You go on, now." Akridge waited until they heard the man's truck start and grind across the gravel. "He's pretty upset, too, Mr. Wager. He was like an uncle to that boy."

"And business is business."

"Well, that's true, too. Now." He settled back in his chair and crossed his hands on the small potbelly. "Ain't nobody here but us cops. Suppose you tell me why you've been interested in the T Bar M ranch."

"I know a couple of the hands there."

"That's not what you told Bob Schrantz. You are the same Detective Wager from Denver who called a while back and asked if we knew of anything going on out there, right?"

"Yes."

"And the river just happens to go through T Bar M property, and you just happened to be there. Why don't you just happen to tell me what's going on?"

He did, starting with the part about Tom wanting him to look into his sons' activities.

"But this Tom Sanchez hasn't found out anything more?"

"Nothing he told me about."

"Where can I get in touch with him?"

"He's dead. He was found beside a road near Salida. The sheriff there calls it a robbery and beating."

"Oh? Now this is starting to get curiouser and curiouser." He splashed more whiskey for both of them. "And you think his boys had something to do with it?"

"As far as I know, they were up in Montana when it happened. But I wanted to check out the ranch."

"You went to the ranch to look it over?"

"Yes. Jo . . . we rode over a week or so ago. To say hello to the boys."

"So they knew you were here."

"Yes."

"And then you took that raft trip to look some more?"

"Yes."

"Did you find anything?"

"No." He gazed levelly into the sheriff's eyes that looked as round and black as two dots on a pair of dice.

"I see. I guess I see." He held a mouthful of whiskey for a few minutes before swallowing. "Did they know you were rafting?"

"John came into camp last night."

"Oh?" Akridge scratched at one wing of his mustache. "You think maybe Ron's got the right idea?"

"I don't know. It might not be him. It might not be anybody."

"Yes, that's true—it's a mean river, this time of year. And there's no motive, either." He looked up. "Is there?"

"No."

Akridge set his glass down. "You know, it sounds to me like you were running an investigation a hell of a long way outside your jurisdiction, Officer Wager."

"We came up here on vacation. I didn't do anything any other civilian couldn't do."

"By law, I suppose that's so. But you're a cop. You know that and I know it, and so do those people out at the T Bar M. Didn't that cross your mind, Wager? Didn't you ever stop to think you were involving that boy and Miss Fabrizio in a criminal investigation? One man's already dead, and now—if Ron's theory is right—two more people have been killed." He leaned forward to stare at Wager. "Didn't it cross your mind that it could be very damned dangerous, and not just for you?"

There wasn't much to say to that; Wager had not thought. He had led them into harm's way and had been careless with their lives.

"Well, we'll leave it at that for now—a theory. I'll list the deaths as accidental drowning."

"I understand."

"But if you turn up any information about the T Bar M or what happened today, I want to be told about it."

"Yes."

Sheriff Akridge said that Wager, too, was welcome to join the search party tomorrow, but advised him against it. Then they drove the few blocks down to the river and Wager's car parked beside the dark Quonset hut of the Foamy Rapids Rafting Company.

"We'll do our best to find Miss Fabrizio, Wager. But like I said, it may not be until September. If ever."

"I understand."

"It's too bad all this happened. I'm mighty sorry about it." His silence indicated that he wanted to say more. "A lot of people come out here thinking they're going to conquer nature or grizzly bears or some such. But it isn't so." He tapped his khaki shirt. "Right here's the real fight—your own self. And I don't think too many people win that one. Goodnight."

Wager stood beside his Trans-Am as the sheriff's boxy vehicle rattled away. In the silence and dim twilight, he could hear the rustle of the river and the dry, chattering rattle of two twigs vibrating against each other in the current. The surface of the water seemed to glow as it gathered the sky's final light into a smooth, broad sheet that looked almost motionless here where the water was deep and the banks sandy. He listened close for any note of sadness in the soft murmur, for a muffled sob or a sigh from the water gliding among the grasses. But there was nothing; there was only the sound of water, and in the distance—from the other side of town—a semi-truck's hard wheels making a tiny, fading scream into the darkness.

.   .   .

Dee Volker insisted that Wager stay at the ranch house instead of the empty cabin. "We already made up the guest bed," she said. "And I've got some supper kept warm in the oven—you must be starved."

"I'm not hungry."

"Of course you're not." She patted his arm gently. "But you should eat anyway."

It helped her to keep busy, so Wager let her sit him down at the kitchen table and pile a plate of food in front of him. Rusty squeezed Wager's shoulder with a calloused hand.

"The sheriff's called out the posse to help search the river tomorrow. I'm going, if you want to come along."

Wager nodded yes, his stomach suddenly aching with hunger as he tasted the food, and he thought ironically of all the routine things that never paused for death—not the river, not his own body; not even John or James, who had probably finished a fine dinner and were now settled down in front of the bunkhouse television set waiting for the regional news.

"Can I use your phone to call Denver? Jo's parents—I don't think anybody's told them yet."

"Sure you can," said Dee. "I guess we should have called, but we don't know their number."

Neither did Wager, but the department would have it in the who-to-notify file. And he wanted someone to tell them personally, someone who could do it with gentleness. Max answered on the first ring.

"Gabe! How's the vacation? Don't tell me you're homesick for this place already."

He told him about Jo.

"Aw, God, Gabe—I'm sorry."

"We haven't found her body yet. I'm going to be out here a while longer. Max, can you tell her parents?"

"Of course. I'll go over there. God, Gabe, I just don't know what to say to you."

"There's not much to say. Tell her parents that her body's still missing—and that I'll call as soon as we know something. And I'll be by when I get back. Tell them . . ." He hesitated. "Tell them it was very quick. An accident."

"I will, Gabe. I'll go over there now. You take it easy, partner, and call me as soon as you get back."

. . .

He did not know if he would sleep, but that was the last thought he remembered until morning when a sharp twinge along his bruised ribs woke him to the renewed knowledge of Jo's death. Somehow, in the warm, clear light of early sun, it seemed even less possible that he would not see her again, would not feel her beside him or see the laughter in her golden eyes at some half-assed thing he said or did. Even as he lay and stared at the ceiling, he could picture her brushing her long hair back from her forehead with a quick, unconsciously graceful movement. Or the way her full lips tightened slightly when she concentrated. Or the tilt of her head up beneath his face when they made love staring into each other's wide eyes. He heard a strangled groan and for a moment didn't realize he had made the noise. But it was enough to pull him back to the sunwashed bedroom with its lacy white curtains moving slightly in the breeze, and the brightly patterned quilt lumped by his body. The cheery, sun-filled room served temporarily for guests, but it really wanted to be a nursery, and some of that persistent hope lingered in the carefully pleated curtains and the waiting, empty chest of drawers.

Everybody had hurt; his was nothing new to the world, and nothing special to anyone but him. Stiffly, his breath catching as things in his body protested, he swung out of bed and dragged on his clothes. He could smell the aroma of coffee and frying bacon, and as he grunted to pull on his boots, a soft knock jiggled the door.

"I'm up."

Rusty's voice asked, "You still want to go this morning?"

"Yes—I'm coming now."

After a quick breakfast, Rusty guided his oversized pickup truck along a ranch road different from those Wager had ridden with Jo. "This is the shortest way—Sheriff Akridge said our bunch should meet up on this side of the river. He'll have his bunch on the other bank."

"Do we cross T Bar M land to get there?"

"Have to, but they won't mind. As long as we close the gates."

The two men fell silent under the drone of the heavy engine and the jolt and lurch of a road that wound over piñon hills patched with red earth and rock. They crossed a cattle guard braced by angle-iron triangles at each end, and then bounced down a two-rut road cut into the black of old lava ash. It fanned out into a level, treeless basin made soft-looking with sagebrush. Ahead, the white flash of an antelope's color darted along a rise, and beyond that, a line of gray, nude humps of powdery clay broke away from the basin into the valley of the Dolores.

"It's that place the rafters call Boulder Field, right?"

"That's right."

They passed scattered cattle, a few of which turned their

white faces toward the truck until a rise of earth blotted them out. At the first of several fences, Wager got out to lift the rusty loop of barbed wire from a skinny post and pull open the sagging strands that formed a gate. After the second fence, Rusty said, "This is T Bar M range. We go across a corner of it." The land looked no different—the same sandy levels broken by occasional wind-stunted trees. Here, no dark shapes of grazing cattle stood against the sage, but Wager knew the reason for that now. By the time it was warm enough to roll down the windows, they had left the T Bar M and begun winding along bluffs high above the river and then down into a canyon that led to a wide shelf of earth thirty feet above the water. They drove in the dust from some vehicle that had gone down the road earlier, and, rounding a cliff of wind-pocked sandstone, saw three other trucks already parked at the loop marking the end of the road. Their drivers stood in a small group at the edge of the cliff and gazed down at the river.

Wager was introduced to the men. Each shook hands and said something about being sorry.

Tod McAlpin, somewhere in his early thirties and with a round chin that stuck out farther than his nose, tipped his ball cap to the back of his head and said, "It's about time to go."

A man with thin red hair brushed straight back from the wrinkles of his sagging face nodded. "Akridge's already started down." He pointed a tobacco-stained finger at a short line of dark figures moving carefully along the rock face of the opposite bank.

Wager fell in behind the men, stopping occasionally to look at the strip of water streaked white by the boulders that choked this narrow section. From here—a rifle shot away—he couldn't tell which of the rocks they had last hit; the river looked different, even peaceful and pretty from this height. But as they drew into the roar and coolness of mist rising from the spray, he felt the weight of yesterday come back with a new, deep ache.

The search took the full day. The parties worked along each bank, peering under rocks and probing with long poles into the holes and swirls that brought the river's spew toward shore. They found bits and pieces: one of the plastic bailing buckets, its handle ripped loose from the line that tied it to the raft; the lid of a cooler that might or might not have been theirs; a frayed oar, its safety line also snapped. But no raft. No body. They scrambled along shore for three or four miles downstream, finally halting where the river shoaled in a series of gravel bars that Wager vaguely remembered passing yesterday. Tangles of tree trunks and other flotsam formed scattered dams where they snagged bottom, and both parties pulled off their boots and waded out along the gravel bars to look carefully among bleached limbs and timber the color of old bones.

"Anything coming down this far—a raft or anything—would hang up here," said McAlpin.

On the other side of the main channel, Sheriff Akridge's Stetson bobbed agreement. "I don't think it's going to do much good to look farther downstream, Mr. Wager," he called.

He, too, nodded.

"All right, boys, let's call it a day—thanks a lot."

Wager thanked them, too. Akridge, drying his feet on a gravel bar across the channel, said they would notify ranchers along the stream to keep an eye out, and that when the river went down they would come back for another search. "I got a call from Miss Fabrizio's parents last night. There wasn't much else I could tell them. I didn't say nothing about Ron or the raft."

"Thanks."

"This won't make it any easier on them."

"No," said Wager. "It won't."

The drive back was as quiet as the morning's ride; the sun had swung low over the mesas west of the river to soften the dry sweep of valley and the sharp faces of the cliffs. Much of the soreness had been driven from Wager's body as he scrambled and stretched to make his way along the riverbank, and weariness and hunger dulled the soreness of his mind. Silently, he watched the sagebrush blur past the window and the occasional line of crooked fence posts that swung in slow pendulum across the gray earth.

"You're welcome to say as long as you want, Gabe. We got no use for that room so far. So you might as well use it."

"I'll be going back tonight, as soon as I pack up. I have to talk to her parents."

"I understand. But you're welcome anyway. I think Dee's got Josephine's stuff together; she said she was going to do that while you were gone today."

She had, and—after supper—tried to force an envelope on Wager, a refund for the time remaining on their cabin.

"You keep it, Dee. Use it to call me if Jo's body turns up."

She refused, saying she couldn't do that, and both of them made him tuck it into his bag. When he reached the highway, he sealed it and scrawled "Thanks" across the envelope and left it in their mailbox.

Turning toward Rimrock, he drove until his headlights picked out the marker he looked for, an oversized mailbox mounted on a post and anchored in a small oil drum. The name, roughly painted in white, said Watkins; below that, nailed to the upright, was the T Bar M branded into a board. Wager turned the Trans-Am onto the dirt road and, careful of the humps and occasional rocks, wound through the night toward the ranch. When the road fell away into darkness, he eased forward and the headlights dipped to a locked gate swung between new timbers. Wager backed and turned, parking on the sandy shoulder, and climbed over the wooden gate.

If the dog heard him, it did not bark. Staying at the edge of the splashes of light from the ranch house, he went toward the bunkhouse. The windows of the long, low structure were dark, and he could make out the shadows of equipment and gear scattered in the yard: the roping dummy with its wide cow horns, a stack of fence posts, a hay rake with the tips of its spidery tines buried in the dirt. He knocked at John's door, the rap loud in the night. No answer, no sound, no light. Trying once more, he went to the windows and peered in; the curtainless panes showed no movement. Wager turned and went to the ranch house.

His boot heels thudded on the porch boards, and finally the dog woke up, its bark coming with a booming yelp from somewhere in the house and then settling behind the door. Wager heard a man's voice say, "Shut up, goddammit," and a moment later the porch light flicked on. The door swung open and the cook, face stubbled in dark beard, looked at him with surprise. "What do you want?"

"John and James Sanchez."

"They ain't here."

"Where are they?"

"I don't know."

"Are they still at the ranch or have they gone?"

"I don't know that it's any of your damned business."

Wager's fist caught the man just above his stomach, the air from his lungs a wheezing grunt as he half bent and stumbled back into the living room. The next was a straight jab landing with the weight of his back and shoulders and mashing the man's nose with that cold little squish that comes when the knuckles break it. The cook tried to cover and swing back, but Wager stepped away and snapped a kick at the side of the man's knee with his boot. The leg gave way to drop him hard in a rolling scramble for a small table. Another kick, this one to the man's lower ribs, and he doubled, grunting loudly, and Wager drove the corner of his heel on an outstretched hand that yanked back under the man with a high squeal. Across the room, lit by the flickering colors of a television set, the dog cowered against the wall with its tail wrapped tightly between its legs and whined a howling note that drowned out the cook. Two or three other chairs sat emptily facing the set, and Wager listened for the sound of running feet from upstairs. But the only noise came from the man and the dog, and the tinny music of the television where two figures traded choreographed punches and took graceful turns being knocked down.

"Are they still at the ranch or have they gone?"

"Gone." The word was breathed out between heavy

grunts, and the cook struggled up to his knees clutching his hand to his chest. "You broke my goddam fingers, god damn you!"

Wager looked in the drawer of the small table and picked up a forty-five. He clicked off the safety with his thumb and worked the slide once to spin a copper blur across the room. Aiming it loosely toward the man, he fired. The orange flash winked on bulging eyes and a smear of bloody lip as the cook crabbed backward across the scarred boards of the bare floor. The dog, howling again, disappeared.

"Where are they?"

"Put that fucking thing down—you almost shot me, you crazy son of a bitch!"

The stinging smell of gunpowder floated through the room, and Wager stilled the weapon on the man's midsection. Under the stained T-shirt, the stomach seemed to shrink and pucker.

"Where are they?"

"A rodeo—where the hell else? A fucking rodeo!"

"Where?"

"I don't know—Denver! They went to Denver—some fucking rodeo in Denver!"

"Where's Watkins?"

Something closed behind the man's eyes, and he shook his head in small twitches. "He ain't here either. I don't know where he is. I swear to God."

"Give me your wallet."

The man's good hand went slowly to his hip pocket, and his eyes said that he knew now what Wager was really after, and that Wager wasn't a damn bit different from any other scumbag in the world.

Wager flipped through the little plastic windows for the driver's license. It said Maynerd L. Riggs, and the tiny colored photograph showed him leaning stiffly away from the glare of the flash. It was a Colorado license, and that meant a set of fingerprints on file with DMV. Wager took it and tossed the wallet back to him.

"What do you want that for?"

"Where's Jerry Latta?"

The head shook again. "Hey—hey, man, I don't know. He lives up in Glenwood—he never comes here." He wiped the blood from his lip with his thumb. "What you want with my driver's license? Why're you taking that?"

"I want to know who to kill if you lied to me."

"I'm not lying—I don't know where Latta is! He never comes here. Who the fuck are you, anyway? I thought you were a goddam cop!"

"I'm a man with a forty-five. If you come out that door, you can be a man with a forty-five hole." He was halfway across the porch when he heard Riggs say, "You sorry son of a bitch, I ought to kill you," and turned back, weapon ready. But the man wasn't talking to Wager; he was glaring at the dog, whose wet muzzle poked cautiously around a doorframe.

CHAPTER 13

He reached Denver about sunup, the harsh glare burning his sleepless eyes as he coasted down the long grades of I-70. One of Jo's favorite views of the city was from up here, where the highway crested the Front Range and you could see almost all the way to Kansas. Out of the broad, shadowed bowl of prairie stretching east from the foot of the mountains, clusters of office towers rose in dusty silhouette against the orange sky. He tried to see it with her eyes, and to imagine her on the empty car seat beside him. But of course she wasn't. During the night when the car was filled with shadow, he could almost believe that she lay sleeping there. But the glaring light angling into the windshield took even that away, and his mind repeated for a countless time: She's gone. Once he could convince himself of that, it would be easier. It might be easier. It did not make any difference whether it was easier or not, she was gone. That was a fact.

There were other facts, and the Sanchez boys were the most important right now. That was the fact he would keep his mind on. Wager, beginning to tangle in the morning traffic that flowed into downtown from the surrounding suburbs, pulled into a diner and bought copies of the *Denver Post* and the *Rocky Mountain News*. As he drank his coffee, he flipped through the pages looking for two things, notice of Jo's death and rodeo ads. The first had not been picked up yet; the second he found in the *News* on a back page near the comics, a large drawing of a cowboy on a bronc. A regional rodeo of the Mountain States Rodeo Association, affiliated with the North American Rodeo Commission—top prize money in all categories, open to all contestants residing in the Mountain States region. Contestants from outside the region must be PRCA members. The shows were at 7:30 p.m., Thursday, Friday, and Saturday—Sunday at 1:30 and 6:30. Location: National Western Arena. Wager tore out the ad and gazed at it as he finished his breakfast.

The sun had moved to its familiar place over the ragged shadow of western mountains when Wager woke late in the afternoon. His visit to Jo's parents had been, as he expected, grim. They still hoped she would be found alive, even though he had to tell them again there was no hope. Unlike Sidney's mother, they did not hate him, though they had better reason. They could have hated him for taking her out there, they could have hated him for not saving her, they could have hated him for destroying the dream that she might still be alive. But they didn't. Instead, soft-spoken and formal, they thanked him for coming by.

"Did she—was it a nice trip before the accident?"

"Yes ma'am."

"That's good. She loved the mountains . . . nature. . . . We want her back, but if . . ."

They didn't hate or accuse. But Wager did, and for reasons he could not tell them: he was the one who had goaded John Sanchez, he was the one who had told Jo there was nothing to worry about, he was the one she reached to in those last terrible moments when he failed her. He was one of those who had contributed to her death.

Kicking off the sweaty sheet, he soaked in the shower for a long time, trying to let the pummel of water erase the feeling of self-disgust that had awakened with him. It did not leave, but at least it sank deeper toward that area of his soul where all his other guilts had been shrugged. There it would fester and rot and, like gas, erupt through his dreams to leave him wide-eyed and numb, and waiting for the dawn and its refuge of daily routine.

·   ·   ·

The National Western Arena was on the north side of town near the old stockyards and across I-70 from the hulking green bulk of the Denver Coliseum. Wager swung off the freeway at the Coliseum sign and followed the flow of traffic toward the unpaved vacant lots that provided parking. Orange-jacketed attendants beckoned the traffic toward lanes marked $2.00, and Wager pulled in between a pickup truck and a station wagon full of bouncing children wearing cowboy hats and jeans tucked into their small boots. A harried woman screamed at one who darted toward the traffic, and her husband, another slung over his shoulder, said, "Stay right here—you kids want to see this damned rodeo, you stay right here with me!"

Wager crossed the busy street to a mesh fence where a cowboy leaned against a metal pole. On this side of the high-walled building, twilight was heavy and arc lights from the elevated freeway filled the sky with blue light and cast a spray of thin shadows from his feet.

"This is the contestants' gate, sir—you with the rodeo?" A badge said "Arena Police."

"No."

"Ticket windows are around that way. Just cross the street and through that parking lot under the vidock, there."

"Have John or James Sanchez come through yet?"

"I don't know them. But they're probably here—most of the contestants are by this time."

"How can I get in touch with them?"

"The arena secretary's office under the grandstand. In the south gate and turn left—it'll be crowded as all get out. You can't miss it."

Making his way under the bed of a ramp leading up to the elevated freeway, he passed a line of tall cattle trailers.

In the mote-filled glare of spotlights high up the arena's wall, he saw the pens filled with broncs and the massive, thick-bodied bulls. The horses stood patiently, chewing and steaming in the cool air. The bulls, their wide horns clicking together occasionally, moved with a slow, steady restlessness that reminded Wager of the river.

"Look at that one, Daddy—he is big!" A boy pushed against his knee to gaze closely at one of the animals, whose thick hump was as tall as Wager's head. "Which one's Jay going to ride?"

"I don't know. We'll find out when we get a program."

Beyond the pens, a sand-colored building housed the tack rooms and stalls for the contestants' animals. Through a partly open door, Wager glimpsed rows of horses' heads and an occasional figure with a bucket or shovel working around the stalls.

"Sorry, sir, contestants only in here." Another arena policeman smiled and propped a casual arm across the opening.

"I'm looking for John or James Sanchez. Do you know if they have a stall here?"

"Sure don't. Do you know what events they're in?"

"No."

"If it's not roping or steer wrestling, they probably wouldn't be here anyway. You know where the arena secretary's office is?"

"I can find it."

He bought his ticket and a program, a booklet bright with the names of rodeo sponsors and the drawing of a cowboy being flung from a saddle bronc. The insert listed the Sanchez names three times in tonight's performance, but that didn't help Wager find them in all this crowd. The arcade under the grandstand was filled with people in western wear who milled slowly past booths that sold shiny commemorative pens or offered comic sketches while you posed. Others displayed saddle equipment and leather wear, and a few had trays of shiny badges and buttons with a variety of slogans. A cluster of cowboys stood in front of a dart game, five dollars for three tosses, and tried to win a GMC pickup truck. Another small crowd studied the samples of lariat rope hanging in one booth. Many wore satiny blue warm-up jackets with "Mountain States Rodeo Association" in white letters across the back, and a number of other colors and rodeo names decorated other jackets. He made his way through the crowd and past a snack bar whose serving line snaked out into the alley; beyond a beer booth, he saw a lit window and a bulletin board filled with thumbtacked notices. From somewhere outside one of the stock entrances that cut across the arcade and slimed the floor with mud and manure, the scream of a whinnying horse knifed through the voices of the crowd.

Wager had to wait to get into the small office where men studied the lists hanging from whitewashed boards. Finally, he caught the eye of the woman hunched behind a small desk and busily scrubbing at something with a worn eraser.

"Can you tell me if John and James Sanchez have registered?"

"I hope so. Registration closed Monday. If they haven't, it's too late now."

"I'm looking for them. It's important to find them."

"The message board's right over there. If they're here, they'll find it."

"I have to tell them personally," said Wager. "It involves a death."

"Oh? Now that's too bad—let me check. Do you know what events they're in?"

"Bareback, bronc, and bulls."

"The rough stock, is it?" She turned to a master list and ran her finger down the names. "Here's James—he's up for saddle bronc riding tonight, on Tough Spot. He drew slack time for bareback and bulls."

"What's that mean?"

She looked up. "It means he already rode. He had his go-round this afternoon. We got too many contestants to pack them all in during the show, so everybody draws and takes their chances on what animal they get and when they ride."

"What about John?"

"He's already rode his bareback. But he's up tonight for saddle and bull. He should be somewhere around the chutes if he's not wandering around looking at the girls."

"Can I get to the chutes without a pass?"

"Not in them, but you can sit right behind them if you want to. This is a good arena for seeing what goes on behind the chutes. Just take the next gate down to your left and that'll put you in the seats closest to the chutes."

Wager thanked her and squeezed his way out of the small office and back into the strolling crowd. A small knot of women in their late teens or twenties studied him as he came through the door, their eyes searching his waist for a championship belt buckle. But he didn't have one, and he wasn't a cowboy, and something about his eyes made them uneasily shift their gaze to someone else. He followed a jacket that said "Holloway Stock Contractor" out through a short tunnel leading to the arena. Here, clusters of cowboys talked and searched the passing crowd for familiar faces; one in a shiny red jacket flung his small saddle over a railing in front of the lower seats and hollered, "Gilbert—Gilbert—over here!"

Turning up the concrete steps, Wager made his way half-way up the green rows of wooden seats and paused to study this end of the arena. He could see behind the first three chutes and into the tunnel that led to the stock pens outside. Three more chutes were on the other side, but his view of them was blocked by the wooden superstructure bracing the announcer's box. Already horses stood nervously in the white-painted chutes, an occasional hoof thudding loudly against a plank. On the packed dirt behind, half a dozen cowboys, their numbers bright squares on their shirts, worked over their bareback rigging to stretch the straps and grind rosin into the handgrip. Others wrapped tape around their arm, the one that would be yanked and jerked by the plunge of the horse's head; and here and there a cowboy went through limbering-up exercises, twisting his torso, bending, pulling the kinks out of cold leg muscles.

High up in the opposite seats, an organist played something that sounded like "You Are My Sunshine," and farther down the grandstands, in the central sections where rows of faces made animated pink dots, vendors picked their way up and down the busy stairs calling, "Cold beer—cold Coors beer!"

He bought one and carried it with him, sipping at its thick foam as he climbed higher and centered himself in the almost empty seats over the tunnel that led from the animal pens and under the announcer's box to the arena. There, a flash of bright colors, the flag bearers were lining up, their horses prancing sideways and the pennants of the rodeo associations and sponsors wagging stiffly as riders anchored the flagpoles in their stirrup sockets. The organ music gave way to a woman singing "How Much Is That Doggie in the Window?" and inviting everyone to say arf-arf. On the platform just below Wager, the arena secretary and a battery of judges shuffled papers and double-checked the contestants' names against the animals they had drawn.

The organ gave three loud chords and the singer thanked everyone and asked them to shift their attention to the announcer's box, where Marvin Sutton would welcome all you cowboys and cowgirls to the second go-round of the fifteenth annual Mountain States Rodeo Ride-Off.

The arena lights brightened and an amplified voice asked, "Is everybody ready to rodeo tonight!" and milked louder cheers and shouts and applause to warm up the spectators. The arena behind the chutes filled with more cowboys as the flags of the Grand Entry galloped in a circle into the arena. At one of the gated chutes, a rider eased his bareback rigging over a nervous animal, and a stock handler fished with a hooked stick for the loose ends of cinch and flank strap. The organ music rose as the final pennants snapped and waved behind galloping riders, and the announcer called the crowd to their feet to greet the American flag and sing the National Anthem. By the time the last flag cleared the arena sands, the announcer was introducing the first rider, and Wager was having trouble making out any of the faces or numbers among the throng that now milled in the dim area behind the chutes.

Gate one suddenly yanked open, and the first bareback rider burst into the arena with a spray of muddy sand and organ music. Judges with clipboards trotted a safe distance from the flying hooves, and the pickup men circled their horses behind the twisting, jolting animal to wait for the eight-second buzzer. But the cowboy, his hat still floating in the air behind him, was yanked forward as the horse doubled, flying from the handgrip to crash loudly into the boards of the arena wall. A wad of black, gummy mud thudded onto Wager's program as one of the pickup men galloped in to yank loose the horse's flank strap, and the animal stopped bucking and turned quickly, head high and ears up, to trot toward the animal pens outside. He ran beneath Wager and out of sight while the rider, staggering slightly and holding his shoulder against movement, squeezed through a fence gate into the crowd behind the chutes. The second bronc rider was racing into the spotlights while the first cowboy sank onto a bench and two men in jackets with "Sports Medicine" across the backs began to feel around the dislocated shoulder.

Saddle bronc riding was fourth on the schedule, and the flow of cowboys milling or talking or leaning on the arena fence gradually changed with each event. John was listed to ride third, and his number was 343. The hometown following his name was Rimrock, Colorado, and his score last night had been a 68. Tonight, he would ride Duster, and the program insert had two blank slots behind his name so spectators could mark his time for the second go-round and the total score so far. James, too, was listed as coming from Rimrock, and he drew thirteenth spot. His horse was Knothead. Wager wasn't sure which chute they would be assigned, but as the steer-wrestling competition—launched from the far end of the arena to gallop toward the announcer's box—moved into its final contestants, he squinted among the restless faces and numbers that moved constantly in the shadowy angles behind the fencing at this end of the arena.

There—612—James's number. It lifted and fell on the back of a checkered shirt that leaned tensely over a plunging horse being locked into chute two. Wager moved down the aisle, edging past contestants who sat on the steps to talk with friends or relatives in the seats. At the chutes, cowboys sat in their saddles on the ground and stretched leather, while others strapped on their gloves with rawhide thongs and rubbed rosin onto sticky fingers.

In the chutes—quick glimpses of hairy legs or tossing heads—the saddle broncs were outfitted and cinched. Wager passed a cowboy who dropped his jeans to anchor a spine pad down the back of his pants; an arena policeman loosely patrolled the alley that opened into the chute area, and Wager saw John, hat jammed down far enough to fold his ears out, clamber up the wooden fences of chute two and straddle them to squat just above the brown heaving motion that was his animal. Face down and staring intently past his leather chaps, John focused all his attention on the horse waiting beneath him. Chute one slapped open to free the horse, and the audience cheered as the announcer howled, "Oh, no! That's too bad, but let's give that cowboy a big hand, ladies and gentlemen—that's the only pay he'll take home tonight, so please be generous."

John nodded at something said by one of the cowboys and then eased quickly but lightly into the waiting saddle. The horse heaved up, white eyes catching the arena glare, and swung its teeth at a cowboy, who jumped away quickly and swore as the others laughed at him. The chute boss said, "Ready?" and John's hat brim nodded and the gate swung open, baring the left side of horse and rider.

Duster leaped and twisted once, then ran in a series of short kicks straight for the arena barrier. It scraped its flank along the boards to brush off the rider, then fishtailed and spun, hooves cracking loudly against the fence. Plunging sideways, the horse lost its balance, and John, one hand high against the glare of spotlights from the arena roof, felt the horse stumble and plunge sideways. He yanked his feet from the stirrups, and as the animal thudded against the sand, he rolled frantically from the tossing head and flailing hooves to come up sprinting for the wall. A pickup man darted his horse between John and the bronc, and another chased after the now galloping animal to yank free the flank strap. The two judges stood talking together as John, slapping dirt from his hat, walked slowly back to the chutes. The crowd began chanting, "Reride, reride!" and the announcer, leaning over the rail of the box to hear the judges, was happy to answer them, "Yes, sir, the men with the clipboards say Johnny Sanchez gets a second chance—he'll be having a reride and another shot at the money!"

Under the applause, Wager moved closer to the gate that swung open to let John back into the dark at the edge of the brightly lit arena. He tried to push close enough to reach the man, but waiting contestants crowded in, and Wager felt a hand tap his shoulder. He turned to see a politely smiling face. "Sorry, sir, contestants only back here. You can see everything real good from the seats up there."

"Thanks."

John's number disappeared behind a wall of shifting cowboy shirts and hats, and a few moments later Wager saw him talking with James, his hands describing the ride. James grinned at something, and the two laughed, their voices unheard beneath the clamor of amplified music and the steady voice of the announcer describing the current contest. John pulled his spine pad and unstrapped his chaps to let James have them, and the two men worked their way to a chute, where James began to lash a riding glove tightly around his wrist.

James stayed on for the full eight seconds of his ride, earning a good seventy-three for his score. At halftime the groundsmen cleared the arena and began raking the sand for the Ladies' Barrel Racing event, and the announcer urged the crowd to stretch and help themselves to some of the good food and beer they could find in the arena arcade. Among the stir and swirl of cowboys, Wager lost sight of them. He climbed to the top row and walked around the edge of the large bowl, searching the tunnels for numbers or faces. But the halftime crowds were too big and constantly shifting. In the arcade it was worse, a carnival of hawkers and gawkers who strolled and stopped and stood talking in loud clusters in the middle of the alley. Once he thought he saw the two flank a girl with curly blond hair, but they were gone before he could elbow through the crowd. Later, he might have seen James disappear behind a pale green post, but he was too far away to be sure. When the distant organ music began to sound over the noise of the crowd, Wager drifted with the flow of bodies back toward the arena. Gradually, he worked his way up and above the chutes to the emptier seating high over the end. His only opportunity now would be the bull riding, the final event.

The team roping started from the far end. The calf ran hard toward the announcer's box, and the horsemen galloped fast behind with their ropes whistling in large loops. Halfway through the event, the first six bulls were run through the tunnel and chuted up for the last contest. John rode eleventh out of fifteen, and Wager, restless, worked his way down to the staging area where the cowboys waited. In the first chute, already mounted, a rider drew his grip rope close under the bull's body and thudded his fist into the animal's ribs to drive air from its lungs and yank the rope even tighter. Legs high on the bull's broad back to keep from being crushed against the fences, the rider listened to the cowboys around him: "You got this one, Gene—ain't no goddam bull mean enough to throw you, boy!" "You can do it, Gene; you can do it, man, you know you can!" "Hang on and give this sucker a ride, Gene. He's a spinner—he likes to go left, remember."

Wager hovered at the edge of the guarded section. A steady stream of cowboys rubbed past, and near the gate to the arena floor the bull-fighting clown and his barrel man gave a few last adjustments to their costumes and props. He searched the faces of the men and boys who pressed toward the chutes, and finally he spotted James. Hatless, the young man paused at the mouth of the tunnel and tried to edge his way around a group of girls flirting with some of the cowboys. He was by himself, and his eyes brushed across Wager without recognition. The crowd opened slightly, and James worked his way through a mob of cowboys who stood and craned up toward the stands for familiar faces.

"James—I want to talk to you."

The boy's heavy eyebrows pulled together in puzzlement. Then he knew Wager and his face went hard and blank.

"Let's go up this way—up the stairs, here."

"I don't want to talk to you."

Wager grasped the wiry arm that tried to pull away. "It's about what's on that ranch—your fall crop—and you'd better hear it." The arm stopped tugging. "Up here—up where it's empty."

Wager could see angry redness streak the back of James's neck, and he stayed close behind as they made their way through lines of spectators filing back to their seats with cardboard trays of beer and sandwiches. When the crowd thinned near the upper rows, Wager said, "This way," and turned him toward the empty seats high behind the announcer's box.

"I'm supposed to help Johnny get ready, dammit."

"You've got plenty of time if you don't waste it."

"What the hell is it you want?"

"First I want you to hear this: I know about your pot patches out on the ranch. And I know that's why your father was killed—because he found out, too."

"What pot—?"

"I saw it, James. The reservoir, the irrigation system, the fences. So don't hand me any crap about not knowing."

The youth's lips tightened, and he stared without seeing at the brightly lit arena where a pair of calf ropers chased their animal and snagged it with ropes. Their horses backed smartly to face each other over the trapped and bawling calf.

"You arresting me? That what you doing?"

"I'm interested in something besides the marijuana."

"Like what?"

"Who killed your father?"

"I don't—"

"You and your brother beat him to death, didn't you? Your own father, and you two beat him to death."

"No! It wasn't Johnny and me—we didn't do it!"

"You two drove over to his ranch and took him for a ride, and then because you were so damned scared he would tell someone about your pot farm, you beat him until you broke his skull and then you tossed him out to die—your own father—like a piece of shit onto the road."

"He was a piece of shit! You don't know nothing about it—you didn't see how he ran off and left Ma with two kids and no money! God, I cried when he left, and that son of a bitch didn't even turn around to look back—he just walked out and climbed into that goddam pickup truck and pulled out of the driveway and never looked back once!"

"So you and John killed him."

"No—hell no! We weren't even there, man. We were up at the Culbertson rodeo, up in Montana. By God you can ask anybody: we rode up there!"

"You knew when it was going to happen. You made sure you'd have an alibi."

Silence.

"Who did it?"

"Fuck you."

"You think Tom didn't give a damn about you and your brother?"

"I don't think it, I know it."

"Tom was trying to help you. He came to me and said he was worried about you. He thought you two were in some kind of trouble, and he asked me to look into it without making things any worse for you."

"We didn't ask for his help. He should have kept his goddam nose out of our business!"

"He was worried about his sons."

"Yeah."

"He told me he never could pull himself together after

Elias got killed. But he couldn't quit rodeoing, either. And that was why he left—your mother blamed him for Elias's death. And he blamed himself."

"That wasn't nobody's fault. The horse rolled."

"Your mother didn't look at it that way. She finally told Tom it was her or the rodeo, so he left."

"Yeah? Well . . . well, he sure as hell didn't try to see us! Johnny and me. He didn't even come back for Johnny's graduation. We damn well expected him to show up for that, at least!"

"He wanted to, but he was afraid."

"What?" James looked at Wager for the first time.

"He was afraid to."

"What for?"

"He didn't know how you two would treat him."

"But we wanted him to come! We thought if anything—"

"He didn't know that."

James's shoulders sagged. "He was always bragging about how well Johnny did in school. About how Johnny would be the first one to get his high school diploma. And then he didn't even come."

"He was proud of John. And of you, too. And worried about both of you."

"Hell, when he didn't come to see Johnny, I figured it wasn't worth it. I quit school and went to work on the ranch."

"Who killed him, Jimmy?"

Silence.

"He found out about the marijuana, but he didn't tell me. Instead, he asked me to back off—he told me there was nothing wrong and wanted me to stop asking around."

"Why?"

"He was trying to protect his sons." Wager waited, but still the youth said nothing. "He wanted to straighten things out without getting you in trouble. And he got killed for it. Who did it, Jimmy? Who beat your father to death?"

His profile stayed motionless and staring toward the arena. The announcer and the clowns were going through a routine that involved a lot of shouting back and forth, and

James, unhearing, began to blink rapidly. "I told Johnny."

"What?"

"I told Johnny. I told him it wasn't no damn good getting mixed up with that bunch."

"The people at the ranch? Watson and Riggs?"

"Riggs and some others. I never met Watson. He owns the place, but he don't come near it."

"What others?"

"You seen them. Up in Leadville—they were at that restaurant where we met you and that lady."

Wager remembered. "Jerry Latta?"

Surprise widened his eyes. "You know him?"

"I have his rap sheet from California."

"Son of a bitch! He always brags about how clean he is—about how nobody knows him."

"They're the ones who market the crop?"

"Yeah. We grow it and harvest it. They bring in the seeds in the winter and give us the money for fertilizers and equipment, then they take it out in the fall."

"And you and Johnny and Riggs and Watkins get a cut."

"Maynerd gets his. Then Johnny and me. I guess Watkins gets a lot; I don't know. I think he put up the money to start with, but I don't know."

"And that's how you pay for rodeoing."

"That's right. Real good money—God, I never heard of so much money. But we weren't in it for that. Good money and free time—it's the only way we could make it rodeoing. These other guys"—his hand wagged toward the crowds behind the chutes—"most of them, they got help. College boys and family and all—they got people helping them pay their way. Me and Johnny, we had to help ourselves."

Wager pulled him back to the subject. "Johnny's the ranch manager. That means if anybody finds out about the marijuana, Watkins stays in the clear and Johnny takes the rap."

"I guess. I don't know. Johnny was hired on as manager, that's all."

"Tom figured that out, didn't he? He saw you two holding the shitty end of the stick, and he wanted you to let go."

"He should have stayed out of it!"

"What does Maynerd Riggs do?"

"He's the cook. But he keeps an eye on things, too. He handles the contacts; we take care of the ranch. Any problems that come up, we're supposed to go through him."

"Did he kill Tom?"

"I don't think so. He never leaves the ranch. He talked to the others . . . and . . . they did it."

"Latta?"

"Him and a couple others. They were all up there in Leadville. But they didn't know they killed him—they were just trying to . . ."

"Why'd they do it?"

"Because of you, for one thing! We told Maynerd about you looking us up at that rodeo and being a cop and all. We'd just planted the seedlings and stood to lose the whole crop if you found out about it."

"But why beat on Tom?"

"They couldn't beat on you, could they? I guess . . ." He sighed and shook his head. "I guess they told Daddy we'd get hurt if somebody tipped the cops to anything."

"And they beat him to show him how?"

"It ain't that simple. That's part of it, but it ain't that simple. Maybe nothing's simple." Anger came back. "Maybe I don't want to tell you no more! Maybe I better talk with Johnny before I talk anymore with you!"

"You've got a little problem, Jimmy. It's called accessory to murder. And by the time you get out of jail, you might be too old to rodeo." Wager let that sink in. "Then again, you might get a suspended sentence. A lot of it depends on what I tell the judge—and that depends on what you tell me."

The boy pressed a knuckle against his lower lip and chewed it. "Johnny too? You're going to help him, too?"

"Sure," said Wager. "I'm going to help both of you."

James's shoulders rose and fell heavily; then, in a tight voice, he told Wager. "Daddy figured something was wrong when he came out to the ranch to visit. I guess all he had to do was look around and see it wasn't no cow outfit. Anyway, he got nosy. And we thought he found an overlay. We thought he took it when he left."

"What overlay?"

"A map of the pot fields. Latta wants us to keep records—the fields, how many plants, fertilizer mixes, so on. He wants to be real scientific about it—always talking about quality control and margins and crap like that. You know the kind of things farmers talk about."

Wager had a good idea. "What about the overlay?"

"We have them for each field. You put it on a map and it tells you where the plants are. After Daddy left, we couldn't find one. We figured he knew what it was, and was going to give it to you."

"I never saw it."

James drew another long, shaky breath. Even in the white glare of the floodlights reflecting from the arena floor, his face seemed to loose much of its hardness; the tight lines around his eyes and across his forehead faded until he looked as young as his seventeen years. "We didn't know that. We told Riggs and he told Latta. They went and tried to make him tell what he did with it. But Jerry didn't mean to kill him—he was as surprised as we were when you told us Daddy was dead."

Wager thought differently, but he let it go. "They took Tom's wallet? They thought he might have the overlay in his wallet?"

"I guess. They went down to his ranch and—ah—talked to him there, and looked through the place but didn't find it. So they took him to . . . ask him some more. But it wasn't on him, either."

"That's why Latta tried to break into our motel in Leadville? He thought I might have it?"

"You knew who that was?"

"I figured it out."

"You knocked the shit out of him. He wanted to go back and blow you away, but me and Johnny talked him out of it. I think it was mostly words, anyway; I think he had enough of you for that night."

"So then you and Johnny went through our cabin out at the ranch."

"Johnny did that, yeah. Why the hell else would you be out there? First you show up in Leadville just after Daddy got beat up, and then you come riding into the ranch hinting around like that. We figured that's why you came, to check out that overlay."

"But Johnny didn't find it either, did he?"

"No. Not there, anyway." He sighed with a mixture of agony and confession. "We found the damn thing a couple days ago when we packed up to come here. It got pushed into a torn seam in Johnny's ditty bag. It was there all along." He wagged his head slowly. "Daddy never even had it."

Wager, too, drew a deep breath and leaned against the creaking slats of the green seat. Below, the arena boss made the final check with the first rider before the handler pulled open the gate. The organ hit a loud note, and the crowd yelled as the contestant exploded into the arena. The bull jerked its narrow hips high into the air and kicked with a speed and grace that made its size even more frightening. Clinging with one hand and with his raking spurs, the rider spun and leaned against the twisting flesh below him, trying to keep balance on the shifting, loose skin that threatened to go in all directions at once. Trying to hook the rider, the bull spun in a tight circle, and the cowboy, teeth glinting between drawn lips, slipped sideways toward the horns and then toward the ground as the bull twisted more tightly. Hand still caught in the rope, the rider was flung off to dangle by one arm in the circle formed by the hooking bull as a clown sprinted forward to slap the bull's muzzle with an orange wiffle-ball bat. The grip rope with its clanging cowbell began to slip and release the dangling cowboy; the bull turned to sprint toward the clown, and its bulging flank tossed the rider like a stuffed doll to roll in the dirt as the other clown, hopping up and down in a bright red barrel, lured the animal away. Two cowboys hopped over the fence and dragged the limp rider toward the gate.

"He fell in the well," said James. "That's what we call it when you're caught on the inside like that and you can't get loose—you're in the well. You can't outrun him. You can't get back on. You can't let go. You just sort of hang there and get beat up until some clown comes along and helps you out."

"You put yourself in the well. You and Johnny both."

"Don't I know it. Us and Daddy, too."

Wager asked quietly, "Which one of you shot out our raft?"

"Who did what?"

"The raft. Who made it sink?"

"I don't know what you're talking about."

Wager studied the youth's dark eyes. The announcer began trading jokes with the clowns as they dashed toward the fence and let the bull run in a slow, heavy trot toward the tunnel and the pens waiting outside. Wager and James watched the animal, light-footed and sinewy despite its size, run beneath them. "Three nights ago. We were at the campground. John came in and saw us."

"Well, he's supposed to—that's part of the rounds, to collect the fees at the campground. We take turns; I make rounds one night, he makes them the next. We check on the plots and chase off the deer. And make sure the damn rafters ain't camping where they shouldn't."

"He didn't tell you he saw us?"

"No. But I reckon he must have shit when he did."

"Why?"

"Because we still thought you had that goddam overlay. We knew damn well you were looking for something, being a cop and all."

"You left Wednesday night?"

"Yeah. We wanted to be here yesterday for the first draw. Why? What's the matter now?"

"You didn't hear about two people being drowned?"

"No. Who got drowned?"

"The kid rowing the raft—Sidney."

"Sid? Aw, damn!"

"Y mi mujer."

In Spanish, the phrase held a lot more echoes, and James blinked as he translated it. "Your woman? The one who was with you at the ranch?"

"Yes."

"I'm real sorry. . . ." The eyes widened. "No—Johnny wouldn't do that! You got that wrong—Johnny wouldn't go killing no woman!"

"They're dead. My woman is dead."

"No, you can't blame him for that!"

"The raft was shot. He did it. He killed her."

James stood up, still staring at Wager, his head wagging from side to side. "He didn't. . . . I'm not going to let you . . ." The fist was quick and knotty and landed solidly beside Wager's eye to blind him for an instant in pain and blossoming explosions of silent light. "No!"

He heard the thump of boot heels against the concrete steps as James pulled out of Wager's grip. Blinking the shock from his vision, Wager stumbled after him, his knees snagging on the seats that filled the row. Below, he saw James leap two and three steps at a time down the aisle on the far side of the announcer's booth. Wager lunged after him, wiping the water from his stinging eye and trying to follow the dark head as it tangled among the throng of spectators and cowboys behind the chutes.

There—pushing his way toward the center chute; Wager sprinted around the upper edge of the arena past the organist's platform.

James dodged between cowboys and climbed up the fencing to the figure hunched above the waiting bull. John's face, a pale oval, turned toward the stands and swung along the rows of seats until he saw Wager running down the aisle toward them. Then the face turned back to James, and they drew together, James saying something urgently to his brother.

Wager elbowed his way through the people standing in the aisle and clogging the narrow stairway to the arena floor. He reached the contestants' area just as the gate slapped open and John, head down tightly against his chest and loose arm snapping high, burst into the arena on the snorting, hooking bull. The crowd cheered as the bull flung itself first one way, then the other, long strings of glistening saliva whipping from its muzzle. Then it plunged hard toward the barrier to send the arena hands scrambling up the fence. A spray of sandy dirt peppered the boards as the announcer's voice rose to a shout and the bull spun and bucked all four feet clear of the ground and landed with a vicious hook at the loosely wagging man on its back. Jaw tight-clenched against the bull's jolting speed, John swayed left, then right, and raked his spurs hard against the sagging gray hide, and the bull once more tossed its head and twisted in a tight circle to gore the rider. The eight-second horn buzzed almost unheard through the shouts and cheers of the crowd, and the clowns came forward to draw the bull away. The rider, slipping his hand from the gummy rope, swung away from the bull's wide back and leaped clear to land on hands and knees in the dirt.

The cheers and applause of the crowd were loud, and the announcer had to shout the score—"An eighty-three for that ride, ladies and gentlemen! The top score so far, and that puts Johnny Sanchez in the lead for the money"—and the yells and clapping and whistles grew noisier. John glanced at the gate, and Wager saw his eyes as they caught his face, and the man turned from the opening to sprint down the animal chute toward the pens outside the arena.

Wager pushed toward the fencing, his arm grabbed by a pair of hands and James's voice at his ear through the still-cheering crowd. "He didn't mean it, Mr. Wager! He was after you, not her—he wanted to keep you off the ranch!"

Wager yanked his arm free and clambered over the fence, swinging his leg high as the bull from the arena lumbered in an agile trot down the narrow alley. Behind him, a voice shouted, "Hey, get the hell off there!" and two or three faces popped up on the other side of the fence to stare at him with wide eyes. Ahead, beyond the bobbing rump of the animal, Wager saw John run toward the white boards. The bull saw him, too; it paused, hesitated, then leaped catlike at the reaching figure.

For a moment, Wager could see nothing but the massive

and bunched muscles of the charging animal. Then he saw John rise above the gray hump, arced backward against the motley glare of spotlights shining down on the pen of suddenly stirring animals and nervously tossing horns. For a long instant, the figure hung outlined by the dark sky, head curved back almost against its heels and face turned toward Wager with the eyes open wide and staring at him. Then the figure dropped into the dirt and, glimpsed between the shuffling legs of the animals, crawled and fought its way toward the fence. The white-ringed eye of the bull feinted quickly at Wager, backing him against the boards; but his real interest was in front. John's face was glimpsed for a moment, still gazing at Wager, and his arm reached out, hand open and pleading. Wager punched at the bull's solid flank with both fists, but the warm, hairy side jiggled slightly and closed against the planks to pinch Johnny out of sight. Then the busy spread of the bull's torso twisted and kicked, and Wager heard men shouting as the other animals bunched toward the spot on the ground and the gray bull rose high and jabbed stiffly with its front legs.

"Get out of there, goddam you now!" a red face screamed at Wager, and through the fence three or four men began jabbing cattle prods to drive the animals from the thing that lay mangled and wet in the mud and manure of the pen. As Wager climbed over the boards, a long hook reached out to snag John's belt and drag him toward the fence, where two men leaped quickly down to hoist him over the barrier and clamber out before the bulls could turn.

CHAPTER 14

That took a lot of guts, Gabe." Max poured a second cup of coffee for them and typed another line into the report. "I've seen those bulls—they scare the hell out of me."

The telephone finally stopped its ringing as most of the reporters quickly filed their stories, stirred by the knowledge that wire services might pick up their words because of the novelty of the death. Max warned Wager that Internal Affairs would have to look into it even though it was an accident, because a police officer was involved. But there shouldn't be any problem about it.

Wager finished his own letter to Sheriff's Detective Charles Allen and enclosed Riggs's driver's license. It was only a matter of time before the police networks located him and Latta. And with James Sanchez turning state's evidence, there was even a good chance of convicting them.

Max rested his large hands on the typewriter and looked at Wager, his eyes baggy and tired and flat. "You know, partner—if it had been me, I'm not sure I would have tried to rescue that bastard."

Like the others, Max assumed that was why Wager went after him—to save him from the animals. In a way it was, but for a different reason. Wager had wanted him. He had wanted him all to himself, but the animals had cheated him of that, too. He sipped at the familiar bitter coffee and tossed Allen's letter on the desk with the one to Sheriff Akridge. Let him notify the DEA and get credit for the drug bust. Wager didn't want any more to do with any of it.

"You got anything you want to add to this?" Max held up his report on the death of John Sanchez.

"I've made my statement."

"Right. Well, come on—I'll walk you down to the parking lot."

"I can find my own way, Max. By myself."

The big man sank back into his chair. "Sure, Gabe. I'll see you next week. We've got the day shift."

"All right."

He went down the short hallway past the office of the bomb unit and the workroom, and on toward the night desk. Goldman, his sport coat open to show a brightly checkered shirt and solid blue tie, lifted a hand to him from the coffee machine. "Gabe—if you're interested, I've got a psychologist friend who specializes in trauma retrieval. It's really effective—what you do is go through it with him, sort of relive it, you know? It helps you to . . . Gabe? Gabe?"

Waiting for him at the sergeant's desk in the lobby was Gargan, his familiar black turtleneck shirt twisted slightly to show damp patches under his armpits. "Wager—hey, Wager, hold up a minute, will you?"

He slowed.

"Listen—ah—about that Molly White Horse story—"

"What about it?"

"I found out from Doyle that it was the DA's office that was pushing for the murder charge."

"That's right."

"Well, I was blaming you for a vendetta against her. You and Max both. I owe you an apology, but you've been on vacation, so I didn't get a chance." He held out a hand on the end of its bony arm. "It hurts like hell to say this, but I'm sorry."

"Fine." Wager turned away.

Behind him, he heard Gargan's voice complain to the desk sergeant, "You see that? I just about kiss his ass and he doesn't even shake hands! The guy's a goddam zombie—he's got a tin badge for a heart!"

FOR THE BEST IN PAPERBACKS, LOOK FOR THE 🐧

In every corner of the world, on every subject under the sun, Penguin represents quality and variety – the very best in publishing today.

For complete information about books available from Penguin – including Pelicans, Puffins, Peregrines and Penguin Classics – and how to order them, write to us at the appropriate address below. Please note that for copyright reasons the selection of books varies from country to country.

In the United Kingdom: For a complete list of books available from Penguin in the U.K., please write to *Dept E.P., Penguin Books Ltd, Harmondsworth, Middlesex, UB7 0DA*

In the United States: For a complete list of books available from Penguin in the U.S., please write to *Dept BA, Penguin, 299 Murray Hill Parkway, East Rutherford, New Jersey 07073*

In Canada: For a complete list of books available from Penguin in Canada, please write to *Penguin Books Canada Ltd, 2801 John Street, Markham, Ontario L3R 1B4*

In Australia: For a complete list of books available from Penguin in Australia, please write to the *Marketing Department, Penguin Books Australia Ltd, P.O. Box 257, Ringwood, Victoria 3134*

In New Zealand: For a complete list of books available from Penguin in New Zealand, please write to the *Marketing Department, Penguin Books (NZ) Ltd, Private Bag, Takapuna, Auckland 9*

In India: For a complete list of books available from Penguin, please write to *Penguin Overseas Ltd, 706 Eros Apartments, 56 Nehru Place, New Delhi, 110019*

In Holland: For a complete list of books available from Penguin in Holland, please write to *Penguin Books Nederland B.V., Postbus 195, NL–1380AD Weesp, Netherlands*

In Germany: For a complete list of books available from Penguin, please write to *Penguin Books Ltd, Friedrichstrasse 10 – 12, D–6000 Frankfurt Main 1, Federal Republic of Germany*

In Spain: For a complete list of books available from Penguin in Spain, please write to *Longman Penguin España, Calle San Nicolas 15, E–28013 Madrid, Spain*

The Penguin Book of Ghost Stories

An anthology to set the spine tingling, including stories by Zola, Kleist, Sir Walter Scott, M. R. James and A. S. Byatt.

The Penguin Book of Horror Stories

Including stories by Maupassant, Poe, Gautier, Conan Doyle, L. P. Hartley and Ray Bradbury, in a selection of the most horrifying horror from the eighteenth century to the present day.

The Penguin Complete Sherlock Holmes   Sir Arthur Conan Doyle

With the fifty-six classic short stories, plays *A Study in Scarlet*, *The Sign of Four*, *The Hound of the Baskervilles* and *The Valley of Fear*, this volume is a must for any fan of Baker Street's most famous resident.

Victorian Villainies

Fraud, murder, political intrigue and horror are the ingredients of these four Victorian thrillers, selected by Hugh Greene and Graham Greene.

Maigret and the Ghost   Georges Simenon

Three stories by the writer who blends, *par excellence*, the light and the shadow, cynicism and compassion. This volume contains *Maigret and the Hotel Majestic*, *Three Beds in Manhattan* and, the title story, *Maigret and the Ghost*.

The Julian Symons Omnibus

Three novels of cynical humour and cliff-hanging suspense: *The Man Who Killed Himself*, *The Man Whose Dreams Came True* and *The Man Who Lost His Wife*. 'Exciting and compulsively readable' – *Observer*

CRIME AND MYSTERY IN PENGUINS

Deep Water Patricia Highsmith

Portrait of a psychopath, from the first faint outline to the full horrors of schizophrenia. 'If you read crime stories at all, or perhaps especially if you don't, you should read *Deep Water*' – Julian Symons in the *Sunday Times*

Farewell My Lovely Raymond Chandler

Moose Malloy was a big man but not more than six feet five inches tall and not wider than a beer truck. He looked about as inconspicuous as a tarantula on a slice of angel food. Marlowe's greatest case. Chandler's greatest book.

God Save the Child Robert B. Parker

When young Kevin Bartlett disappears, everyone assumes he's run away . . . until the comic strip ransom note arrives . . . 'In classic wisecracking and handfighting tradition, Spenser sorts out the case and wins the love of a fine-boned Jewish Lady . . . who even shares his taste for iced red wine' – Francis Goff in the *Sunday Telegraph*

The Daughter of Time Josephine Tey

Josephine Tey again delves into history to reconstruct a crime. This time it is a crime committed in the tumultuous fifteenth century. 'Most people will find *The Daughter of Time* as interesting and enjoyable a book as they will meet in a month of Sundays' – Marghanita Laski in the *Observer*

The Michael Innes Omnibus

Three tensely exhilarating novels. 'A master – he constructs a plot that twists and turns like an electric eel: it gives you shock upon shock and you cannot let go' – *The Times Literary Supplement*

Killer's Choice Ed McBain

Who killed Annie Boone? Employer, lover, ex-husband, girlfriend? This is a tense, terrifying and tautly written novel from the author of *The Mugger*, *The Pusher*, *Lady Killer* and a dozen other first class thrillers.

CRIME AND MYSTERY IN PENGUINS

Call for the Dead John Le Carré

The classic work of espionage which introduced the world to George Smiley. 'Brilliant . . . highly intelligent, realistic. Constant suspense. Excellent writing' – *Observer*

Swag Elmore Leonard

From the bestselling author of *Stick* and *LaBrava* comes this wallbanger of a book in which 100,000 dollars' worth of nicely spendable swag sets off a slick, fast-moving chain of events. 'Brilliant' – *The New York Times*

The Soft Talkers Margaret Millar

The mysterious disappearance of a Toronto businessman is the start point for this spine-chilling, compulsive novel. 'This is not for the squeamish, and again the last chapter conceals a staggering surprise' – *Time and Tide*

The Julian Symons Omnibus

The Man Who Killed Himself, *The Man Whose Dreams Came True*, *The Man Who Lost His Wife*: three novels of cynical humour and cliff-hanging suspense from a master of his craft. 'Exciting and compulsively readable' – *Observer*

Love in Amsterdam Nicolas Freeling

Inspector Van der Valk's first case involves him in an elaborate cat-and-mouse game with a very wily suspect. 'Has the sinister, spell-binding perfection of a cobra uncoiling. It is a masterpiece of the genre' – Stanley Ellis

Maigret's Pipe Georges Simenon

Eighteen intriguing cases of mystery and murder to which the pipe-smoking Maigret applies his wit and intuition, his genius for detection and a certain *je ne sais quoi* . . .

FOR THE BEST IN PAPERBACKS, LOOK FOR THE 🐧

PENGUIN CLASSIC CRIME

The Big Knockover and Other Stories Dashiell Hammett

With these sharp, spare, laconic stories, Hammett invented a new folk hero – the private eye. 'Dashiell Hammett gave murder back to the kind of people that commit it for reasons, not just to provide a corpse; and with the means at hand, not with handwrought duelling pistols, curare, and tropical fish' – Raymond Chandler

Death of a Ghost Margery Allingham

A picture painted by a dead artist leads to murder . . . and Albert Campion has to face his dearest enemy. With the skill we have come to expect from one of the great crime writers of all time, Margery Allingham weaves an enthralling web of murder, intrigue and suspense.

Fen Country Edmund Crispin

Dandelions and hearing aids, a bloodstained cat, a Leonardo drawing, a corpse with an alibi, a truly poisonous letter . . . these are just some of the unusual clues that Oxford don/detective Gervase Fen is confronted with in this sparkling collection of short mystery stories by one of the great masters of detective fiction. 'The mystery fan's ideal bedside book' – *Kirkus Reviews*

The Wisdom of Father Brown G. K. Chesterton

Twelve delightful stories featuring the world's most beloved amateur sleuth. Here Father Brown's adventures take him from London to Cornwall, from Italy to France. He becomes involved with bandits, treason, murder, curses, and an American crime-detection machine.

Five Roundabouts to Heaven John Bingham

At the heart of this novel is a conflict of human relationships ending in death. Centred around crime, the book is remarkable for its humanity, irony and insight into the motives and weaknesses of men and women, as well as for a tensely exciting plot with a surprise ending. One of the characters, considering reasons for killing, wonders whether the steps of his argument are *Five Roundabouts to Heaven*. Or did they lead to Hell? . . .'